Aunt Dimity and the Buried Treasure

Also by Nancy Atherton

Aunt Dimity' Death
Aunt Dimity and the Duke
Aunt Dimity's Good Deed
Aunt Dimity Digs In
Aunt Dimity's Christmas
Aunt Dimity Beats the Devil
Aunt Dimity: Detective
Aunt Dimity Takes a Holiday
Aunt Dimity: Snowbound
Aunt Dimity and the Next of Kin
Aunt Dimity and the Deep Blue Sea
Aunt Dimity Goes West
Aunt Dimity: Vampire Hunter
Aunt Dimity Slays the Dragon
Aunt Dimity Down Under
Aunt Dimity and the Family Tree
Aunt Dimity and the Village Witch
Aunt Dimity and the Lost Prince
Aunt Dimity and the Wishing Well
Aunt Dimity and the Summer King

Aunt Dimity and the Buried Treasure

NANCY ATHERTON

VIKING

VIKING
An imprint of Penguin Random House LLC
375 Hudson Street
New York, New York 10014
penguin.com

ISBN 9781101981290 (hardcover)
ISBN 9781101981306 (ebook)

Printed in the United States of America
1   3   5   7   9   10   8   6   4   2

Set in Perpetua Std
Designed by Cassandra Garruzzo

For Gillian Weavers,
whose friendship I treasure

Aunt Dimity and the Buried Treasure

One

*F*t was a warm and sunny day in late October. My husband was at work, my sons were at school, and my daughter was teething. Thankfully, Bess had made it clear that she'd outgrown her original source of nourishment, so her new teeth didn't pose a hazard to my health.

They didn't bother her much, either. While other infants ran fevers and fussed as each new tooth erupted, Bess seemed content merely to chew and dribble copiously on any object that came within her reach. Those objects included, but were not limited to, plastic dinosaurs, cricket bats, Wellington boots, table legs, and a dog's ears. The dog in question was a gentle old basset hound who'd tolerated Bess's attentions until I'd become aware of his plight and rescued him. I'd rescued the dinosaurs, cricket bats, and Wellington boots as well, but not before Bess had coated them liberally with drool.

Bess's teething adventures had taught my nine-year-old twins, Will and Rob, the inestimable virtue of tidiness. Toys left lying on the floor or scattered on the coffee table were fair game for Bess, who would, despite my best attempts to preempt her, invariably leave her mark on them, a mark that was always damp and occasionally indented.

Though my husband, Bill, had christened our daughter "Jaws" after he'd found her gnawing on the handle of his leather briefcase, Will and Rob were as tolerant of her incursions as the old basset hound had been. They'd never seen a child grow her own teeth before, and they thought it a very clever thing to do.

And Bess was very clever. To keep my sons' morale from dipping, I refrained from telling them that their almost-eight-month-old sister was sailing through her developmental milestones with a rapidity that made their early accomplishments seem . . . infantile.

Bess had rolled over, sat up, scooted, crawled, and demanded solid food much earlier than the twins had, and as incredible as it might seem, I was willing to swear that she was on the verge of producing intelligible speech. Bill disputed this last claim, declaring that the standard definition of *intelligible* did not include words like *gug*, *pah*, and *wahbah*, but he couldn't deny that, by every other measurement, our girl was ahead of the curve.

We hadn't done anything special to push Bess along. We hadn't played Mozart to her before she was born or showered her with toys guaranteed to increase her IQ. I credited her speedy progress to her desire to catch up with her brothers and to the abundance of love and attention she received from the tight-knit community we called home.

Bill, Will, Rob, Bess, and I lived in a honey-colored cottage near the small village of Finch, a postcard-pretty hamlet set amid the rolling hills and the patchwork fields of the Cotswolds, a rural region in England's West Midlands. Although Bill and I were Americans, as were our children, we'd lived in England long enough—and watched enough county cricket—to know the difference between a googly and a yorker.

Our sleek black cat, Stanley, was one hundred percent English, but he'd had no trouble adjusting to our alien accents and our curious turns of phrase. I was convinced that we could have spoken to him in Welsh, and he wouldn't have cared, as long as we scratched his ears and filled his food bowl.

While Stanley divided his time between eating, sleeping, and keeping out of Bess's reach, the rest of us had slightly busier schedules. Bill ran the European branch of his family's venerable Boston law firm from an office overlooking the village green, Will and Rob attended Morningside School in the nearby market town of Upper Deeping, and I juggled the myriad roles of wife, mother, friend, neighbor, and community volunteer. Even so, none of us were as busy as Bess, whose learning curve made ours look pancake flat.

Our cottage was two miles away from Finch, up a narrow, twisting lane lined with tall hedgerows. We shared our little lane with a handful of other families, but the vast majority of our neighbors lived in the village proper. Their homes and their small business establishments stood on either side of the village green, between St. George's Church and the ancient humpbacked bridge that crossed the Little Deeping River.

From an outsider's perspective, Finch was an insignificant speck of a village, a sleepy backwater in which nothing of note had ever happened. There were no blue plaques to mark the birthplaces of the great and the famous in Finch because no one great or famous had been born there. Apart from its pastoral beauty and the medieval wall paintings in St. George's, Finch had very little to recommend it to the world beyond its borders. It was and had always been an ordinary place where ordinary people lived ordinary lives, yet I found it extraordinary.

Despite its sleepy appearance, Finch was, in fact, a buzzing hive of activity. The lengthy time gaps between baptisms, weddings, and funerals were filled with flower shows, sheep dog trials, church fetes, jumble sales, art shows, harvest festivals, gymkhanas, and Nativity plays. When my neighbors weren't organizing and participating in village-wide events, they ran businesses, tended gardens, pursued hobbies, bickered passionately over trifles, and savored the serenity of the surrounding countryside.

Their favorite pastime, however, was the passionate pursuit of local gossip. The villagers paid no attention to so-called celebrity news and very little to world events, but they had an encyclopedic knowledge of one another. Weight gains and losses, new haircuts, altered clothing, and sudden mood swings were observed minutely and discussed endlessly wherever two or more villagers met. Sally Cook's tearoom was a popular conversation spot, but so, too, were Peacock's pub, the greengrocer's shop, the church, the bridge, the village green, the bench near the war memorial, the old schoolhouse that served as our village hall, Peggy Taxman's well-stocked general store, and every kitchen table in every cottage.

Those craving anonymity would have found my neighbors' nosiness intolerably intrusive, but it gave me a strong sense of security. If privacy was all but unknown in Finch, so, too, was crime. The villagers could spot a suspicious stranger faster than a kestrel could spot a field mouse, and they were quick to alert others to the sighting. I knew that my children were safe in Finch because I knew how many eyes were trained on them.

Bess was the belle of the ball in Finch, which was understandable, given that she was the only baby in a village populated primarily by retirees and middle-aged working folk. Though the villagers were quite fond of Will and Rob, there was something about an infant that turned even the most curmudgeonly of curmudgeons into a baby-talking pile of mush.

Bess's most devoted fan, however, was Bill's father. William Arthur Willis, Sr., was a courtly, old-fashioned gentleman who'd made our lives complete when he'd retired from the family law firm and moved to England to fulfill his role as his grandchildren's only surviving grandparent. Willis, Sr.'s patrician good looks, impeccable manners, and hefty bank account had made him the most eligible widower in Finch until he'd made his own life complete—and broken many a heart—by marrying the well-known watercolorist Amelia Thistle.

Willis, Sr., was utterly besotted with Bess, and Amelia had filled several sketchbooks with pencil drawings that captured Bess's essence in a way that made photography seem obsolete. Happily for all concerned, Willis, Sr., and Amelia lived up the lane from us, in Fairworth House, a graceful Georgian mansion surrounded by a modest estate.

The wrought-iron gates guarding the entrance to my father-in-law's estate were a short stroll away from the humpbacked bridge. The gates were a bit farther away from our cottage, but Bess and I were hearty souls and we enjoyed the walk almost as much as we enjoyed spending time with Grandpa and Grandma. We'd visited Fairworth House daily since the newlyweds had returned from their honeymoon.

On that golden day in late October, though, my footsteps were guided not so much by familial affection as by an unabashed and irrepressible curiosity. A momentous event was about to take place in Finch, and it would take place virtually on Willis, Sr.'s doorstep.

Ivy Cottage, which sat directly across the lane from my father-in-law's wrought-iron gates, was about to receive new tenants. In a big city, such an event might go unnoticed, but not in Finch.

My neighbors had already ascertained a few basic facts about the newcomers, having engaged them in conversation when they'd visited Finch to view the property. I hadn't been on hand to join in those friendly chats, but thanks to the village grapevine, which operated at speeds that put the Internet to shame, I felt as if I'd eavesdropped on them.

Sally Cook and several other reliable sources had been quick to inform me that our soon-to-be neighbors, James and Felicity Hobson, were retired schoolteachers with an unmarried son who worked in finance in Singapore and a married daughter who lived with her architect husband and their two young children—a boy and a girl— in Upper Deeping, where she ran a firm that specialized in high-end interior decoration. It was through the decorator daughter in Upper Deeping, I was told, that the Hobsons had learned of Ivy Cottage.

To someone unfamiliar with Finch's funny little ways, it might have seemed like an awful lot of information to glean from a handful of friendly chats, but I was well aware of my neighbors' prowess in the fine art of interrogation. The only thing that surprised me was that they hadn't nailed down the son's gross annual income, the grandchildren's school scores, and the daughter's views on the vexed question of curtains versus drapes.

Tidbits gleaned from a few casual conversations would not, however, be enough to satisfy the most inquisitive villagers. To learn more, they would almost certainly participate in an information-gathering ritual that was, as far as I knew, unique to Finch. Bill called it "the moving van vigil."

My neighbors prided themselves on their ability to judge people by their possessions. They were as adept at reading armchairs and lamps as a fortune-teller is at reading palms. Since they were also incurable snoops, they never missed a chance to watch a moving van as it was unloaded. They attempted to do so discreetly, of course, because no self-respecting villager would gawk openly at another person's personal belongings.

Had Ivy Cottage been located on the village green, it would have been child's play for the villagers to observe the Hobsons' moving van. They could have surveilled it covertly from the pub or from the tearoom or even through the lace-curtained windows in their own homes. As it was, they would have to cross the humpbacked bridge and amble a short distance up my lane to nab a viewing spot.

I couldn't wait to join them. I was every bit as nosy as my neighbors. I, too, wanted to know more about the Hobsons. I wanted to know if they could be counted on to participate in village life or if they would spurn our neighborly advances, draw their drapes—or curtains—and keep themselves to themselves. I wasn't as skilled as the villagers at reading dining room tables, but I could usually deduce a thing or two from a well-used armchair.

My frequent visits to Fairworth House gave me a reasonable excuse to be in the lane when the moving van arrived. I planned to linger near my father-in-law's wrought-iron gates and eye the van surreptitiously while I fiddled with Bess's bonnet or rummaged through her diaper bag, but I wasn't sure what strategies my neighbors would employ to disguise their true intentions.

"I hope we haven't missed the best bits," I said to Bess as I steered her pram along the narrow lane.

Bess rattled off a string of syllables that, to my ears, came very close to sounding like, "Be reasonable, Mummy. We had to drive Will and Rob to school, then drive back home to move me from my car seat to the all-terrain pram Daddy bought for me. And don't forget the diaper incident, which we've agreed never to mention in polite company. We really couldn't have set out for Ivy Cottage any sooner than we did."

Bill wouldn't have understood her, but I did.

"You're right," I agreed. "But I'll walk faster to make up for our slow start. Hold on to your hat, baby girl!"

We'd already passed the curving drive to Anscombe Manor, where my best friend, Emma Harris, lived, and the mellow redbrick house young Bree Pym had inherited from her great-grandaunts. We were less than ten minutes away from Willis, Sr.'s wrought-iron gates, but I broke into a trot as we rounded the final bend, then came to a full and deeply appreciative stop.

The tableau that met my eyes was better than any I had imagined. The moving van was there, parked in front of the tall hedgerow that concealed Ivy Cottage from view, and two burly men were unloading it, but I scarcely noticed them. I was too busy studying my neighbors, who'd devised a complex tapestry of reasons to loiter in the lane, some of which were more believable than others.

Dick Peacock, our local publican, appeared to be cleaning the wrought-iron gates with a white cloth and a spray bottle filled with the mysterious blue liquid he used to clean the tables in his pub. Mr. Barlow, the retired mechanic who served as our church sexton as well as our general handyman, had clambered up one of his ladders to oil a wrought-iron hinge. Charles Bellingham and Grant Tavistock, who ran an art appraisal and restoration business from their home in Finch, were walking their small dogs Goya and Matisse *very slowly* up and down the verge.

Opal Taylor, Elspeth Binney, Millicent Scroggins, and Selena Buxton—whom Bill had dubbed "Father's Handmaidens" because of their devotion to Willis, Sr.—had elected to appear in the guise of artists, which made a certain amount of sense, since they attended art classes taught by a Mr. Shuttleworth in Upper Deeping. Predictably, their easels sat at angles that would allow them to watch the van while pretending to be absorbed in their work.

Tearoom owner Sally Cook hovered near the Handmaidens, as if fascinated by their paintings, but she abandoned them without a second glance when she spotted me. The others also seemed to be distracted by my arrival because they tore their gazes away from a rather interesting leather sofa the burly men were maneuvering through the gate in the tall hedgerow and followed hot upon Sally's heels as she darted up the lane in my direction.

Bess and I were accustomed to drawing a crowd in Finch, but the crowd we drew usually clamored for Bess's attention rather than mine. I was vaguely alarmed, therefore, when the oncoming horde ignored my darling daughter and addressed themselves exclusively to me.

"Lori!" Elspeth Binney cried. "At last!"

"Where have you been?" demanded Opal Taylor.

"We thought you'd never get here!" Charles Bellingham exclaimed.

"Bess and I had to take the boys to school—" I began.

"No time for explanations," said Sally Cook, waving me to silence. She glanced furtively toward the moving van, then stepped closer to me and murmured, "We have a serious problem with our new neighbors, Lori. And you're the only one who can solve it."

Two

F wasn't sure why Sally Cook had lowered her voice. Our little group of gawkers couldn't have been more conspicuous if we'd waved flags and shot off fireworks. Short, grandmother-shaped Sally wore a gray cardigan over a loose-fitting white blouse and an everyday pair of black stretch pants, and Mr. Barlow was dressed in his usual work shirt and twill trousers, but they were the only villagers whose attire might have gone unnoticed in a country lane.

The Handmaidens looked like a pastel rainbow in their flowing painters' smocks—soft pink for Selena Buxton, baby blue for Elspeth Binney, primrose yellow for Opal Taylor, and mint green for Millicent Scroggins—while Dick Peacock had chosen a blindingly bright paisley waistcoat from his collection of waistcoats, as if he wished to call attention to his massive girth.

Tall, portly Charles Bellingham had covered his balding pate with a rather dashing black fedora he'd adorned with a crimson hatband. Grant Tavistock, by contrast, had evidently decided to accentuate his healthy headful of salt-and-pepper hair by winding a long silvery scarf around his neck.

I'd worn faded blue jeans and a navy blue pullover for the express purpose of blending into the shadows, but it didn't seem to matter. The movers appeared to be too absorbed in their work to take any notice of my colorful neighbors.

"How on earth can you have a problem with the Hobsons?" I

demanded. "They haven't even finished moving in. Did they storm out of their new home and tell you to go away?"

"No," Sally admitted. "None of us have spoken with them since they came to Finch to view the cottage."

"We saw them arrive this morning," Dick Peacock added helpfully. "They were here before the removals men."

"Mr. Hobson drives an old Fiat Panda," Grant Tavistock informed me.

"And Mrs. Hobson was in a blue hatchback," said Charles Bellingham.

"They parked their cars in the garage," said Elspeth Binney, "and we haven't seen them since."

"It's hard to see anything through the hedgerow," said Millicent Scroggins, with the disappointed air of one who'd tried.

The tall but tidy hedgerow that blocked our view of Ivy Cottage also blocked our view of the garage. The Hobsons could have bunny-hopped from their cars to their front door, and no one in the lane would have been any the wiser.

"If you've had only a glimpse of the Hobsons," I said patiently, "and you haven't spoken with them recently, how can you have a problem with them?"

"We saw the boxes," said Opal Taylor.

"What boxes?" I asked.

"The boxes marked MUSEUM," Sally said, as if it were obvious. "The removals men carried dozens of them into the house."

"No, they didn't," countered Elspeth. "I saw no more than ten boxes labeled MUSEUM."

"I saw twelve," said Opal.

"That's odd," said Grant. "Charles and I saw nine."

"There were five museum boxes," Mr. Barlow stated flatly and since he was as precise as the others were prone to exaggeration, no one contradicted him.

"Does it matter?" Sally said irritably. "The point is: The boxes prove that the Hobsons intend to open a museum."

"A museum?" I said, bewildered. "What kind of museum would a pair of retired schoolteachers open?"

"Blackboards through the ages?" Charles suggested.

"A collection of inkwells might be interesting," said Selena.

"I wouldn't mind looking at old copybooks," Dick said thoughtfully. "Handwriting has changed a lot since we were in school."

"It certainly has," said Mr. Barlow. "It's become a lot less legible."

Everyone laughed except Sally, who seemed to be distinctly out of sorts.

"There's no reason to suppose that the museum will have anything to do with the Hobsons' teaching careers," said Grant. "They may have a collection of model airplanes or music boxes or exotic insects."

"Will and Rob would go bananas over an insect museum," I said. "My boys love bugs."

Bess chose that moment to let out a squawk. I knew that she was agreeing with me about her brothers' entomomania, but the others seemed to think that she was reproaching them for ignoring her.

The discussion of museums was immediately put on hold while the villagers endeavored to redeem themselves. Bess was scooped up, passed around, cuddled, kissed, and lavishly praised until I returned her to the pram, where she promptly fell asleep. Adoration, however well deserved, could be exhausting for an almost-eight-month-old.

"All right," I said, once order was restored. "You saw the movers carry five boxes labeled MUSEUM into Ivy Cottage. You assume, therefore, that the Hobsons intend to open a museum of some sort." I raised my hands, palms upward. "I still don't see what the problem is."

A deafening wave of noise reverberated through the lane as everyone spoke at once. The burly movers glanced in our direction, rolled their eyes, and got on with their work.

"Pipe down!" Sally barked. "You'll wake the baby!"

My neighbors peered at Bess contritely, and the clamor was replaced by a whispered chorus of apologies. Since I wanted to get to the bottom of their issue with the Hobsons, I didn't tell them that my clever daughter could sleep through a brass band concert.

"Let's talk one at a time, shall we?" Elspeth proposed primly.

"I'll go first," said Sally, and the glint in her eye warned the others to back off. "Ivy Cottage is in a residential zone, Lori. The Hobsons would have to get a special permit and all sorts of special licenses from the county to run a business from their place of residence."

"If they do get the permit and the licenses," said Opal, "where will the museum visitors park?" She swept an arm through the air to indicate the narrow lane. "You can see for yourself that there's no space for parked cars here. Mark my words: We'll have cars parked helter-skelter on the village green."

"They'll ruin the grass," said Grant. "If it rains, the green won't be a green anymore. It'll be a muddy mess."

"Goya and Matisse don't care for mud," said Charles, gazing indulgently from his Golden Pomeranian to his partner's Maltese.

"I don't care for mud, either," Millicent chimed in.

"Nor do I," said Elspeth. "No one cares for mud."

"They'll drop sandwich wrappers and soda cans all over the village," Selena said with a disapproving sniff. "I don't know about the rest of you, but I don't wish to spend my spare time picking up after a pack of strangers."

"A museum might be good for business," Dick pointed out. "I wouldn't mind seeing a few more seats filled in the pub."

"It won't be good for *my* business," Sally grumbled, finally revealing the reason for her ill humor.

"Why not?" I asked.

"Museums *always* have tearooms, Lori," she replied. "My tearoom barely turns a profit as it is. A second tearoom in the village could wipe me out."

Mr. Barlow, ever the voice of reason in Finch, spoke up again.

"If you ask me," he said, "you're getting yourselves wound up over something that might never happen. We don't really know what those boxes mean, do we?"

The villagers fell silent as they turned his question over in their minds. Elspeth Binney was the first to concede that he might be on to something.

"You're quite right," she said. "Perhaps the Hobsons bought the boxes *from* a museum."

"Or they could be storing them *for* a museum," said Millicent.

"Or they might be taking them *to* a museum," said Opal. "After they settle into their new home, of course."

"Or we might be right," Sally said darkly. "The Hobsons may be planning to run a museum of their own, with a tearoom, in Ivy Cottage."

"Only one way to find out," Mr. Barlow said briskly. "Ask them. Go in there right now and ask them straight out: Do you intend to open a museum?"

"My thoughts exactly," said Sally. She turned to me. "That's where you come in, Lori."

The rest of the villagers nodded encouragingly.

"Sorry?" I said, baffled. "Where do I come in?"

"We'd like you to ask the Hobsons if they intend to open a

museum in Ivy Cottage," Elspeth explained. "And we'd like you to ask them as soon as possible."

"Within the next five minutes would suit me," said Sally, tapping her foot impatiently.

I gaped at Sally and Elspeth, as if they'd made a subversive suggestion. In a way, they had. It was customary in Finch to allow newcomers three days to recover from the initial shock of moving. To knock on the Hobsons' door any sooner would be considered extremely impolite, as it would put undue pressure on them to be hospitable in the midst of chaos. To intrude on the Hobsons on the very day of their arrival, while their moving van was still being emptied, would, under normal circumstances, be seen as a descent into barbarism.

"B-but what about the three-day rule?" I stammered.

"We're willing to waive the three-day rule," Sally replied.

"We *have* to waive it," said Mr. Barlow. "If we don't, certain people"—he gave Sally a sidelong glance—"will let their imaginations run away with them. Before you know it, those five boxes will become hundreds, and Ivy Cottage will become the Finch branch of the British Museum."

"Don't be ridiculous," Sally snapped, having caught Mr. Barlow's glance. "No one said a word about the British Museum. But even a *small* museum, with a *small* tearoom—"

"You've made your concerns perfectly clear, Sally," Grant interrupted gently. "You won't get a wink of sleep until you know what the Hobsons intend to do with Ivy Cottage."

"We'd all like to know," said Millicent. She raised her eyebrows, then added portentously, "We wouldn't want alarming rumors to reach Peggy Taxman's ears, would we?"

The villagers' eyes widened in dismay, and I had no trouble

understanding why. Peggy Taxman was a broad-shouldered, buxom bossyboots, a natural commander who ruled the village with an iron hand and a voice that could pulverize granite. Peggy ran the post office, the general store, and the greengrocer's shop, and she chaired every committee meeting in Finch. Village life would have ground to a halt without her organizational skills and her seemingly boundless energy, but most of us would have preferred a ruler who was less overbearing, officious, and opinionated than the one we had.

I looked toward the humpbacked bridge and asked, "Why isn't Peggy here?"

"Delivery day," replied Millicent. "She's restocking the shelves in the Emporium."

Finch's general store had been known as the Emporium from time out of mind. It was an aptly grandiose name, as the Emporium stocked everything from hay bales to freckle cream.

"Why didn't she send Jasper in her place?" I inquired.

Jasper Taxman, Peggy's soft-spoken, mild-mannered husband, was the only person on earth who could curb his wife's wilder excesses, but even he chose his battles wisely.

"Jasper's working the till," Millicent informed me, "but they'll hear about the museum soon enough."

"God forbid," Dick groaned. "If Peggy gets wind of it, we'll be stuck in committee meetings for the next three days. She'll want to get up a petition and hold a protest rally. Either that, or she'll want to run the museum herself, which means that she'll volunteer *us* to run it."

"A committee meeting once a week is bad enough," Charles said, looking appalled. "If I have to attend three in three days, I'll go mad."

"And deaf," Grant added glumly.

"We need to stop the rumors before they start," Mr. Barlow said decisively. "The only way to get our facts straight is to speak directly with the Hobsons."

My neighbors gazed at me imploringly.

"I'm willing," I said, taking the leaden hint, "but I don't know why it has to be me. Why can't one of you speak with them?"

"Because you have a baby and we don't," Sally replied bluntly. "Bess is your passport into Ivy Cottage."

"Have you no shame?" I said, eyeing her reproachfully. "Do you really want me to use my infant daughter as a prop in an underhanded scheme to trick an innocent couple into revealing secrets they might wish to keep to themselves?"

"We do," said Sally.

"Hole in one," said Grant.

"She got there in the end," Dick said complacently, and the others nodded.

"What a great idea," I said, grinning. "I should have thought of it myself. Wish me luck!"

"You won't need it," said Sally. "You have Bess."

Three

The villagers were urging me onward when a loud *bang!* made everyone jump. The burly movers, having completed their task, had slammed the van's swinging doors shut. The sound of their laughter as they climbed into the cab suggested strongly that they'd enjoyed startling us.

"Well, really," Elspeth said indignantly. "The manners of some people."

No one joined Elspeth in berating the movers as they drove off. I suspected that the others were remembering, as I was, a certain proverb concerning glass houses and thrown stones. People who spied on moving vans couldn't in all honesty claim the high ground when it came to practicing good manners.

The slamming doors didn't make my dozing daughter jump, but they did wake her. She opened her eyes, blinked slowly, and yawned lazily, then smacked her lips to indicate that she was ready for the midmorning snack I'd tucked into the diaper bag.

"Brilliant," I said, beaming at her. "We'll ask the Hobsons if we can warm your puréed carrots in their kitchen."

"I hope they've unpacked their pots and pans," said Sally.

"We'll soon find out," I said cheerfully, and steered the pram toward the arched wooden gate in the tall hedgerow.

I couldn't believe my luck. Despite our late arrival at the moving van vigil, Bess and I had managed to score better-than-front-row seats. Thanks to the museum mystery, we wouldn't have to listen wistfully while our neighbors described the Hobsons' tables, chairs, and lamps. Instead, we'd be the first locals—the very first!—to see their possessions up close, *inside Ivy Cottage*. I felt as though Christmas had come early.

I strode through the gateway in an excess of high spirits, but my steps slowed, then stopped as a wave of memories washed over me. Ivy Cottage was a pretty place, two stories tall, its walls cloaked in the climbing vine that had given the cottage its name. Shaggy strands of ivy framed a pair of bay windows on the ground floor, tall chimneys bracketed the slate roof, and a shallow porch sheltered a front door made of weathered oak. A well-kept garden grew on either side of the smooth brick path that led from the arched gate to the front door.

I could remember a time, however, when Ivy Cottage hadn't presented such a pretty picture to the world. Its previous tenant, the late Hector Huggins, had allowed his garden to engulf his home. When I'd first seen it, I'd been reminded of Sleeping Beauty's castle. Fortunately, the overgrowth had been tamed and the cottage updated by Mr. Huggins's heir, a young Australian named Jack MacBride.

Although Jack had lived in Ivy Cottage during its lengthy renovation, he'd recently moved in with Bree Pym, who, after a few miscues, had fallen as deeply in love with him as he had with her. The villagers had accepted the new arrangement grudgingly, not because they disapproved of it but because it deprived them of the pleasure of attending another wedding at St. George's.

Since I'd helped Jack with the renovation, Ivy Cottage was as familiar to me as my own cottage. I felt a touch of pride as I surveyed the neatly clipped vines, the sparkling windowpanes, and the carefully tended garden, and I hoped the Hobsons would take good care of their new home, whether they used it as a museum or not.

Bess ended my reverie with a powerfully worded request for food. With a hasty apology, I cut short my stroll down memory lane and made my way up the brick path without further delay.

I'd scarcely finished knocking on the front door when it was opened by a tall, slender woman dressed in a Fair Isle sweater, brown corduroy trousers, and sensible brown suede shoes. Her eyes were an interesting shade of powder blue, and she wore her gray hair in a short, chic style that flattered her oval face. She had a pencil tucked behind one ear, a pair of reading glasses perched halfway down her nose, a piece of paper in her hand, and a puzzled frown creasing her brow.

The woman peered at me over her reading glasses, then held the piece of paper out to me. It appeared to be a checklist.

"Any idea what this scribble might mean?" she asked, pointing to the second item on the list. "You'd think I'd be able to read my own handwriting, but I can't make head nor tail of it. That's what comes of making to-do lists at the last minute."

" 'Empty . . . coolbox'?" I ventured, after studying the scrawl.

"Good Lord, yes," she said, clapping a hand to her forehead. "I hope the ice hasn't melted. We'll need the butter for our toast tomorrow morning. There's nothing so dispiriting as dry toast." She gestured for me to follow her as she hurried into the cottage.

I lifted Bess and the diaper bag from the pram, carried them across the threshold, closed the door behind me, and paused to scrutinize the large rectangular room that stretched from the front to the back of the cottage. The late Hector Huggins had used it as both living and dining room, but it looked as though the Hobsons would use it exclusively as a living room. I was tempted to open the door to the dining room, to see if they planned to put it to its intended use, but decided against it. I didn't want to push my luck too far.

I liked what I saw in the living room. Upon closer examination, the leather sofa I'd noticed earlier appeared to be neither cheap nor outrageously expensive. It was comfortably worn as well, like a favorite pair of bedroom slippers, and the rest of the furnishings were equally unpretentious. There were a few antiques scattered here and there, but I sensed that, once the furniture was arranged properly, the finer pieces would blend in nicely with the more modest ones.

Satisfied, I entered the kitchen, where I found the gray-haired woman transferring the contents of a large red cooler to the stainless steel refrigerator Jack MacBride had installed. The kitchen was crowded with boxes, some half empty, others unopened, none of them labeled MUSEUM.

"You arrived in the nick of time," the woman said over her shoulder. "One more hour, and our butter would have been soup." She tipped a stream of half-melted ice cubes into the sink, then set the cooler aside, with its lid open, to air dry. "I really can't thank you enough," she went on, turning to extend a damp hand to me. "I'm Felicity Hobson, by the way, and your baby is beautiful."

Mrs. Hobson couldn't have chosen a better way to endear herself to me. I looked down at my daughter's silky dark ringlets, her velvety brown eyes, and her rose-petal complexion, and I had to agree that she was indeed beautiful. My boys were good-looking, too, but there was something about an infant . . .

"I'm Lori Shepherd," I said, shaking Mrs. Hobson's hand. "And my daughter's name is Bess. We live up the lane from you, just past Anscombe Manor."

"Anscombe Manor," Mrs. Hobson repeated reflectively. "Is that the place with the riding school?"

"That's right," I said. "My sons take lessons there."

"I know," she said. "The woman who owns the tearoom told me."

"Did she?" I said, wondering what else Sally Cook had told our new neighbors about me.

"Oh, yes," said Mrs. Hobson. "Our estate agent introduced us to quite a number of villagers when we came to Finch to view Ivy Cottage. Everyone we met seemed eager to speak with us."

"Talking is the most popular form of exercise in Finch," I told her.

"I'm rather fond of it myself," said Mrs. Hobson.

The twinkle in her eye suggested that she'd learned as much about the villagers as they'd learned about her during her first visit to Finch. It was a promising sign. Mrs. Hobson, I thought, would have no trouble holding her own in a community of snoops.

Bess repeated her request for food.

"Diaper?" Mrs. Hobson guessed.

"Hunger," I said. "Bess usually has a bite to eat right about now."

"I'm afraid we didn't bring any baby food with us," said Mrs. Hobson. "Our children outgrew it some thirty years ago."

"Not to worry," I said, patting the diaper bag. "I never leave home without a jar of puréed carrots."

"Would you like me to warm it for Bess?" Mrs. Hobson asked. "I do have a saucepan here, somewhere."

She began to shift boxes from one place to another, and in no time at all, I was seated at a cleared kitchen table, feeding Bess spoonfuls of her favorite midmorning snack. Mrs. Hobson's saucepan search had produced a teakettle, a sturdy brown teapot, a squashed packet of tea, and a pretty set of blue-and-white cups and saucers as well as the saucepan. While I fed my ravenous daughter, Mrs. Hobson made a pot of Earl Grey tea and set the table with three cups and saucers. She then left the kitchen to stand at the bottom of the staircase leading to the upper floor.

"James!" she called. "Come down! We have guests!"

She returned to the kitchen and took the chair opposite mine, placed her reading glasses on the table, and rubbed her eyes.

"My husband will be with us shortly," she said. "Unless he becomes distracted, in which case I'll go upstairs and haul him down bodily."

"Please don't," I protested. "He must have a lot to do—you both do—and you've already gone to so much trouble—"

"It's no trouble," she broke in, filling her cup. "I needed a sit-down, and you gave me an excuse to have one."

I heard the sound of footsteps descending the stairs, and a moment later James Hobson strode into the kitchen. He was a head taller than his wife, and his face was more weathered than hers, but he had the same slim build. His bright blue eyes peered at me from behind a pair of wire-rimmed spectacles, and his iron-gray hair stood up in random wisps, as if he'd just finished running his hand through it. He was dressed as casually as I would have expected him to be, in a plaid flannel shirt, a somewhat grubby pair of chinos, and sneakers.

"Lori?" said Mrs. Hobson. "Please allow me to present my husband, James. James, say hello to Lori Shepherd and her daughter, Bess. Their timely arrival saved our butter."

"Hello and thank you," he said, smiling down at me. "I'd offer my hand, but yours appear to be fully engaged."

"I'm very pleased to meet you, Mr. Hobson," I said.

"Please don't call me Mr. Hobson," he said with a groan, sinking into the chair next to his wife's. "Felicity and I have been addressed as Mr. and Mrs. Hobson for so long that we've nearly forgotten our Christian names."

"The schoolteacher's curse," said Mrs. Hobson. "One of them, at any rate."

"Among grown-ups," said her husband, "we're James and Felicity."

"And I'm Lori," I said. "I'm familiar with schoolteachers' curses. My mother taught third and fourth graders back in the States."

"I thought I detected an American accent," said James. "Is your mother still in the States?"

"She died a year before I moved to England," I replied.

"I'm sorry," said James. "And your father?"

"James," Felicity said, frowning at him, "you're prying."

"It's okay, Felicity," I said. "I'm used to people prying. To answer your question, James, my father died shortly after I was born."

"It must be a comfort to have your father-in-law living nearby," said James. "He owns the estate across the lane from us, doesn't he?"

"Another tidbit from the tearoom?" I inquired.

"Not at all," James replied. "We heard about your father-in-law from the man who owns the pub. He sounds like quite a nice chap."

"William is wonderful," I said. "You couldn't ask for a better neighbor."

"I don't suppose we could borrow a blender from him," said Felicity, with a wry smile. She kicked a nearby box, and it made a faint tinkling noise. "Ours didn't survive the move."

"I'll bring one over tomorrow," I said. "My husband and I were given six blenders as wedding presents, and we've only ever used one. The rest are stashed in our attic. They may not have the latest bells and whistles, and their warranties are definitely out of date, but they're as good as new."

"I was joking," Felicity said, "but if you wouldn't mind . . . It would save us a trip to Upper Deeping."

"It would be my pleasure," I said. "We'll call it a housewarming gift."

Bess had finished inhaling her carrots, and although she found our conversation fascinating, she was ready for some exercise. I cleaned her up, then scanned the cluttered floor for a safe place to put her, but there was none. Her body language—and mine—must have spoken to James because he proposed a simple solution.

"Shall we repair to the back garden?" he said. "Your daughter can play among the leaves while we chat."

"Are you sure we're not taking up too much of your time?" I asked.

"Let's see," said James, feigning concentration. "Unpack another box or sit idly in the garden on a fine October morning? Difficult choice, but . . ." He stood. "I choose the garden!"

"So do I," said Felicity, standing. "A breath of fresh air will make a nice change from breathing dust. James, you bring the diaper bag, and I'll bring the tea."

Jack MacBride had, with ample help from my friend Emma Harris, transformed Ivy Cottage's back garden from a tangled jungle into a tranquil haven. No garden was at its best in late October, but I'd seen the trellis covered with roses, the boundary wall shaded by the pergola's profusion of grape leaves, and the blooming beds of wildlife-friendly flowers that had been cut back but not uprooted during the renovation. James and Felicity, I thought, had a lot to look forward to.

Whatever the season, the garden's most noteworthy feature was the old well that stood at its center. It was known throughout the village as the wishing well, and it looked the part. The wellhead was round and constructed of smooth river stones, with a shingled roof resting on a pair of wooden posts. An oak bucket hung from a rope wound around the wooden spindle that spanned the posts. I remembered the day Mr. Barlow had given the rope and the bucket to Jack MacBride.

Although the sight of the old well revived vivid memories, I pushed them aside. I'd been so disarmed by the Hobsons' hospitality that I'd forgotten the reason for my visit, but it was time to get down to business. I was fairly sure that the villagers would look upon me with disfavor—and possibly growl at me—if I left Ivy Cottage without learning the truth about the museum boxes.

The movers had deposited a simple teak table and four matching chairs on the back garden's brick patio. I placed Bess and a few of her toys on the soft grass at the edge of the patio and kept an eye on her as the Hobsons and I took our places around the table. I didn't mind Bess playing with dead leaves. I just didn't want her to fill her mouth with them.

I was about to turn the conversation toward the mysterious boxes when James spoke.

"Tell me, Lori," he said, "were you deputized by the lurkers in the lane, or did you visit us of your own volition?"

I blushed to my roots. A feeble denial sprang to my lips, but I couldn't bring myself to insult James's intelligence.

"I suppose it was too much to hope that you wouldn't notice our little gathering," I said with a sigh.

"We're tired, but we're not *that* tired," said Felicity. "Does it happen every time someone new comes to Finch?"

"I'm afraid so," I said apologetically. "The arrival of newcomers is a big event in a small village. Since Finch is a very small village, your arrival is a very big event."

"We aren't complaining," James assured me. "It's rather flattering to be the center of so much attention. Were you sent, by the way? Or did you volunteer?"

"A bit of both," I admitted. "The villagers are curious about you."
I was too embarrassed to meet his gaze, so I kept my eyes fixed on
Bess as I added, "So am I."

"We thought as much," said James, nodding. "And we're prepared
to give you a few morsels of information to take back with you."

"We won't reveal our deepest secrets," said Felicity. "We plan to
be here for a long time, and we'd like to save something for later."

"But we'll tell you enough of our life story to satisfy our audience," said James.

"Please feel free to break in with questions," said Felicity.

Their graciousness had robbed me of the desire to ask any questions of them, ever, on any subject, but I'd lived in Finch for too long
to put my fingers in my ears as James began.

Four

"Let's start with why we came to Finch, shall we?" James proposed. "It's a dramatic tale, filled with pathos, danger, and near-tragedy. I'm sure the lane lurkers will gobble it up."

"Behave yourself, James," Felicity scolded. "The 'lane lurkers,' as you call them, are our new neighbors."

"I stand corrected," James acknowledged. "I'm sure our *new neighbors* will gobble it up." He took a small sip of tea, adjusted his spectacles, and gazed out over the meadows beyond the garden's boundary wall. "I suppose you could call us climate-change refugees."

"It's an accurate description," Felicity agreed, "but I think we'll have to turn the clock back a bit to explain why." She refilled my cup, then went on. "After James and I retired from teaching, we sold our house in North London and bought a cottage in a small village near Eastbourne."

"Our cottage had been built in 1820," James said, "and it sat high on a cliff overlooking the Channel. We'd hoped to spend the rest of our days there, savoring the sea air and the glorious sunsets."

"It was our dream home," Felicity said, "until it turned into a nightmare."

"A nightmare?" I echoed, and my reluctance to ask questions went straight out the window. "What happened?"

"The southeast coast has always been battered by winter storms," James said, "but over the past few decades, the storms have become bigger and stronger and more frequent than any in recorded history. As a result, the cliffs have begun to erode at an alarming rate."

"The sea is reclaiming the land," said Felicity, "and it was happening before our very eyes. Cliffs that had been fifty meters away from our back door were suddenly forty meters away, then thirty." She shook her head. "It was like watching a disaster film."

"It was like being *in* a disaster film," James countered. "We couldn't let our grandchildren play outside when they came to visit because we never knew when the next section of cliff would collapse. We couldn't stroll on the beach because falling rocks might land on our heads. The stress and the uncertainty began to take a toll on our health. We had trouble sleeping, eating, concentrating. It was, as Felicity said, a nightmare."

I left my chair to persuade Bess to chew on a teething toy instead of a pinecone, then returned to it, breathless with anticipation.

"I'm so sorry," I said. "About your nightmare, I mean. It must have been awful."

"We were certainly filled with awe," James said dryly. "But we could see the handwriting on the wall."

"Once we faced the fact that our dream home's days were numbered," said Felicity, "we revised our dream and began to look for another home."

"We should mention here that our daughter lives in Upper Deeping," James interjected.

"I know," I said, with a half smile in Felicity's direction. "I also know that your daughter is an interior decorator and that she's the one who told you about Ivy Cottage." I shrugged. "Word gets around."

"Naturally," said Felicity, smiling back at me. "Yes, Jessica did tell us about Ivy Cottage. She'd be here helping us today if her children weren't under the weather."

"Both of them sick?" I said. "That's tough." I smiled sheepishly as Felicity's eyebrows rose. "As I said, word gets around. Rumor has it that your daughter has two school-aged children, a boy and a girl."

"And our son?" Felicity asked.

"Unmarried, works in finance, lives in Singapore," I said unhesitatingly.

"Remarkable," said Felicity.

"Typical," I said. "If you let something slip, the villagers will remember it. And pass it on."

"I'll bear it in mind," said Felicity, "and I'll watch what I let slip."

"So will I," said James.

"A wise decision," I said.

"Where were we?" said Felicity. "Ah, yes . . . our daughter learned of Ivy Cottage from a client who knew the estate agent handling the property."

"Felicity and I drove up from the coast to view the cottage," said James, "and decided on the spot to up stakes and move inland. It wasn't an easy decision, but it was the right one."

"I imagine you'll miss the sea air and the sunsets," I said sympathetically.

"We can drive back to the coast whenever we like," said James. "And we won't miss the tension and the fear. Our grandchildren will be able to visit us more often, and we'll allow them to play outside when they do."

"The Little Deeping floods from time to time," I said, in the interest of full disclosure.

"We know," said Felicity, with another smile. "Grant and

Charles—the chaps who live in Crabtree Cottage—told us. But they also told us that the floodwaters have never reached Ivy Cottage."

"If our nightmare taught us anything," James said philosophically, "it's that no place on earth is entirely safe. We believe, however, that we're safer here than we were on our crumbling cliffs."

"Ivy Cottage suits us perfectly," said Felicity. "It's on solid ground, it has a magnificent garden, and it has plenty of room for James's hobby."

"My wife is a keen gardener," James informed me.

"A decent-sized garden was the one thing our cliff-top cottage lacked," said Felicity. "Well," she temporized, "that, and solid ground."

"I'll introduce you to my friend Emma Harris," I said. "She worked on the garden while the cottage was being renovated. I know for a fact that she still has a three-ring binder filled with her drawings, diagrams, and plant lists. I'm sure she'll be willing to pass it on to you."

"I look forward to meeting her," said Felicity, sounding impressed.

"We look forward to meeting everyone we haven't already met," James put in. "That's the point of village life, isn't it? Getting to know one's neighbors?"

Bess crawled across the brick patio to join in the discussion, but before I could reach for her, James picked her up, parked her in his lap, and gave her his key ring to play with. When she made no objection, I knew beyond a shadow of a doubt that the Hobsons would make a fine addition to Finch. Bess was a shrewd judge of character.

"If you're looking for neighbors who take an interest in one another," I said, "then you've come to the right place. As a matter of fact, the villagers sent me in here to ask you about some boxes that piqued their curiosity. They think you're planning to open a museum in Ivy Cottage, and they've worked themselves into a lather over the extra traffic, the parking, the litter, the zoning laws, and just about anything that could be remotely connected to the opening of a museum."

"A museum?" Felicity said. "Why would they think . . ." An arrested expression crossed her face, and she looked accusingly at her husband. "It's your fault, James. The villagers saw those boxes of yours and got the wrong idea."

"Seems likely," said James, nodding. "They must have excellent eyesight."

"Nothing goes unseen in Finch," I told him. "If you leave a scone uneaten in the tearoom, you'll hear about it later in the pub."

James rounded on his wife and said sternly, "No more topless sunbathing."

"No more joyriding," she retorted, shaking an index finger at him.

"We're joking," James clarified, when my eyes widened.

"Of course you are," I said with a belated chuckle, "but I'd go easy on the jokes until the villagers get to know you better. They tend to take things literally. When they see boxes labeled MUSEUM, for example . . ." I left the sentence hanging, but Felicity answered my unspoken question.

"James collects odds and ends," she said, "and he keeps them in a room he calls his museum."

"There's a splendid shelf-lined room upstairs," said James. "We assume it was used as a library, but I've claimed it for my collection."

"Please assure the villagers that we have no plans to open a real museum," said Felicity.

"I will," I said. "Thank you. They'll sleep easier tonight." I turned to James. "What sort of odds and ends do you collect?"

"All sorts," he said. "I'm a metal detectorist."

"I see," I said, recalling a newspaper article I'd read on the subject. "You have one of those wand things that goes beep when it passes over metal."

"That's right," said James. "I use a metal detector to search for buried treasure."

"Have you found any?" I asked.

"It depends on your definition of treasure," said Felicity, rolling her eyes.

"I haven't found my Viking hoard yet," James admitted, "but I have a rather nice collection of old coins."

"And old cutlery and old tins and old belt buckles," Felicity put in.

"My wife thinks I'm daft," said James, "but it's good healthy fun, and it can be quite educational. I never know what I'll dig up."

"It sounds exciting," I said.

"It can be," said James. "Sometimes, when the going is slow, I'm more of a bird-watcher than a detectorist, but I enjoy watching birds. I enjoy being outdoors." He cast a sidelong glance at Felicity. "As my wife will tell you, my hobby has the added benefit of getting me out from under her feet."

"There's such a thing as too much togetherness," said Felicity, laughing, "especially when a couple has retired." She held out her arms to Bess. "Let me have a go, James. It's been an age since I cuddled a baby."

Bess was duly passed from husband to wife and given a teaspoon, which she happily pounded on the teak table. The Hobsons had evidently developed selective deafness during their years in the classroom, because they seemed unfazed by the racket.

"I don't suppose . . ." I hesitated, then started again. "After you and Felicity have fully recovered from your move, James, and after you've put your house in order, would you be willing to give a talk in the village about your hobby? I, for one, would find it fascinating, and I'm sure the others would, too."

"Why wait until we've settled in?" said James, sitting upright. "I can speak with the lane lurk—that is, I can speak with our new neighbors right now, if you like."

"Any excuse to avoid unpacking," Felicity said, but she didn't look upset.

"It's a rather good excuse," James argued. "It's clearly the best way to calm their fears about the museum."

"They won't expect tea, will they?" Felicity asked me.

"They won't even expect chairs," I assured her. "You'll score big points with them by simply inviting them into the garden for a chat."

"I'd put the tea things away nevertheless," James advised, getting to his feet. "We wouldn't want them to get their hopes up."

"Very well." Felicity stood and passed Bess to me. "While I clear the table and Lori changes Bess's nappy, James can invite our new neighbors into the garden for a brief introduction to metal detecting." She caught her husband's eye and repeated pointedly, "A *brief* introduction, James."

"I shall be the soul of brevity," he promised, but there was a definite bounce in his step as he strode off to speak with the lurkers.

The back garden looked as though it had burst into bloom. The Handmaidens' pastel smocks, Dick Peacock's paisley waistcoat, Charles Bellingham's crimson hatband, and Grant Tavistock's silvery scarf brightened the somewhat dreary retreat as those who'd participated in the moving van vigil gathered before the wishing well to listen to James Hobson's impromptu lecture.

It must be admitted that some of the villagers craned their necks to peer through the cottage's uncurtained windows, but most contented themselves with deceptively casual glances. Sally Cook regarded James with undisguised suspicion, but the others wore slightly smug expressions, as if they were anticipating the pleasure of informing Peggy Taxman that she'd missed out on a golden opportunity to be among the first locals to receive a personal invitation to visit the newcomers. My neighbors were good people, but they weren't saints.

James stood behind the teak table, with his hands resting lightly on one of his museum boxes. Felicity and I stood on either side of him, having agreed that it would be inconsiderate to sit when the villagers were forced to stand. Bess crawled among her admirers, toying with their shoelaces, tugging on their trousers, and talking to herself.

"I feel as if I'm back in the classroom," James announced. "But I promise not to assign any homework."

The villagers acknowledged his quip with polite smiles, as if they were reserving judgment.

"As I told you in the lane," James went on, "Lori thought you might like to hear a little something about my hobby."

"What is your hobby?" asked Mr. Barlow, who was always willing to cut to the chase.

"I'm a metal detectorist," James replied.

"You use one of those long, beeping stick things to find stuff that's buried underground," Dick Peacock said knowledgeably. "My wife and I read an article about chaps like you in the paper not long ago."

"We all read the article, Dick," said Sally Cook. "It was the only thing worth reading in the paper that day."

"The sports section is always worth reading," Dick protested.

An argument about what parts of the newspaper were worth reading might have ensued, but James knew how to bring a classroom to order.

"It's a worthwhile topic," he said very quietly.

The villagers instantly shut their mouths and cocked their ears to hear him.

"Metal detectors aren't used only to find objects buried underground," James continued, resuming his normal tone of voice. "They're used to detect concealed weapons at airports and to locate hidden pipes and cables in construction. Metal detectors have many uses, but I use mine to explore the past."

He opened the museum box and took a large bronze coin from it, then held the coin high in the air for all to see.

"I'm sure I don't have to tell you what this is," he said.

"It's an old penny," said Mr. Barlow. "The kind we used before decimalization."

"That's right," said James. "It's a 1957 bronze penny."

"Why would you want an old penny?" Opal Taylor asked. "You can't use it in the shops anymore. It's worthless."

"Is it?" James said, gazing up at the coin. "I found it in a field where a traveling fair once pitched its tents. If it could speak, imagine the stories it would tell."

Every eye, including mine, was suddenly fixed on the penny.

"When I look at my penny," James continued, "I can almost hear children laughing as they ride a merry-go-round or gorge themselves on candy floss or win a prize at a carnival game. I imagine the child who lost it, the desperate search, and the tears that followed."

I wasn't sure about the others, but I found myself hoping the coin hadn't slipped from a sticky little fist.

"Some metal detectorists," James went on, "focus on the monetary value of a find. Simply put: If it isn't gold, it isn't worth keeping. Others, like myself, enjoy the story each object tells. It's like holding a piece of history in my hand. I can't help imagining who made it, who owned it, who left it behind, and why. With a lot of research and a little imagination, I can reconstruct the world that produced my coin. A 1957 bronze penny may not be valuable in material terms, but every find connects me to another time and place."

"Have you found any gold?" asked Millicent Scroggins.

James's hand disappeared into the box again. When it came out, he was holding a round brooch made of pearls inset in gold to mimic a daisy's petals. An awed murmur ran through his rapt audience.

"Sorry," he said, responding to the murmur. "In this case, all that glitters *isn't* gold. The pearls are fake and the metal is painted brass, but when I dug it up, I thought I'd found a treasure. And I was right. Although my brooch turned out to be a tatty piece of mid-twentieth-century costume jewelry, I'll never forget the thrill I felt when I first saw it, and I've never stopped weaving stories around it. Who made it? Who owned it? Was it lost, or was it cast aside?"

"Why would someone throw away a perfectly good brooch?" demanded Selena Buxton.

"I can think of many reasons," James replied. "If you put your mind to it, you can, too."

The villagers became thoughtful, as though they were concocting scenarios ranging from temper tantrums to broken engagements to failed marriages. James Hobson was clearly a gifted teacher. My mother, I thought, would have approved.

Elspeth Binney was the first to break the spell.

"You could have put an advertisement in the paper," she suggested, bending to lift Bess into her arms, "saying you'd found something of value in such and such a place. The brooch's owner might have come forward to claim it."

"I did place an advert in the paper," said James, "but no one came forward. I like to think I've given it a good home in my museum."

"So," Sally Cook said slowly, "it's a . . . a private museum, is it? Not open to the public? No tearoom?"

Felicity pressed a hand to her mouth, presumably to keep herself from laughing, but James responded to Sally's questions without betraying a hint of amusement.

"My museum is nothing more than the room in which I display my finds," he explained. "I display them for my own pleasure, but once I've unpacked and organized them, you'll be welcome to view them, free of charge, whenever you like—within reason."

The villagers smiled broadly this time, and Sally Cook's worried frown vanished.

"I'll be happy to make a cup of tea for anyone who stops by," James added, "but if you want a really good cup of tea, I suggest that you continue to patronize Mrs. Cook's charming establishment."

Sally beamed at him.

"I'm sure we'll all enjoy viewing your finds and listening to the stories you've invented about them, James," she said. "But we've taken up enough of your time this morning. You must have better things to do than to stand around in your garden, talking to us."

"I'm afraid we do," said Felicity, stepping forward. "We've hardly begun to unpack. I'll probably spend the next half hour hunting for dishes so James and I can have our lunch."

"Don't you worry about cooking," said Opal. "We'll fill your fridge before you can say snap."

"If there's any heavy lifting to be done, I'm your man," said Mr. Barlow.

"I'll bring a keg of ale along," said Dick, "to spare you the walk to the pub."

"There's no need—" Felicity began, but Sally silenced her polite protest.

"Of course there's a need," said Sally. "Moving house is no joke. We'd be ashamed of ourselves if we left you two to fend for yourselves."

"Well, then . . . thank you," said Felicity, admitting defeat with a grateful smile.

"When you've got your place sorted out, James," said Mr. Barlow, "I'd like to take a look at this detector gizmo of yours."

"So would I," said Charles Bellingham.

"I think we all would," said Grant Tavistock. "I don't suppose you'd consider giving a demonstration, would you? We could hold it in the old schoolhouse—it's our village hall."

"It'd make more sense to hold it on the village green," Mr. Barlow pointed out. "There's nothing under the schoolhouse but a stone foundation. The green might have anything buried in it."

"A truer word was never spoken," said James. "All right, then . . . In response to popular demand, I'll give a demonstration on the village green as soon as our home is presentable." He bent his head toward Mr. Barlow. "How does one make announcements in Finch?"

"Church bulletin board," Mr. Barlow replied.

"Then you can look for an announcement on the church bulletin board very soon," said James.

"Much obliged," said Mr. Barlow. "We'll be off, then."

With a jerk of his head, Mr. Barlow signaled to the others to follow him along the brick path that would take them back to the lane. Elspeth Binney paused only to return Bess to me.

"I hope you like casseroles," I said to the Hobsons after the villagers had departed. "Because you're about to receive quite a few."

"We'll take whatever's given and be thankful for it," said Felicity. "It'll be a luxury to have someone else cook for us. We'll use the spare time to shop for a new blender in Upper Deeping."

"I forbid it," I said adamantly. "If you manage to carve out some free time over the next few days, put your feet up and relax. I'll bring you a blender."

"You're a generous lot, aren't you?" James observed.

"No more generous than you," I said. "You did very well, James. The villagers won't forget it."

"It truly was my pleasure," said James. "I could talk about my hobby for hours on end."

"And yet," said Felicity, "you were the soul of brevity." She kissed her husband on the cheek.

"I wouldn't worry about brevity when you tell the villagers the tragic tale of your cliff-top cottage," I said. "You're right, James. They'll gobble it up."

"You've reminded me that it's lunchtime," said Felicity, pressing a hand to her stomach. "Will you share our casseroles with us, Lori?"

"Thanks, but Bess and I will follow our neighbors' example and get out of your hair," I said. "You must be longing to have the cottage to yourselves."

"Let me drive you home," James offered.

"No, thanks," I said. "A quiet walk will be better for Bess after her action-packed morning."

The couple accompanied Bess and me to the pram, then to the gate, where they waved us off. I returned the friendly gesture, then set out for home, convinced that Ivy Cottage was in very good hands indeed.

"Remind me to look for the blender," I said to Bess, but she was too busy chewing on her blanket to respond.

As I strolled up the leaf-strewn lane, thinking of crumbling cliffs, bronze pennies, tatty brooches, and my lunch, I couldn't have known that my search for a simple appliance would take me on a journey through space and time. I couldn't have known that it would mark the beginning of my very own treasure hunt.

Five

The blue sky had vanished behind a heavy blanket of clouds by the time Bess and I reached the cottage, but the rain was unusually considerate. It waited until we were indoors to come bucketing down.

I said hello to Stanley, who was in the living room, curled snugly in Bill's favorite armchair, and wheeled the pram down the hallway to its parking place in the solarium. Bess was entranced by the rain cascading down the glass walls, so we stayed put for a while, watching the world through a glimmering waterfall.

Bess stayed awake long enough for a hearty lunch, a diaper change, and a spirited game of peekaboo, but she nodded off shortly thereafter, worn out by the fresh air and her burgeoning social life. I carried her upstairs to the nursery, settled her in her crib, turned on the baby monitor, and left her to dream about a world filled with teething rings.

"Next stop, attic," I murmured as I closed the nursery door.

I clipped the baby monitor's mobile receiver to a belt loop on my blue jeans, then took a short pole from the linen closet and used its hooked end to open the trap door in the hall ceiling and to pull down the attic's folding ladder. It wasn't a smooth operation—it never was—but I knew that the thumps, bumps, and grumbling wouldn't bother my sleeping beauty.

The roar of rain battering the slate roof surged into the hallway when I opened the trap door, reminding me that the day had gone from sunlit to stygian. Since the attic was illuminated by one dim, dusty lightbulb and two small, grimy windows, one at each gable end, I took a flashlight from a drawer in my bedside table and brought it with me as I climbed the ladder.

When Bill and I first moved into the cottage, the attic had been empty, apart from a light coating of dust and an old leather trunk that had been tucked away in a dark corner by the cottage's previous owner. Before the twins had come along, the wide floorboards had been clutter free, and nothing had concealed the hand-hewn roof beams, the burly tie beams, or the slender laths beneath the slate tiles.

The attic had changed a lot since then. The beams and the laths were still visible, and the old trunk was still tucked away in its dark corner, but the dust had become omnipresent and the floorboards could no longer be described as "clutter free." After more than a decade of use, our attic had come to resemble a badly organized garage sale.

The dangling lightbulb revealed a maze of storage boxes overflowing with Christmas ornaments, Halloween decorations, Easter paraphernalia, camping gear, picnic supplies, wrapping paper, toys the boys had outgrown but couldn't quite part with, miscellaneous odds and ends I'd saved for rainy-day crafts projects, the quilting squares I'd temporarily set aside after the twins had been born, and an embarrassing array of sports equipment—tennis racquets, golf clubs, badminton sets—that rarely saw the light of day.

Some of the boxes contained nothing but packing material. Bill had stowed them in the attic in case he had to return an electronic device in its original packaging. Though he'd never returned a single device, he'd accumulated an outstanding collection of boxes.

As I picked my way through the maze, ducking under a tie beam and stepping over a fluffy purple stegosaurus that had escaped from its storage container, I made the same vow I made whenever I visited the attic.

"You've got to clean this place up, Lori," I muttered. "It won't take more than a day or two to get it organized. Next week. I'll do it next week."

I meant it every time and forgot it just as often.

Our surplus wedding gifts—unopened, untouched, and still in their original boxes—had been the first of our possessions to find a home in the attic. Bill and I had stacked them neatly next to the old trunk in the corner, intending to wait for a decent interval to pass before we donated them to the thrift store in Upper Deeping.

The decent interval had passed so long ago that it had become indecent, but the Crock-Pots, coffeemakers, juicers, rice cookers, toasters, bread-making machines, and all but one of the blenders hadn't gone anywhere. Though their colorful boxes were now furred with dust and linked by cobwebs, they remained in their neat stacks.

I switched on my flashlight as I approached the dark corner, feeling like an appliance archaeologist. A reminiscent smile curled my lips when its beam picked out the boxes Bill and I had toted up the ladder after we'd returned from our honeymoon. He'd volunteered to tackle the chore himself, but I'd told him that we'd tackle it together or not at all. My somewhat belligerent offer of help had provoked a highly memorable kiss that had been repeated several times while we were in the attic.

With a happy sigh, I moved forward to continue my search. I knew which blender I wanted to give to the Hobsons—it was an exact duplicate of the one I used— but I couldn't remember its precise location. As I squatted before the wall of wedding gifts, I murmured a brief word of thanks to the world's appliance manufacturers for packaging their wares in illustrated boxes. I could barely make out the written descriptions, but the colorful photographs showed me that the model I sought was at the very bottom of the blender stack. To make matters worse, the blender stack was in the middle of the wedding gift wall.

With a less happy sigh, I placed the flashlight on the floor and began to dismantle the blender stack. Though I handled each box as gingerly as a bomb disposal expert, I couldn't avoid stirring up a cloud of dust. When the dust hit my nostrils, the inevitable happened.

My sneeze didn't topple the wedding gifts, but a violent jerk of my hands did. One brain-rattling sneeze followed another as the dusty boxes tumbled pell-mell to the floor, knocking me onto my bottom but doing no real harm until a plummeting juicer struck the flashlight and sent it spinning around the old trunk and into the dark corner.

After the dust settled—more or less—and my sneezing fit stopped, I pulled a crumpled tissue from my pocket, blew my nose, and took stock of my situation. On the plus side, the Hobsons' blender was lying at my feet. On the minus side, the surplus wedding gifts were in disarray and the flashlight was beyond my reach.

"Drat," I said.

By the dim and distant light of the dangling bulb, I picked up the blender and put it behind me, then patiently restacked the gifts, vowing under my breath to donate them to the thrift store by the end of the week.

"If Bill offers to bring them down, I'll let him," I grumbled. "I've had my fill of the attic."

I put the last coffeemaker back in place, then crawled around the reconstructed wall to retrieve my flashlight. It had come to rest in the narrow gap between the old trunk and the attic's stone wall, with its beam pointing in an entirely useless direction.

I was so eager to leave the attic that I stuck my arm into the narrow space without a second thought. I felt a sense of relief when my groping fingers bumped into the flashlight, but I quickly snatched them back as its beam swung around to reveal a gleaming row of beady red eyes peering at me from the shadows.

I recoiled with a horrified squeal.

"Mice," I breathed, my heart racing.

Though I wasn't abnormally fearful of mice, I didn't relish the thought of sticking my fingers into a nest filled with them. I sat back on my heels and listened for the pitter-patter of tiny clawed feet that would signal a rodent retreat, but it was an exercise in futility. I couldn't hear anything through the rain's constant din, except for the baby monitor and my thundering heart. I contemplated beating a hasty retreat of my own until I imagined the look on Bill's face when I told him that I'd been chased out of the attic by a handful of beady-eyed mice.

I made a mental note to have a serious talk with Stanley about a feline's household duties, reminded myself that I was a big girl, and looked cautiously into the shadowy gap.

The red eyes were still there, and so, presumably, were the mice. They seemed to be frozen in place, as if the poor creatures were too terrified to move. I banged on the trunk, hoping to release them from their paralysis, but they didn't even blink.

"I just want my flashlight," I explained, raising my voice to be heard above the rain.

Nothing happened. Puzzled, I leaned forward and realized with a mixture of relief and embarrassment that I'd been completely mistaken. I hadn't discovered a mouse family hiding behind the old trunk. I'd discovered a piece of jewelry. Chiding myself for being both a ninny *and* a nincompoop, I rescued the flashlight and the glittering trinket, then sat back to examine my find.

It was a cuff bracelet, about two inches wide, and designed to fit a wrist much bigger than mine. There was nothing tatty about it. The bracelet appeared to be made of solid gold inlaid from one edge to the other with an intricate, intertwining pattern of small, simply cut garnets that gleamed in the flashlight's beam like drops of wine.

"Mouse eyes," I scoffed, running a fingertip over the garnets.

Despite James Hobson's cautionary tale about the monetary worth of his brooch, I was confident that my bracelet was the real deal. I'd seen enough antique jewelry to distinguish between the warm glow of old gold and the harsh shine of plated brass, and I doubted that fake gems could mimic the garnets' rich, deep shade of burgundy.

I wondered how such a precious object could have lain undetected in the shadows for so many years, but when I recalled the rosy haze of newlywed bliss that had filled the attic when I'd last approached the old trunk, I understood. On that day, Bill and I had been so absorbed in each other that a shower of gold coins could have rained down on us and we wouldn't have noticed. It had certainly never occurred to us to look behind the trunk for lost jewelry, and once we'd constructed the wedding gift wall, the trunk had been effectively concealed.

Though I was certain that I'd found a treasure, I was also certain that it didn't belong to me. Bill had given me quite a few pretty baubles and I'd purchased some for myself, but I had nothing to compare with the bracelet. If it had fallen out of the old trunk, however, then

I knew exactly who owned it. I wasn't sure how I would return it to her, but I could at least tell her I'd found it.

I rose creakily to my feet, stuffed the bracelet into my pocket, picked up the blender, and began the long journey from the attic's outermost reaches to a comfortable chair in the study.

I needed to speak with Aunt Dimity.

Six

*F*descended the ladder, restored order to the hallway, and looked in on Bess, who was still in dreamland. Though I was in desperate need of a shower, I gritted my gritty teeth, bypassed the bathroom, and went downstairs. I left the Hobsons' blender on the table in the front hall and brought the glittering bracelet with me into the study.

The study was quieter than the attic had been, but it wasn't much brighter. Rain pummeled the strands of ivy that crisscrossed the diamond-paned windows above the old oak desk, and the autumnal gloom sent a chill through me that had nothing to do with the room's actual temperature. In self-defense, I knelt to light a fire in the hearth. I waited until the flames were leaping high enough to warm me inside and out, then stood to greet my oldest friend in the world.

"Hi, Reginald," I said, pulling cobwebs from my hair. "Yes, I know I'm a mess. I've been up in the attic. You won't believe what I found there."

Reginald was a small, powder-pink flannel rabbit with black button eyes and beautifully hand-sewn whiskers. My mother had placed him in my bassinet shortly after my birth, and he'd been by my side ever since. A sensible woman would have put him away when she put away childish things, but I wasn't a sensible woman. My pink bunny sat in a special niche in the study's tall bookshelves, where I could see him and speak with him and let him know that he was not forgotten.

Reginald's black button eyes blushed crimson when I held the garnet bracelet up for his inspection.

"I found it behind the old trunk in the attic," I informed him. "I'm pretty sure it belongs to Aunt Dimity, but I won't be one hundred percent certain until I ask her."

I wiped my hands carefully on my jeans before I gave Reginald's pink flannel ears an affectionate twiddle, then reached for a book that sat on the shelf next to his. The book was a journal bound in blue leather and filled with blank pages. Though I had no intention of writing in it, I took it with me to one of the tall leather armchairs that faced the hearth.

I'd inherited the blue journal from my late mother's closest friend, an Englishwoman named Dimity Westwood. The two had met in London while serving their respective countries during the Second World War. Together they had endured bombing raids, firestorms, and the constant fear of an enemy invasion, and their shared experiences—good and bad—had created a bond of affection between them that was never broken.

When the war in Europe ended and my mother sailed back to the States, she and Dimity maintained their friendship by sending hundreds of letters back and forth across the Atlantic. After my father's sudden death, those letters became my mother's refuge, a peaceful retreat from the daily pressures of working full time as a teacher while raising a rambunctious daughter on her own.

My mother was very protective of her refuge. She told no one about it, not even her only child. When I was growing up, I knew Dimity Westwood only as Aunt Dimity, the redoubtable heroine of a series of bedtime stories told to me by my mother. I had no idea that my favorite fictional character was a real woman until after both she and my mother had died.

It was then that Dimity Westwood bequeathed to me a comfortable fortune, the honey-colored cottage in which she'd spent her childhood, the precious postwar correspondence she'd exchanged with my mother, and a curious book bound in blue leather. It was through the blue journal that I finally met the real Aunt Dimity.

Whenever I opened the journal, Aunt Dimity's handwriting would appear, an old-fashioned copperplate taught in the village school at a time when plow horses could still be seen in furrowed fields. I'd nearly fainted the first time it happened, but once I'd recovered from the shock, I'd realized that Aunt Dimity's intentions were wholly benevolent.

I couldn't explain how Aunt Dimity's spirit managed to remain in the cottage long after her mortal remains had been laid to rest in the churchyard—and she wasn't too clear about it, either—but the love I felt for her needed no explanation. She was as good a friend to me as she'd been to my mother. I simply refused to imagine life without her.

By the light of the flickering flames, I placed the garnet bracelet on the ottoman, seated myself in the tall leather armchair, and opened the blue journal.

"Dimity?" I said. "I have a question to ask you."

I smiled as the familiar lines of royal-blue ink began to curl and loop across the blank page.

Only one, my dear? I have at least a thousand questions to ask you. Was there a good turnout for the moving van vigil? Was it instructive, or did you arrive too late to see anything of interest?

"The moving van was nearly empty by the time Bess and I reached William's gates," I replied, "but it didn't matter. Thanks to the villagers' paranoia and my skill at deciphering Felicity Hobson's handwriting, I was allowed to walk straight into Ivy Cottage. I spent half the morning chatting with Felicity and her husband, James."

You broke the three-day rule? And lived to tell the tale?

"The villagers waived the three-day rule," I said.

Congratulations, Lori. You have succeeded in astonishing me. Why did the villagers waive the three-day rule? What triggered their paranoia? Why did you have to decipher Felicity Hobson's handwriting? Do you like the Hobsons, or will you need more than half a morning to decide? I'll let you know when I reach my thousandth question, but the ones I've asked just now are enough to be going on with.

I lowered the journal to look at the garnet bracelet, then put it out of my mind while I told Aunt Dimity about the museum boxes, the villagers' fears, and my unexpectedly smooth entry into Ivy Cottage. I told her about the illegible checklist, the reheated carrot purée, and the coastal erosion that had driven the Hobsons from one dream home to another. I mentioned Felicity's love of gardening as well as James's passion for metal detecting, and I confessed to warning them about their sense of humor. Finally, I described the talk James had given about his hobby and the interest it had aroused in the villagers.

"James plans to give a metal-detecting demonstration on the village green as soon as he and Felicity have finished unpacking," I concluded. "It should draw a big crowd. He's an excellent teacher."

High praise, coming from the daughter of another excellent teacher. It sounds as though the Hobsons will be a definite asset to Finch.

"They will," I agreed. "Bess and I like them very much."

When will you see them next?

"Tomorrow morning," I said. "Their blender was broken during the move, so I'm giving them one of our spare wedding gifts."

One of the gifts you haven't yet donated to the charity shop?

"It's just as well I haven't," I retorted. "If I were an efficient housekeeper, I wouldn't have had a blender on hand to give away."

Fair point.

The clock on the mantel shelf chimed the quarter hour, and I realized that the afternoon was slipping away. Since I wanted to take a quick shower before getting Bess up for the school run, I began to talk a little faster.

"While I was in the attic, looking for the blender," I said, "I found something I wasn't looking for."

I imagine you found quite a few things you weren't looking for. Spiders, for example. And moths.

"If there were spiders and moths up there, I didn't see them," I said, thanking God for small favors. "I thought I'd found a nest of mice, but it was a false alarm."

Of course it was. Stanley is a hardworking cat.

"Stanley spends most of his time asleep in Bill's chair," I pointed out.

True, but when he's not sleeping, he works very hard.

I laughed and pressed on.

"To return to the attic," I continued. "What I thought was a mouse's nest turned out to be a splendid piece of jewelry. It was hidden behind your old trunk."

There was a pause before the handwriting resumed.

A splendid piece of jewelry? What sort of jewelry?

"A gold and garnet bracelet," I said. "I've never seen anything like—" I broke off as a few brief words appeared on the page.

Oh, dear. Oh, no. The graceful lines of royal-blue ink stopped flowing. When they began again, they were shaky and faint. *Forgive me, Lori, but I must go. I must compose myself before we continue.*

"I'm sorry, Dimity," I said in dismay. "I didn't mean to upset you."

It's not your fault, my dear. You couldn't have known. Come back later. We'll speak then.

I waited for Aunt Dimity's handwriting to fade slowly from the page, as it always did, but it vanished in an instant, like a snuffed candle flame. Bewildered, I closed the blue journal and stared at the bracelet through narrowed eyes. The garnets glittered in the firelight like drops of blood.

Only once before had Aunt Dimity ended a conversation so abruptly. It had happened soon after our first meeting, when I'd unknowingly touched on a subject too tender for her to discuss.

"Bobby," I whispered.

Bobby MacLaren had been the great love of Aunt Dimity's life. She'd met him during the war, a few weeks before she'd met my mother. He'd been a dashing young fighter pilot, and like so many dashing young fighter pilots, he'd been shot down over the English Channel. His body had never been recovered.

Had I blundered again? I wondered. Had Bobby given the bracelet to Aunt Dimity? Had its reemergence reawakened memories she found hard to bear?

"Reginald," I said, looking up at my powder-pink bunny, "what have I done?"

A somber gleam lit his black button eyes. With a heavy heart, I rose slowly to my feet and returned the blue journal to its shelf. Almost as an afterthought, I placed the garnet bracelet in Reginald's niche.

"Look after it for me," I told him. "I think it has a tale to tell."

If it hadn't been for Bess, I would have gone through the rest of the day in a distracted daze. Babies tend to concentrate the mind, however, and my maternal responsibilities prevented me from dwelling on what had happened in the study.

My concentration didn't slip until we were halfway through

dinner. Will and Rob laughed uproariously when I filled my water glass with gravy, and Bill didn't even try to hide his mirth. I left the dinner table knowing that the hilarious story of Mummy's glassful of gravy would be told for decades to come.

After the boys went to bed, I retrieved the garnet bracelet from Reginald's niche in the study and joined Bill, Bess, and Stanley in the living room. Bill was sitting in his favorite armchair, Bess was asleep in her father's arms, and Stanley the hardworking cat was snoozing on the bay window's cushioned window seat. I stirred the fire Bill had lit in the hearth, then sat on the chintz sofa, curled my legs beneath me, and put my thoughts in order.

"You were in another world during dinner," Bill observed. "What's on your mind? If you're thirsty, I can get you a cup of gravy."

"No, thanks," I said with a rueful smile. "As a matter of fact, I do have something on my mind. I haven't had a chance to tell you yet, but Bess and I met the new people in Ivy Cottage—James and Felicity Hobson."

"I know," said Bill. "I know all about the Hobsons, too."

"How?" I asked.

"I had a late lunch in the pub," he replied.

"Dick Peacock," I said, as understanding dawned. "Dick filled you in on the Hobsons after he brought them the keg of ale."

"It wasn't just Dick," said Bill. "Everyone who dropped into the pub had something new to say about the Hobsons. It sounded as though half the village had been in and out of Ivy Cottage, delivering food and drink, helping to arrange the furniture, and poking their noses into every closet, cabinet, and drawer. The ladies repaired to the tearoom to compare notes, but Charles, Grant, and Mr. Barlow came to the pub to talk things over." He shrugged. "It's a small pub. I couldn't help overhearing."

Bill wasn't as interested in gossip as I was, but he understood its role in village life, and he made no attempt to avoid it when it was handed to him on a plate.

"So you know about the cliff-top cottage?" I inquired.

"Yes," said Bill.

"And the sick grandchildren in Upper Deeping?"

"Yes."

"And the metal detecting?"

"*Especially* the metal detecting," said Bill. "Charles, Grant, Dick, and Mr. Barlow kept talking about the things they'd seen in James Hobson's museum room. They can't wait to get their hands on one of those gadgets."

"James showed them his finds?" I said with a touch of envy.

"It sounds as though he showed them a world-class collection of junk," said Bill, "but you know the old saying: One man's trash . . ."

"Is another man's treasure," I said, completing the bromide. "There's one piece of trash James won't display in his museum room. I'll bet your pub pals didn't tell you about the broken blender."

"They didn't," Bill acknowledged, "but Opal Taylor did. She came to my office to let me know that you were replacing the Hobsons' broken blender with one of ours. She thought it was a very neighborly thing to do."

"I should have guessed," I said. "Opal regards it as her duty to organize other people's kitchens. Felicity must have mentioned the broken blender while Opal was rearranging her pantry."

"Sounds about right," said Bill, chuckling.

"Okay," I said. "Since you're up to speed on the Hobsons, I can skip them and go directly to the strange thing that happened this afternoon."

Bess gave an undignified snuffle, and Bill made soft crooning noises to soothe her. Since he'd looked after her from the day she was born, he didn't need my help to calm her when she was fussy.

"You were saying?" he said after Bess settled down.

"I was up in the attic, looking for the replacement blender," I told him, "when I thought I saw some mice hiding behind Aunt Dimity's old trunk."

Bill's sly grin made me happier than ever that I hadn't fled the attic, screaming for help, like a dim-witted damsel in distress.

"Yes," I said stoically, in response to his implied question, "I did have a brief moment of panic, but no, I didn't give in to it. I stood my ground, took a second look, and found . . . *this.*"

I pulled the garnet bracelet from my pocket and held it out for Bill to see. He studied it in silence, then gave a low whistle.

"Beautiful," he said. "Was it Dimity's?"

My husband was one of the scant handful of people who were in on the secret of Aunt Dimity and the blue journal. Unlike me, he'd had the privilege of meeting Dimity Westwood before her death. He'd been a young boy at the time, and the meeting had been relatively brief, but he'd never forgotten it.

"I think so," I replied hesitantly, lowering my hand. "Well, it must be hers, right? I've never owned anything like it, and I doubt that a stranger would sneak into our attic and drop it behind Dimity's old trunk just for the heck of it." I frowned at the bracelet for a moment, then returned it to my pocket. "It must belong to Aunt Dimity."

"There's a fairly reliable way to find out," said Bill. "Ask her."

"I did," I said. "I came down from the attic and went straight to the study to tell her about the bracelet, but when I mentioned it, she cut our conversation short and asked me to come back later, after she'd had time to compose herself. It really upset her, Bill."

"And upsetting her, upset you," he said gently. "That explains the gravy."

"I'm lucky I didn't pour it in my lap," I admitted.

"Do you think Bobby MacLaren gave the bracelet to her?" Bill asked shrewdly. "Do you think it touched a nerve?"

"I do," I said. "I wish I'd thought of Bobby sooner. If I had, I would have revealed the bracelet gradually instead of springing it on her. I feel as if I ripped open an old wound."

"If you did, I'm sure Dimity will forgive you," said Bill. "Cheer up, Lori. It's not as if she'll never speak to you again. She asked you to come back later, didn't she?"

"Yes," I said, "but I don't want to upset her again."

"She's had time to compose herself," Bill pointed out. "Go ahead. I'll look after Bess." He gazed down at his little princess and heaved a contented sigh. "I've looked forward to looking after her all day."

Seven

The rainstorm had stopped just before sunset. The study was dark and silent. I lit the mantel lamps, then knelt to light a fire in the hearth. The somber gleam in Reginald's black button eyes seemed to soften in the firelight. I took it as a sign of encouragement, reached for the blue journal, and carried the slender volume with me to the armchair I'd occupied earlier.

I stared into the fire, wondering what would happen when I opened the journal. Would its blank pages remain blank? Would they be covered with exclamation points and angry words written in BIG LETTERS? Would Aunt Dimity be cold and distant? Would she pretend that nothing had happened? I didn't know what to expect.

I was so worried about saying the wrong thing that my voice trembled slightly as I opened the journal and said, "Dimity?"

My entire body relaxed when her handwriting appeared, flowing smoothly across the blank page without a moment's hesitation.

Please forgive me, my dear.

"You're asking me to forgive you?" I said in surprise. "Shouldn't it be the other way around?"

No, it shouldn't. It was thoughtless of me to leave you hanging, without a word of explanation. You must have felt as though you'd done something to offend me.

"I thought I'd reopened an old wound," I said cautiously.

You did reopen an old wound, Lori, but it isn't the wound you're thinking of. You helped me come to terms with Bobby MacLaren's death. When I remember him now, I'm at peace.

"Then why did you shut down when I told you about the bracelet?" I asked.

The bracelet you found in the attic wasn't given to me by Bobby but by someone else.

I leaned forward, hardly believing what I was reading.

"Someone else?" I said. "I didn't know there'd been someone other than Bobby."

How could you? I've never told you about him. I haven't thought of him in years, but the garnet bracelet brought it all back—every word, every look, every smile. It's somewhat disorienting to have distant memories rekindled unexpectedly. I had to regain my balance before I could speak with you again.

"I didn't mean to upset you," I said earnestly. "And if you'd rather not talk about . . . him . . . I'll understand."

Don't be absurd, Lori. You're a Finch-trained snoop. If I dangled a tantalizing hint in front of you, then refused to talk about it, you wouldn't understand. You'd go stark, staring mad.

"I probably would," I acknowledged. "But I'd rather go mad than cause you the smallest amount of pain."

You can ease my pain by listening.

"I'm all ears," I said readily.

It's rather a long story.

"The boys are in bed, and Bess is with Bill." I leaned back in the chair and stretched my legs out on the ottoman. "I have all night."

The handwriting paused, as though Aunt Dimity were marshaling her thoughts, then continued to unfurl across the page in graceful lines of royal-blue ink.

I was seventeen when England declared war on Germany. My parents thought I was too young to enlist, but I was determined to do my duty. I joined the Auxiliary Territorial Service as a volunteer, not as a conscript. Though university had been beyond my reach, I'd taken a secretarial course in Upper Deeping. My qualifications led to my assignment as an extremely junior clerical worker in the War Office. As your mother used to say, "We also serve who only type and file."

My mother had said the same thing to me, though in the past tense, when describing her contributions to the war effort. To see the familiar phrase appear in Aunt Dimity's familiar handwriting reminded me of how close the two had been.

Two other ATS recruits and I were billeted in a flat in Soho. A single gas ring served as our cooker. We had no icebox, no hot water, and barely enough room to dress, but we spent so much time at the War Office or huddled in air raid shelters that none of it really mattered. We were willing to live without home comforts because we knew we were doing something of value.

Aunt Dimity had never before spoken so fluently of her life in wartime London. I was keen to hear more.

"What was it like," I asked, "living in London during the Blitz?"

It should have frightened us out of our wits, but it didn't. We weren't naïve. We walked to work through streets piled high with debris. The whole city reeked of charred wood and burning rubber, and there was so much ash and dust floating about, it was like a fog. We saw dead bodies almost every day—some lying in the open, others discreetly draped, all awaiting transport to the overcrowded morgues—but though they saddened us, they didn't frighten us. We learned very quickly to accept death and destruction as the price of war. I suppose we became fatalistic. I remember your mother saying once, "If a bomb has my name on it, there's nothing I can do to stop it, so why worry?" It made all the sense in the world to me.

"Even after you lost Bobby?" I asked carefully.

I lived under a black cloud after I lost Bobby, but your mother's friendship brought me into the light again. She made me want to work harder than ever to end the war. And it did end, eventually, though we felt its aftereffects for many years. The war nearly bankrupted Great Britain. Cities as well as lives had to be rebuilt at a time when basic resources were scarce. There was a housing shortage, a petrol shortage, a coal shortage, a clothing shortage, every kind of shortage you can imagine. When people saw a queue, they joined it on the off chance that it would lead to something they needed. Food rationing didn't come to a complete end in Britain until 1954—nearly ten years after peace was declared.

"Ten years?" I exclaimed. "I had no idea."

It's not something that's taught at school. History books describe the euphoria of VE Day and VJ Day—the street parties, the bonfires, the parades—but they seldom mention what came after. We were utterly exhausted, body and soul, yet we had to find the strength to repair a shattered world. It was as if we'd climbed a mountain, only to find ourselves on a false summit, with the highest peak still beyond our reach. When the giddiness wore off, many of us were depressed, disillusioned, and desperately frustrated.

A log fell on the fire, sending up a shower of sparks, and the handwriting paused again. I neither knew nor cared whether Aunt Dimity had forgotten about the garnet bracelet. I had no intention of interrupting her.

My flatmates went home after the war ended, as did your mother. I chose to remain in London, but I had to give up the Soho flat when I was demobbed. Fortunately, I had another friend, a nurse who'd worked at Great Ormond Street Hospital during the war, when it was used as a casualty clearing station. She'd taken a year's leave of absence to study nursing in America, and she allowed me to use her flat in Bloomsbury while she was away. I moved from Soho to number sixteen Northington Street and wondered what to do next.

"Did you know about Bobby's will by then?" I asked. "Did you know that he'd named you as his sole heir?"

Oh, yes. His brother had carried out his wishes and transferred the bequest to me. I was a comparatively wealthy woman when I moved into my friend's flat, but I didn't know what to do with my wealth. I'd grown up in a modest home in a small village. I'd had a good, basic education, but it hadn't taught me how to deal with large sums of money.

"Sounds familiar," I said dryly. "I was living from paycheck to paycheck when I found out that I was your sole heir. It took a bit of getting used to."

You had Bill and his father to guide you, Lori. I had no one.

"You had your own good sense," I said.

You're very kind, Lori, and you may even be right. I certainly had no desire to spend my inheritance on fripperies. It would have been shameful to buy hats and shoes and dresses for myself when so many people were going without. I wanted to use Bobby's bequest in a way that would honor his sacrifice. He'd given his life for his country. He'd set an example of selflessness I wished to emulate.

I said nothing, but I already knew what Aunt Dimity had done with Bobby's bequest. She'd used it to create the Westwood Trust, a charitable organization that was still going strong more than half a century after its founding. Though I was the trust's titular head, I knew little about its history. I'd never paused to ask myself, or Aunt Dimity, how a young woman from a small village had managed to establish such an enduring institution. I settled more deeply into my chair and gazed at the blue journal with renewed fascination. I suspected that a hitherto untold story was about to unfold before my eyes: the story behind the founding of the Westwood Trust.

A statue wouldn't do, nor would a marble slab inscribed with praise for Bobby's valor. He would have hated the attention—and the pigeons! I turned many ideas over in my mind, and I began to take long walks through London, searching for inspiration. *My walks always ended at the Rose Café on St. Megwen's Lane, a tiny byway just around the corner from my friend's flat. The café wasn't fancy—no place was, in those days—but it was popular among the locals because its proprietor, Mr. Hanover, overcame the rigors of rationing and served a decent cup of tea. That's where I met Badger.*

"Badger?" I said. I squinted at the page to make sure I'd read the word correctly.

That's how he introduced himself to me after I accepted his invitation to take a seat at his table. The café was crammed with customers when I arrived. If it hadn't been for Badger's gallantry, I would have had to drink my tea standing up, an unpleasant proposition for a woman who'd spent the day walking.

"Why did he call himself Badger?" I asked. "It wasn't his given name, was it?"

He explained that "Badger" was a nickname given to him by his father when he was a young boy.

"Was he bad tempered?" I inquired. "Badgers can be pretty feisty."

Badger wasn't at all feisty. He was thoroughly good-natured, and he had a wonderful sense of humor. A bad-tempered man wouldn't have offered me a seat at his table.

"It'd be a good nickname for a church sexton," I said, thinking of Mr. Barlow and the graves he'd dug in St. George's churchyard. "Badgers do a lot of digging."

I have no idea what Badger's profession was. He never revealed his given name, either. I knew him only as Badger, the nice young man I met from time to time at my neighborhood café.

"Did he look like a badger?" I asked interestedly. "Did he have white streaks in his hair and a long, pointy nose?"

He bore not the slightest resemblance to a badger, Lori. He had a beard and a mustache and a headful of dark, tousled curls—like yours, only darker. He had large, lovely dark eyes, and his nose was no longer or pointier than Bill's.

"How old was he?" I asked, with a villager's thirst for details.

I'm not sure, but he couldn't have been much older than I—in his late twenties or early thirties. His clothes were dated and a bit threadbare— patched elbows on his tweed jacket and pleats in his trousers—as if he'd purchased them from a secondhand shop or inherited them from an elderly relation. I assumed he was a gardener.

"Badger would work as a nickname for a gardener," I said. "Gardeners do even more digging than church sextons."

He certainly looked as though he worked outdoors. He was fit and trim and very brown, and he had a gardener's strong, rough hands. I doubted that he was an ordinary jobbing gardener, though. He had the accent and the vocabulary of a well-educated young man.

I gave a small snort of exasperation.

"Guesswork," I said. "Speculation. It's not your style, Dimity. Forgive me, but I'm not the only Finch-trained snoop here. I find it hard to believe that you didn't have Badger's life story down pat within five minutes of introducing yourself to him."

But I didn't introduce myself to him. Not properly. I would have, but Badger stopped me.

"Why?" I asked.

He said that, once we started down the road of conventional conversation, there would be no turning back. We'd inevitably end up rehashing the war years, and he, for one, had no desire to go through them again. We could, he proposed, discuss the war with everyone else, everywhere else, but while we were together, in the café, we would put it out of our minds, along with our jobs, our families, our backgrounds, and every other predictable topic of conversation. He would be Badger, and I would be . . . well, I had no nickname, so I had to be Dimity, but we would check our surnames at the door, dismiss formality, and chat freely about whatever took our fancy.

"And you went along with it?" I asked.

I did. I found his suggestion delightfully liberating. Until that moment, I hadn't realized how completely the war had dominated every conversation I'd had for the past five years. It was a relief to put it aside and make room for other things.

"Such as?" I prompted.

Art, music, literature, architecture—the first hour I spent with Badger was one of the most enjoyable I've ever spent with anyone, and I'm happy to report that it wasn't the last. We shared a table at the café two or three times a week for the next three months.

"You spent three months talking to a stranger about art, music, literature, and architecture?" I said doubtfully.

Among many other things. My conversations with Badger inspired me to visit art galleries and museums, to attend plays and concerts, to broaden my cultural horizons. The war had shown me man's capacity for destruction. Badger reminded me of man's capacity to create. When I studied a painting or listened to a symphony or stood beneath St. Paul's magnificent dome, I felt a renewed sense of hope for the future. Though much had been destroyed, much remained, and much would be restored. Civilization would endure.

"Wow," I said ruefully. "Your conversations with Badger make my small talk seem pretty trivial. A cure for diaper rash doesn't really compare to the survival of civilization."

There's nothing trivial about nappy rash, Lori. If I'd had children, my small talk would have mimicked yours. Since I didn't, I could turn my thoughts in other directions.

"Did you tell Badger about your inheritance?" I asked.

Yes, but I didn't tell him about Bobby. Had I mentioned Bobby's death, I would have broken the bargain I'd made with Badger, so I said only that I'd come into an unexpected inheritance and that the dearest wish of my heart was to use it in a meaningful way. Badger suggested that I invest it. If I invested it wisely, he said, I would be able to fund a charity that would, with luck, continue well into the future. I told him that I knew nothing about investments. He challenged me to educate myself.

"And you took up the challenge," I said.

I couldn't resist it. I threw myself into learning everything I could about finance and I discovered, much to my surprise, that I had a knack for investments. Eventually, I created the Westwood Trust. I'd hoped to call it the Robert MacLaren Memorial Trust, but Bobby's family wished to reserve the name for a scholarship they had created.

"Badger must have been proud of you," I said.

I don't know whether he was proud of me or not. Badger was no longer part of my life by then.

"What went wrong?" I asked.

Toward the end of those three magical months, during one of my long walks through London, I saw a cuddly toy in a street market. It was a badger, and although it was somewhat bedraggled, I bought it and brought it to the café. I presented it to Badger as a silly gift, a small token of my gratitude for the many wonderful hours we'd spent together. The next day he presented me with the garnet bracelet and a passionate declaration of love.

"Oh, dear," I murmured.

I gave him a trifle, and he gave me his heart. I was stunned.

"You didn't see it coming?" I asked.

I didn't suspect for one moment that Badger felt anything for me but a playful sort of brotherly love. If I'd seen it coming, I would have done everything in my power to avert it. Unfortunately, I was having too much fun to be on the alert for signs of serious affection.

"You'd spent the entire war being alert," I said. "You can't blame yourself for letting your guard down with Badger. You'd earned the right to kick back and enjoy yourself."

I hadn't earned the right to hurt Badger. He'd changed my life for the better in more ways than I can count, but when he declared his love for me, I could do nothing but gape at him like an addled goldfish. He must have read rejection in my eyes, however, because he thrust the bracelet into my hands and left the café without another word. I'll never forget the look on his face as he left.

"Was he angry with you?" I asked.

Worse. He was angry with himself. He was ashamed of himself for daring to hope that he could ever be as dear to me as I was to him. It was as if he believed that he was unworthy of me. I would have told him how wrong he was, but I didn't have the chance. I never saw him again.

"Never?" I said.

I haunted the café for several weeks, but he never, to my knowledge, returned to it. I asked the other customers, the regulars, if they knew where he lived, but they had no idea. Mr. Hanover—the café's owner—didn't know, either. Before we'd met, Badger had rarely spoken to anyone, preferring instead to bury his head in a book while he drank his tea.

"Why did you want to know where he lived?" I asked. "You didn't intend to chase after him, did you? Wouldn't it have been kinder to let him go?"

Would it have been kinder to let him go, believing that he'd offended me? That his tenderest feelings had repulsed me? That he wasn't good enough for me? I think not. I wanted to tell Badger that he had no reason to reproach himself. I wanted to explain to him that I was and always would be incapable of loving anyone but Bobby. Our friendship might not have survived the revelation, but it wouldn't have ended so brutally.

"Badger might have absorbed the blow better if he'd known how devoted you were to Bobby," I conceded.

I should have tried harder to find him. I would have, but my life had become so busy by then, so filled with purpose, and so peripatetic—I moved seven times before finding a place of my own—that I let Badger fall by the wayside. I let him go without even learning his proper name. It was a poor way to repay a man who'd given me so much.

"Do you really think he expected repayment?" I asked.

I'm sure he didn't, but he deserved it all the same. He certainly didn't deserve to be tucked away in a distant corner of my memory like a plaything I'd outgrown.

"I suppose not," I said. "But there's no point in beating yourself up about it now. What's done cannot be undone."

I've never been overly fond of that particular quotation. It's hardly ever true, you know. What's done can very often be undone.

"Maybe, but I don't see how you can undo what you did to Badger," I said, eyeing the journal uncertainly. "It's a bit late in the day to go looking for him. Even if you could conduct a door-to-door search, I doubt that you'd find him at home. I hate to say it, Dimity, but your old friend is probably dead by now."

He's not. I don't know where he is, but he's definitely alive. If you put your mind to it, you could find him.

"I could what?" I said, startled.

You could find Badger. You could use the garnet bracelet as a calling card, to prove that you'd once known me. You could tell him how deeply I regretted the manner of our parting. You could explain why I couldn't return his love or anyone else's. It would put his mind at ease, I know it would.

My jaw dropped. It was, without exception, the most harebrained scheme Aunt Dimity had ever proposed. I didn't have to think hard to come up with several excellent reasons not to go through with it.

"If I were Badger," I said, "I'd be a little reluctant to discuss my private affairs with a total stranger."

He won't be reluctant, if he knows that I asked you to do this for me.

"What if he doesn't remember you?" I asked. "If he was thirty when you met him, he'd be pushing ninety now. He might not remember his own name, much less yours."

You won't know unless you meet him.

"What if he's happily married?" I demanded. "What if he never told Mrs. Badger about you? I don't think she'd be too pleased to hear that he was once madly in love with another woman."

You may have to make a few judgment calls, my dear. But I'm certain you'll make the right ones.

"Thanks," I said weakly, "but . . . it's a pretty tall order, Dimity. I don't know Badger's real name. I don't know where he lived. I don't know where he worked. He could have joined the Foreign Legion or emigrated to Brazil or become a melon farmer in Transylvania. How on earth am I supposed to follow his tracks when there are no tracks to follow?"

You'll think of something.

I wasn't accustomed to being the voice of reason in my exchanges with Aunt Dimity, but someone had to make her see sense.

"I wish I could help," I said. "I wish I could find Badger for you, Dimity, but it's too late. The trail went cold long before I was born. We all have regrets." I eyed the journal sympathetically. "Sometimes we just have to live with them."

No . . . I suppose you're right. It was selfish of me to ask you to do something I should have done. I'm sorry. I won't ask it of you again.

I shifted uncomfortably in my chair. I felt like a complete heel. Aunt Dimity was the least selfish person I'd ever known. I couldn't remember the last time she'd asked me for a favor. She was always too busy calming me down or cheering me up or giving me the benefit of her vast stores of wisdom to think about herself. Though the task she'd set for me was patently impossible, didn't the blue journal prove that the impossible was sometimes possible? I glanced at Reginald and saw a reproachful glint in his black button eyes. With a heavy sigh, I resigned myself to my fate.

"Okay, Dimity," I said. "I'll give it a shot."

Aunt Dimity's graceful script danced across the page.

I knew I could count on you!

"I wouldn't get your hopes up too high," I cautioned. "I'll give it a shot, but it's a long shot."

A long shot, my dear, is better than no shot at all.

Eight

returned to the living room, resumed my seat on the couch, and stared wordlessly at Bill, who was tapping away at his laptop while comfortably ensconced in his favorite armchair.

"I put Bess to bed," he said, without lifting his gaze, "and I looked in on the boys. All's quiet upstairs. How'd it go with Aunt Dimity?"

"She's not angry with me," I replied.

"I knew she wouldn't be," Bill murmured, with the distracted air of someone whose mind was somewhere else.

"She asked me to do something for her," I said.

"What's that?" Bill asked, still absorbed in his work.

"Nothing much," I said. "She wants me to look up a guy who fell in love with her in London about a thousand years ago and explain to him why she couldn't fall in love with him."

"She . . ." Bill stopped typing and peered at me uncomprehendingly. "I'm sorry, Lori. What did you say?"

Slowly and methodically and with a growing sense of how stupid I'd been to give Aunt Dimity any hope whatsoever, I recounted everything she'd related to me in the study. I described her experiences in wartime and postwar London, her search for a meaningful way to use Bobby MacLaren's bequest, and her fortuitous meeting with the bearded young man she'd known only as Badger.

I explained to Bill how important Badger had been to Aunt Dimity, how he'd opened her eyes to a world of beauty the war hadn't destroyed, restored her faith in the future, and enabled her to have enough confidence in herself to create the Westwood Trust. Finally, I described Badger's stunning declaration, Aunt Dimity's dumbfounded response, and Badger's swift and sorrowful exit from her life.

"He ran out of the café before she could explain herself," I concluded. "He didn't give her a chance to tell him that she could never love anyone but Bobby. She's convinced that she made him feel like a particularly repulsive form of pond scum, and she wants me to put him straight. So all I have to do is run down to London, knock on Badger's door, wave the garnet bracelet under his nose, and tell him that Dimity couldn't love him, not because he was a jerk, but because she'd pledged herself to Bobby for all eternity. Easy peasy."

I rested my chin in my hand and groaned.

"Did you agree to do it?" Bill asked, closing his laptop.

"Of course I did," I said. "I couldn't say no to Aunt Dimity. Not after everything she's done for me."

"You don't intend to drive to London, do you?" Bill asked, regarding me warily.

I usually bristled when Bill questioned my driving skills, but in this case, I shared his concerns. Tootling along Finch's leafy lanes was poor preparation for coping with motorway madness.

"I'm not suicidal," I replied. "I'll drive to Oxford and take the train into London."

"And once you get there . . . ?" Bill asked. "How are you going to find Badger? What's the plan?"

"Plan?" I said hopelessly. "I don't have a plan. I don't even know where to start."

"You could try to locate the Rose Café," Bill suggested. "Dimity said that it was patronized by locals, didn't she? Maybe Badger was a local. Maybe he lived in the surrounding neighborhood—maybe he still lives there."

"I think it's more than likely that the Rose Café went out of business decades ago," I said.

"You could find its original location," said Bill, "and work outward from there."

"How am I supposed to do that?" I asked. "I have a tourist's knowledge of London, Bill. I'm familiar with the big shiny sights, but I hardly ever go off the beaten track. I have no idea where the Great Ormond Street Hospital is, let alone a tiny byway called St. Megwen's Lane."

"They're both in Bloomsbury," Bill pointed out.

"Well, okay, then," I said peevishly. "Problem solved."

"Hold on." Bill opened his laptop, tapped a few keys, and nodded. "St. Megwen's Lane is just off Lamb's Conduit Street, which runs between Guilford Street and Theobalds Road," he informed me. "Generally speaking, it's behind the British Museum. You shouldn't have much trouble getting to the British Museum. We've taken Will and Rob there often enough."

"I can find the British Museum," I said with a distinct lack of enthusiasm. "But you know me, Bill. I'm not the world's greatest explorer. I'll probably get lost the minute I lose sight of the museum."

"I'll arrange for a driver to meet you at Paddington Station," Bill offered. "You can leave the navigating to him."

"Thanks," I said. "A native guide might be useful." I nodded at the laptop. "Is there, by any chance, a Rose Café on St. Megwen's Lane?"

After executing a few more keystrokes, Bill shook his head.

"No Rose Café," he said, "but there is a coffeehouse—Carrie's Coffees." He cocked his head to one side and said thoughtfully, "A coffeehouse would be a logical successor to a café that served a decent cup of tea."

"I hate coffee," I said petulantly.

"You don't have to drink it," said Bill.

"I'd have to smell it," I grumbled.

"A small price to pay for Aunt Dimity's peace of mind," Bill observed with admirable patience.

"What do I do when I get there?" I expostulated. "Ask the twenty-somethings manning the espresso machine if they serve low-fat lattes to an extremely senior citizen who calls himself Badger?"

"It's worth a try," said Bill. "If the locals are as loyal to Carrie's Coffees as they were to the Rose Café, you might run into someone who knows Badger or knows what became of him."

"I might run into the queen, too, but I doubt that I will," I said irritably. "The whole thing is ridiculous, Bill. How can I go to London when I have so much to do at home? There's no way I'm taking Bess with me. It would completely disrupt her routine."

"I hope you're not implying that I'm incapable of looking after our children," Bill said stiffly.

I could tell by his tone of voice that I'd stomped on a sore spot. My husband was a reformed workaholic. Though he'd missed great swaths of his sons' infancy, he hadn't missed much of his daughter's. For the past eight months, he'd done everything for Bess but nurse her, and he'd spent quite a lot of everyday time with Will and Rob as well. No one could accuse him of being an absentee dad and get away with it.

"I know you can take care of Bess and the boys," I said hastily, "but what about the cooking, the cleaning, the laundry, and the shopping? What about the Hobsons' blender? If I don't bring it to them, who will?"

Bill rolled his eyes heavenward.

"I know I'm new around here," he said with an exasperated sigh, "but I'm fairly sure I can find my way to Ivy Cottage."

"Very funny," I muttered. "I'll probably be the only person in Finch to miss James Hobson's metal-detecting demonstration."

"For pity's sake, Lori," Bill said, laughing, "you're not going on safari. You're popping down to London for the day."

"It'll take more than a day to find Badger," I said, "and I have no intention of camping out in London until I track him down."

"You can stay with my cousins," said Bill. "Gerald and Lucy would love to see you. Or you could stay at the Flamborough. It's your favorite hotel and one of the finest in London."

"I don't want to impose on your cousins," I said moodily, "and I don't want to stay at a hotel."

"Limit your search to one day at a time, then," Bill said. "Go there, come home, go there again. If commuters can do it, so can you."

"I don't want to be a commuter," I snapped.

Bill closed his laptop, placed it on the coffee table, and crossed to sit beside me on the couch.

"You've told me what you don't want," he said, putting his arm around me. "Why don't you tell me what you do want?"

"I want to put the garnet bracelet back in the attic," I said, "and pretend I never found it."

"Why?" Bill asked.

I heaved a forlorn sigh, leaned my head against his shoulder, and gazed into the fire.

"I'll be looking for a needle in a haystack," I said despondently. "I'm afraid I'll come back empty-handed." I swallowed hard as a lump rose in my throat. "I'm afraid I'll disappoint Dimity."

"You can't disappoint her," Bill said, giving me a gentle shake. "Even if you don't find Badger, she'll know that you tried. That's the important thing, isn't it? That you tried?"

"But she's counting on me to succeed," I said dolefully.

"She believes in you," said Bill. "What's wrong with that? I believe in you, too. If Badger can be found, you'll find him."

"Do you honestly think so?" I asked, looking up at him.

"I honestly think so," he replied. "Let's face it, Lori. You're too stubborn to fail."

"True," I agreed without rancor. "My mother didn't call me her bullheaded baby girl for nothing."

"Maybe I should start calling you Badger," said Bill.

I chuckled in spite of myself.

"It might be fun to explore Aunt Dimity's old stomping grounds," Bill continued. "The flat in Northington Street will probably be off limits, but you could stroll past the building. If Dimity mentions it again, you'll have a clear image of it in your mind. You'll know what St. Megwen's Lane looks like, too," he went on. "You'll walk where she walked, see the sights she saw. Aunt Dimity learned some pretty important things about herself while she was living in Bloomsbury. Your Badger hunt might help you to understand her better."

"With luck," I said, "I'll learn a few things about Badger, too."

"That's the spirit," said Bill.

Bolstered by his pep talk and intrigued by the notion of retracing Aunt Dimity's footsteps, I sat up and swung around to face him.

"You know what?" I said. "Forget about the driver. Aunt Dimity didn't have a guide to steer her through her new neighborhood. She explored it on her own, and so will I. If I get lost, I get lost. I'll bet she got lost every day."

"Yes, but she knew London well enough to get herself unlost," said Bill. "You don't. As you said before, a native guide might be useful. Without one, you could end up in the Outer Hebrides."

I laughed out loud.

"Okay," I said. "Hire a driver for me."

"Consider it done," said Bill. "I'll print a map of Bloomsbury for you as well. Will you start your search at the coffeehouse?"

"I'll have to," I said. "It's the closest thing I have to a lead."

"Then I'll circle it on the map," he said. "I'll circle number sixteen Northington Street as well, to make it easier for you to find Aunt Dimity's flat."

I gazed at him in grateful silence for a moment, then ducked my head.

"Sorry I was so ratty when I first came in here," I said. "If I'd thought things through before I left the study, I wouldn't have wasted time whining at you."

"Were you whining?" Bill asked airily. "I didn't notice."

"You're a terrible liar," I said, snuggling up to him, "but a very nice husband."

"I'm quite a catch," Bill agreed. "When do you leave?"

"The sooner, the better," I said. "Badger's not getting any younger. Plus, it's October—the days are drawing in. If I don't make hay while the sun shines, I'll need a flashlight to read your map. Would tomorrow morning be too soon?"

"Tomorrow morning will be just fine," said Bill. "I'll need the Range Rover for the school run, but you can use my car to catch an early train out of Oxford."

"I'll be home by dinnertime," I assured him. "London's a great place to visit, but I'd much rather spend the night here, with you."

Bill pulled me into his arms and for quite a long while made it clear that the feeling was mutual. He was, without doubt, quite a catch.

Nine

*T*he sky was a gloomy shade of battleship gray the following morning, but I felt as bright as a daisy. Bill's confidence-building campaign had continued late into the night, and it had had its intended effect. Although I remained convinced that my quest for Aunt Dimity's long-lost admirer was doomed to failure, I was ready to give it my all.

After arranging for a driver to meet me on the train platform in London, Bill insisted on taking charge of the children's morning routine. I left him to it and enjoyed the rare luxury of dressing in peace. To ward off the nip in the air, I pulled on a dove-gray cashmere sweater and a pair of merino wool trousers. My old walking shoes were the obvious choice for footwear. They weren't in the least stylish, but I could rely on them to keep my feet blissfully blister free on city pavements.

Armed with Bill's well-marked map of Bloomsbury and swathed in a voluminous black raincoat, I kissed Will, Rob, Bess, and Bill good-bye, tucked the garnet bracelet and a compact umbrella into my shoulder bag, and drove Bill's Mercedes to the train station in Oxford. I reached London's Paddington Station at ten o'clock.

My walking shoes had scarcely touched the train platform when I was approached by a young man who was, at a guess, in his late twenties. I wasn't sure who he was, but he didn't look like a chauffeur. He was tall and slender and dressed like a university student, in black jeans, black leather boots, and a scruffy black rain jacket. Though his attire was depressingly monochromatic, his face had a fresh, rosy glow, his eyes were the color of cornflowers, and his blond hair fell over his brow in a loose golden wave.

"Lori Shepherd?" he said, raising his voice to be heard above the station's clamor. "I'm Adam Rivington. Your husband asked me to meet you. He said you wouldn't mind if I dispensed with the suit and tie. Forgive me . . ." He gripped my elbow and steered me away from the flood of detraining passengers to the relative sanctuary of a newspaper kiosk before adding brightly, "I'll be your guide for the day."

"My guide?" I said in surprise. "I was expecting a driver."

"I *can* be your driver," he allowed, "but to be perfectly honest, a car isn't your best mode of transport in London. The tube is. I've taken the liberty of purchasing an all-day pass for you, but if you'd rather not use it . . ." His voice trailed off as he awaited my pronouncement.

"I'm fine with the tube," I assured him. "It's better than battling traffic and hunting for parking spaces."

"Much better," he agreed, looking pleased.

"How did you know I was me?" I asked somewhat incoherently.

"Mr. Willis sent a photo," he said, showing me his cell phone. "He also instructed me to address you as Lori, because—"

"—everyone does." I finished the sentence for him and smiled wryly. "It's true. I hang up on anyone who asks for Mrs. Willis because it's a sure sign that I'm about to hear a sales pitch. May I call you Adam?"

"I'd prefer it to 'Mr. Rivington,'" he said, smiling. "I've worked for your husband's firm many times, driving out-of-town clients to and from Heathrow and around town, but I've never been asked to give a walking tour. I'm looking forward to it."

"Did my husband tell you why I'm here?" I asked.

"He said you were looking for someone," Adam replied, "and he gave me an outline of your itinerary. Our first stop will be Carrie's Coffees in Bloomsbury." He glanced at his watch, then extended his arm in a courteous, sweeping gesture. "Shall we?"

My young guide ushered me safely through the tangled torrents of commuters to the Underground station and onto a dank, crowded tube train. I was content to let him lead the way when we changed trains at Piccadilly Circus, and I followed him like a devoted puppy when we disembarked at Russell Square. I emerged from the tube station, longing for a breath of fresh air.

The air I breathed was fresher than I expected. A crisp breeze plastered my flapping raincoat to my body, and ominous clouds hung low in the sky. Adam thrust his hands into his jacket pockets while I pulled a silk scarf from my shoulder bag and wrapped it around my neck.

"To tell you the truth," I said as I closed my bag, "I prefer buses to the tube. The view from the top deck of a double-decker bus is a whole lot more entertaining than the view from an underground train."

"It is," Adam agreed. "On the other hand, you don't have to stand in the rain while you're waiting for the tube. And the tube is faster. Unless there's a transport workers' strike, in which case all bets are off. Would you like to take the scenic route to Carrie's Coffees, or would you prefer a more direct route?"

"Scenic, please," I said, thinking of Aunt Dimity's long walks through London. "I'll take scenic over direct every time."

"Me, too," he said happily.

Adam adapted his long stride to my shorter one as we strolled down a side street and crossed a busy thoroughfare. As we quick-stepped from curb to curb, I felt myself ease into the rhythm of city life. Though I'd lived in the country for more than a decade, I'd grown up in Chicago and hadn't yet lost my urban chops. I could shoulder my way through a crowd without bumping into anyone too vigorously, and I knew how to manage the stuttering sidestep required to dart out of the bustling throng when a shop or a restaurant beckoned.

I'd also retained the ability to take in my surroundings while dodging lampposts, mailboxes, large dogs, small children, and inattentive grown-ups. Bloomsbury struck me as an understated, expensive, and surprisingly eclectic neighborhood. A plethora of tidy Georgian row houses gave the streetscape a pleasant sense of cohesion, while dashes of Victorian, Edwardian, Regency, and Art Deco architecture kept it from becoming monotonous. The few modern eyesores seemed to be medical centers of one sort or another.

"I'm not too keen on them, either," Adam admitted when I commented on the drab modern buildings. "Many of them occupy bomb sites, though—places where buildings were destroyed during the war—so I try to think of them as battle scars. Paris may be prettier, but London was braver."

I'd never compared the two cities in quite that way before, but I suspected most Londoners had. I tried to envision the street strewn with rubble, clouded with smoke, and scarred by bomb craters, but my pensive imaginings were cut short when we entered the tranquil precincts of a small park dotted with venerable trees.

The severe iron railings surrounding the park were softened by shrubs and flower beds, and a row of weathered but serviceable wooden benches faced the leaf-littered central lawn. It was easy to imagine Aunt Dimity sitting on one of the benches, kicking off her shoes, and giving her tired feet a breather.

"Queen Square Gardens," Adam announced.

"Lovely," I said. "Though not as lovely as it will be when the lilacs are in bloom. Thanks for bringing me here, Adam. It's the perfect antidote to the Underground."

"Your husband told me that you might need a few doses of greenery to get you through the day," said Adam.

"A little greenery never hurts," I conceded, "but I'm doing okay. I haven't been to London for years—not on my own, at any rate. I'm enjoying it more than I thought I would."

"Even in this weather?" Adam queried.

"If I wanted sunshine every day," I said, "I wouldn't live in England." I caught sight of a statue half hidden by the branches of a towering lilac bush. "Who's that?"

"Good question," said Adam.

He led the way along a curving path to a plinth topped by the statue of a plump, round-faced woman. Since the woman wore an elaborate gown and an odd, muffin-shaped crown, I assumed that she was the queen in Queen Square Gardens, but I didn't know which queen she was. As it turned out, I wasn't alone.

"No one is absolutely sure who she is," Adam informed me, gazing up at the statue. "The statue was erected in 1775, we think. Its subject has, at various times, been identified as Queen Charlotte, Queen Anne, Queen Mary, and Caroline, King George the Third's consort. General consensus pegs her as Queen Anne, but it's a mystery that may never be solved."

I felt a rush of affection for the plump little queen. If my search for Badger proved to be as fruitless as I expected it to be, I would, I decided, console myself with the knowledge that scholars much cleverer than I had been equally unsuccessful in their bid to identify Queen Whatshername.

"How wonderful," I said. "In an age when everything is counted and measured and recorded in triplicate, it's nice to know that a few mysteries remain beyond our reach."

"I'm afraid there's no mystery at all to our next point of interest," said Adam, "except that most people miss it because it's so difficult to see."

I followed him to a bronze plaque lying flat in a circular patch of stone paving set into the lawn. The words on the plaque were almost too worn to read, but Adam saved me the trouble of deciphering them by reading the inscription aloud.

"'On the night of the eighth of September 1915 a zeppelin bomb fell and exploded on this spot,'" he recited. "'Although nearly one thousand people slept in the surrounding buildings no person was injured.'" He squatted to brush some stray leaves from the plaque. "The Queen Square zeppelin bomb was the first high-explosive bomb to detonate in central London."

"Too bad it wasn't the last," I said. "The Blitz would make zeppelin raids look pretty tame."

"Are you interested in the Second World War?" Adam asked, straightening.

"I am," I said. "I have—" Since I had no intention of explaining Aunt Dimity's equivocal state of existence to my guide, I checked myself and began again. "I *had* a friend who lived in London during the war. She's gone now, but her stories have stayed with me."

"Here's a story your friend may not have told you," said Adam. "Approximately two thousand people took refuge from the Blitz in an air raid shelter"—he pulled his hand out of his pocket and pointed at the ground—"beneath your feet."

"Is the shelter still there?" I asked, looking down in amazement.

"As far as I know," Adam replied. "Let's hope we never need it again."

I looked from a pair of women chatting animatedly as they crossed the park to a red-haired man throwing a ball for a very excited wire-haired terrier, and I shook my head.

"It's hard to believe that it was needed in the first place," I said.

"Not for me," Adam said. "I grew up hearing my granddad's stories." He gazed at the bronze plaque in silence, then raised his head and smiled. "One more stop before we leave the gardens. There's someone I'd like you to meet."

He took off across the park and I trotted after him until he stopped before another, more modern memorial: a bronze cat peering down from a freestanding, four-foot-tall segment of redbrick wall, as though entranced by a sudden movement in the wind-whipped leaves.

"Please allow me to introduce you to Sam the Cat," said Adam. "Sam was placed here in 1997 to honor his owner, the late Patricia Penn, a defender of historic buildings and—needless to say—a cat lover."

"A brick wall and a bronze cat," I said. "Very appropriate." I stepped forward to give Sam's head a rub. "I would have walked right past him if you hadn't pointed him out. For someone who doesn't give many walking tours, Adam, you seem to know an awful lot about Bloomsbury."

"I should," he said. "I've lived here all my life."

I blinked at him in surprise, then burst out laughing.

"No wonder Bill called you," I said. "You're not just a guide. You're a *native* guide—a bona fide Bloomsbury-born bloke."

"Guilty as charged," Adam acknowledged. "I'm the fourth generation of my family to live here. My great-grandfather witnessed the zeppelin attacks, my grandfather served as an air raid warden during the Blitz, and my parents work at the British Museum. I hope to work there, too, after I get my postgraduate degree."

"I'm not tearing you away from your studies, am I?" I said.

"Not at all," he replied, and his blue eyes twinkled mischievously as he added, "You're helping me to pay for them." He tilted his head toward the busy street beyond the park's railings. "Next stop, Great Ormond Street Hospital."

"Bill really did brief you well," I marveled as we exited the park. "I suppose Carrie's Coffees is your local hangout."

"It's one of them," he said.

"Of course it is," I said, feeling as though I were covering ground Bill had already covered. "Would you happen to know if Carrie's Coffees replaced an older hangout called the Rose Café?"

"To be accurate," Adam said, "Carrie's Coffees replaced the place that replaced the place that replaced three other places that replaced the Rose Café."

"But it would have been the Rose Café in your grandfather's time," I said thoughtfully. "Has he ever mentioned it?"

"No," said Adam, "but he wouldn't. Granddad prefers pubs to tearooms. A few pensioners meet up at Carrie's, though, to chat about old times."

I came to an abrupt standstill, and Adam yanked me out of the way of a gaggle of teenagers that was bearing down on us.

"What's up?" he asked.

"If you know an elderly gentleman who calls himself Badger," I said, staring hard at him, "prepare to catch me because I'll probably faint."

"You're safe," Adam assured me. "The name doesn't ring a bell. Is he the man you're hoping to find?"

"He is," I said, and we resumed walking. "My friend got to know Badger just after the war. They used to meet at the Rose Café. She asked me to . . . to give him a message."

"A dying wish?" Adam inquired.

For a split second I was tempted to tell him that Aunt Dimity's request had, in fact, been a post-dying wish, but I resisted the urge and answered evasively, "Something like that. I don't know much about Badger, except that he had a beard, a tan, and strong, rough hands. My friend thought he might have been a gardener."

"A gardener would have had no trouble finding work around here," Adam observed. "Bloomsbury is dotted with garden squares: Russell Square, Red Lion Square, Tavistock Square, Bedford Square—"

"Queen Square," I interjected.

"Exactly," he said, nodding. "Gray's Inn and Lincoln's Inn have their own gardens as well, and they're a stone's throw from here." He hesitated, then explained carefully, "Gray's Inn and Lincoln's Inn aren't hotels, you understand. They're professional associations that provide barristers with office space and living quarters, among many other amenities."

"I'm familiar with the Inns of Court," I assured him. "My husband is an attorney, remember. He gave me an Inns of Court tour shortly after we moved to England. As I recall, the gardens were pretty impressive."

"Barristers can afford impressive gardens," Adam said dryly.

I recalled the opulent dining halls Bill had shown me and said, "I hear they dine impressively, too."

Adam laughed as we crossed another busy street. When we reached the other side, he gestured for me to stand with my back to a shop front and pointed across the street to the building facing us.

"That's it," he said. "Great Ormond Street Hospital. The first children's hospital in London."

Although I was sure that the work carried out within the Great

Ormond Street Hospital was both praiseworthy and essential, it wasn't the prettiest place of healing I'd ever seen. It looked as though a long row of dull brown wings had been grafted onto a fairly flamboyant Victorian corner building.

"In 1929 J. M. Barrie gave the hospital the story rights to *Peter Pan*," Adam went on. "The royalties have been rolling in ever since. His gift has saved thousands—perhaps hundreds of thousands—of young lives."

"What a legacy," I said, making a mental note to buy a copy of *Peter Pan* for every child in my sons' school. "My friend told me that the Great Ormond Street Hospital was used as a casualty clearing station during the war."

"It was," Adam confirmed. "My grandfather was brought here after a wall fell on him during the Blitz."

"A wall fell on your grandfather?" I said in dismay. "Was he badly injured?"

"Broken leg, cracked skull," Adam replied matter-of-factly. "He reported for duty three days after he was discharged. Did his rounds on crutches."

"They don't make 'em like that anymore," I said. "A hangnail puts me out of commission for months."

"I somehow doubt it," Adam said, giving me a sidelong look. "If you're anything like my mother, you report for duty every day, regardless. Would you like to go into the hospital?"

"No, thanks," I said. "I just wanted to fix an image of it in my mind."

"You can try," Adam said doubtfully, "but the building is constantly changing. It may look quite different the next time you see it."

"Which means," I said, feeling a bit deflated, "that it would have looked quite different when my friend was here."

As if sensing my disappointment, Adam said helpfully, "The Victorian bit hasn't changed."

"I'll fix that bit in my mind, then." I studied the redbrick corner building in silence, then nodded. "Image fixed. Let us move on."

An ominous sprinkling of fat raindrops struck the pavement as we turned off the busy street and onto a street that was virtually traffic free. Shiny black bollards separated its wide walkways from a narrow lane laid with paving stones.

"Lamb's Conduit Street," said Adam. "No cars allowed, except delivery vehicles."

"Another reason to take public transportation," I commented.

Lamb's Conduit Street was an unostentatious and delightfully old-fashioned shopping district. The four-story apartment buildings that lined the little lane housed ground-floor shops that offered everything from hand-painted china to hand-printed fabrics. Window displays—some rather dusty, but all tastefully arranged—featured the wares of cobblers, tailors, shirtmakers, jewelers, booksellers, and florists. It heartened me to see so many independent small businesses swimming valiantly against the corporate tide.

The street's eating establishments were as varied and attractive as the small businesses. I spotted a classic fish-and-chips shop, a splendid Victorian pub, and a tempting tearoom as well as some elegant high-end eateries, but there wasn't a chain restaurant in sight. Although many of the cafés and coffeehouses had outdoor dining areas, the increasingly grubby weather had evidently driven their patrons indoors.

As the fat raindrops gave way to a gusting downpour, I opened my umbrella, and Adam pulled up his rain jacket's hood.

"Why is it called Lamb's Conduit Street?" I asked as we splashed along side by side. "Did it funnel sheep into London's meat markets?"

"Sorry?" Adam asked in a polite shout. He pointed to his hood. "Couldn't hear you."

I repeated my questions in a roar reminiscent of Peggy Taxman's.

"It's nothing to do with sheep," Adam explained. "Lamb's Conduit Street was named after Sir William Lambe, a civic-minded gentleman who paid for the restoration of a derelict Elizabethan conduit in order to supply water to the City—the oldest part of London. I'd take you to see the conduit's remains, but—"

"But they're probably flooded," I interrupted, tipping my umbrella forward to keep the wind from turning it inside out. "There's a time for sightseeing, Adam, and a time to get the heck out of Dodge. Let's save Mr. Lambe's conduit for another day, shall we? How close is Carrie's Coffees?"

"We're nearly there," he said. "The next left turn will take us into St. Megwen's Lane."

Aunt Dimity's tiny byway lived up to its billing. St. Megwen's Lane was so narrow that I could have stretched out my arms and touched the buildings on either side of it. After a few claustrophobic steps, however, the passage opened up into a kind of half courtyard where a cheerful blue-and-white-striped awning announced that we had arrived at our destination.

"Carrie's Coffees," Adam bellowed.

"I see," I bellowed back, but beneath my breath I murmured, "Aunt Dimity's Rose Café."

Ten

F should have been overcome by a flood of emotions as I stood on the spot where Aunt Dimity had once stood. I should have paused to drink in every detail of the coffeehouse's charming exterior in order to describe it to her later. At the very least, I should have thanked Adam for guiding me unerringly to a place I would have had trouble finding on my own.

I was, alas, too wet and windblown to do and feel what I should have done and felt. What might have been a momentous moment passed in a damp blur as Adam and I put our heads down and hurried through the front door. To my relief, the warmth that enfolded us wasn't polluted by the detested stink of coffee. Coffee, it seemed, was something of a sideline at Carrie's Coffees.

Though an espresso machine took up more than its fair share of space behind the counter directly in front of us, a set of shelves next to it held an impressive array of tea tins. Better still, the glass case beside the counter contained a tantalizing assortment of pastries, quiches, sandwiches, and colorful salads. The warm air was perfumed with the delectable aromas of fresh-baked bread and pungent herbs mingled with the heady scents of cinnamon, nutmeg, hazelnut, and vanilla, with the merest hint of coffee to legitimize the Rose Café's newest name.

"Adam!" called the stout, middle-aged redhead behind the counter. "What in God's name are you doing out in such filthy weather? You look like a drowned rat!"

"It's good to see you, too, Carrie," said Adam, lowering his hood and pushing his wet hair back from his forehead.

"Who's your friend?" the woman asked, eyeing me with great interest. "You haven't broken it off with Helena, have you?"

Adam's rosy complexion deepened to crimson.

"I'm flattered," I interceded, "but I'm also old enough to be Adam's mother. Helena has nothing to fear from me."

"More's the pity," said Carrie. "Helena's not the right girl for our lad, as I keep telling him. She takes too much and gives too little."

"Maybe he has to figure it out on his own," I suggested.

"Wish he'd hurry up," said Carrie. She looked me up and down. "Who are you, then? You're a Yank, so you can't be a relative, and you don't look daft enough to be a bone bagger."

I had no idea what a bone bagger was, but I was glad that I didn't look daft enough to be one.

"I'm Lori Shepherd," I said. "Adam works for my husband. He's showing me around Bloomsbury."

"Silly day to choose for an outing. But I'm pleased to meet you, Lori." Carrie pressed a hand to her expansive bosom as she continued, "Carrie Osborne, proprietor. Don't mind my teasing. I'm in the running for Bloomsbury's Most Colorful Character, and I have to keep up appearances. I want to see my buns immortalized in Russell Square."

Carrie didn't strike me as the sort of woman who'd make a double entendre accidentally, but I didn't know her well enough to laugh, so I turned instead to Adam and asked, "Is there really a Most Colorful Character competition in Bloomsbury?"

"No," he said, "but if there were, Carrie would win it."

"I should think so," Carrie said emphatically. "What can I get for you, Lori?"

"I'd love a cup of Lapsang souchong," I told her, "but I don't suppose—"

"Cup or pot?" Carrie interjected.

"A pot, please," I said readily. "And a glass of water. And one of the baguette sandwiches—the one with the brie and the tomatoes. And . . ." I paused to study the pastries before making a tough decision. "And a blackberry tart."

"And soup?" Carrie said coaxingly. "Nothing warms the soul on a rainy day like a nice bowl of soup. I have butternut squash soup today, made from scratch."

"Yes, please," I said. I needed no coaxing. My brief but chilly walking tour of Bloomsbury had sharpened my appetite to a razor's edge.

"I'll pay," said Adam and he pulled out a company credit card, as if to prove to Carrie that ours was a business arrangement.

"Have a seat while I deal with Mr. Moneybags," Carrie instructed me.

It would have been a gross understatement to say that the coffeehouse wasn't busy. Adam and I were Carrie's only customers. While he hung his jacket, my raincoat, and my dripping umbrella on wooden pegs just inside the door, I selected a table near the white-framed, multipaned café window that stretched from one end of the shop front to the other.

Before Adam could join me, he was waylaid by two new arrivals who were clearly old friends. He bussed the young woman on each cheek and clapped the young man on the shoulder, then stood chatting with them while they divested themselves of their rain gear.

I took the opportunity to pull my cell phone from my shoulder bag and call Bill. A small, mean-spirited part of me hoped to find him in a down-to-the-last-clean-diaper panic, but he sounded downright jolly when he answered the phone.

"I delivered the blender," he said before I could ask. "The Hobsons send their thanks. I also delivered the boys to school on time, emptied the dishwasher, changed Bess's diaper, and did a load of laundry."

"You're a star," I said.

"How's your search going?" he asked. "Did Adam meet you at Paddington?"

"He did and he's fantastic," I said. "He knows more about Bloomsbury than I know about Finch. I assume that's why you chose him."

"He seemed like the right man for the job," said Bill. "Any luck finding Badger?"

"We've only just arrived at Carrie's Coffees," I explained. "I thought I'd touch base with you before we launch the next phase of our search."

"Which will be . . . ?" Bill asked.

"Lunch," I replied, and he laughed.

"Bess and I have already had lunch," he informed me. "How does lentil stew sound for dinner?"

"Scrumptious," I said. "Do you know how to make lentil stew?"

"It's simmering on the stove as we speak," Bill answered smugly. "Bess helped me by chewing on a wooden spoon. At the moment, she's using it to drum on a saucepan. Would you like to say hello?"

"Let her play," I said, "but give her a hug from me."

"I'll give her a hug and a kiss and a cuddle from you," he said. "Oh, and I'm pleased to report that you haven't missed James Hobson's metal-detecting demo. He's holding the first session tomorrow morning on the village green, weather permitting."

"Tomorrow morning?" I said, surprised. "He and Felicity must have broken the land speed record for unpacking."

"They had lots of little helpers," said Bill. "The villagers descended on Ivy Cottage en masse this morning to empty boxes and fill shelves."

"Because the sooner the Hobsons are settled," I said, "the sooner James can give the demonstration."

"Uh-oh," said Bill. "I'd better run. Jaws is making a break for the hallway."

"Head her off at the pass," I told him. "We'll catch up when I get home."

"I'll have dinner on the table," he promised, and we ended the call.

I shoved my cell phone into my bag, ignored a twinge of home-sickness, and looked out the window. Since the view of the truncated courtyard was less than inspiring, and since Adam was still chatting with his friends, I turned my attention to the coffeehouse's decor.

Carrie's Coffees was a sunny place to stop on a rainy day. The polished plank floors gleamed in the diffused light shed by the blue-shaded ceiling lamps that hung, one apiece, over each table. The walls were painted a soft buttercup yellow, trimmed with white woodwork, and hung with framed watercolor paintings of Georgian row houses brightened by flower-filled window boxes.

The day's menu had been handwritten in a florid but legible script on a wall-mounted whiteboard above the espresso machine. The menu's blue ink matched the blue lampshades as well as the stripes on the coffeehouse's awning.

The dining tables and chairs were modern in design and made of pale wood, but Carrie had created a cozy seating area at the far end of the room by arranging three compact leather armchairs around a trompe l'oeil painting of a stone fireplace filled with burning logs. To add to the verisimilitude, someone had affixed a roughhewn board to the painting, to serve as a mantel. A carriage clock and a row of well-thumbed paperbacks on the "mantel" completed the picture.

I wondered what the place had looked like when it had been the

Rose Café. Aunt Dimity's comments about rationing and scarcity led me to believe that it hadn't been as bright and airy as Carrie's Coffees. I envisioned scratched wooden tables on wobbly legs, straight-backed wooden chairs, scuffed floorboards, dingy wallpaper, cracked windowpanes, and dim lamps that were used only after dark.

"But they served a decent cup of tea," I allowed in an undertone.

My one-sided conversation was mercifully curtailed by Adam, who arrived at the table carrying a heavily laden plastic tray.

"Sorry about that," he said, nodding at his friends, who were placing their orders with Carrie Osborne. "Fellow students."

"No need to apologize," I assured him. "We're on your turf. I'd be surprised if you didn't run into someone you know."

"Your lunch and mine," he announced, placing the tray on the table. "I've asked Carrie to join us after the lunch rush. I thought you might like to speak with her about Badger."

"That's why I'm here," I said. "Thanks."

I transferred the tray's contents to the table, and Adam returned the tray to the front counter. He'd made good use of the company card, ordering a bowl of soup, a chickpea salad, a wedge of bruschetta, a focaccia sandwich, a small vat of black coffee, and two bottles of water for himself, but a brief glance at my own dishes revealed a glaring omission.

"Where's my blackberry tart?" I demanded as he took his seat.

"There wasn't enough room on the tray for your tart," he explained. "Carrie will bring it over."

"Bless her," I said, and dug in.

I was halfway through my soul-warming bowl of soup when the lunch rush began. Carrie's assistant, a wiry, gray-haired woman called Dizz, emerged from a back room to help her boss field orders from the dozens of customers who streamed in and out of the coffeehouse. I kept a close watch on Carrie's patrons, but they were either young or middle-aged. Not one was old enough to be Aunt Dimity's very old friend.

Though the tables filled rapidly, the three armchairs before the faux fireplace remained empty.

"Are the leather chairs contaminated?" I asked.

"No," said Adam. "They're reserved for Carrie's old dears—the pensioners I told you about, the ones who come here to chat about old times. She gives them free coffee and tea as well. She says it's the least she can do for her Battle of Britain boys."

"Were they fighter pilots?" I asked.

"I'm not sure," said Adam. "I never know whether Carrie's joking or not, but if you ask her a straight question, she'll probably give you a straight answer. I believe she knows the old boys quite well."

"What happens if someone sits in their chairs?" I asked.

"A first-time offender gets a polite warning and a lecture about what we owe the brave men who stepped up to defend our country in its hour of need," he explained. "Repeat offenders are told to leave and never come back."

"I can see why the chairs are empty," I said. I finished my soup, then glanced toward the front counter and lowered my voice. "I'm almost afraid to ask, but what is a bone bagger?"

"It's Carrie's pet name for an archaeologist," he explained with a martyred air. "I'm working toward a postgrad degree in archaeology, you see, and since you were with me . . ."

"Got it," I said, starting in on my sandwich. "Have you bagged many bones?"

"None," he replied. "I turned up a bone comb at a dig in Kent, but I haven't yet uncovered human remains."

"I'd rather find a bone comb than a ribcage," I said with a dainty grimace, "but I'm not an archaeologist. What period are you study-ing?"

"Early Anglo-Saxon," he said decisively.

"I thought Anglo-Saxon was a language," I said. "*Beowulf* was writ-ten in Anglo-Saxon, wasn't it?"

"It was," said Adam, "but Anglo-Saxon is also the name of the culture that produced *Beowulf*, a culture created by the Germanic tribes that invaded, settled, and ruled Great Britain from the fifth century to 1066."

"That would be . . . after the Romans, but before the Norman conquest?" I said tentatively.

"Close enough," said Adam, grinning. "But if you mention the Dark Ages, I'll have to deduct points. The Anglo-Saxons weren't bullet-headed barbarians, Lori. They were fierce warriors, yes, but they were also artists, artisans, poets, and architects." He leaned for-ward on his elbows, his face alight with a scholar's passion. "Have you seen the Sutton Hoo ship burial exhibition at the British Museum?"

"No," I admitted. "My sons tend to gravitate to the arms and ar-mor. And the bugs. Will and Rob are crazy about bugs."

"Well, if you and your boys ever want a guided tour of the world's greatest collection of Anglo-Saxon treasures, ring me." He raised his hand, palm outward. "No fees involved. It would be my pleasure."

"That's very kind of you, Adam," I said. "I may take you up on your offer, once I finish my Badger hunt."

We had plenty of time to savor our meal, and each part of it was worth savoring. The soup's complex flavor had been deepened by a dash of curry, and the brie-and-tomato baguette had been sprinkled with microgreens and drizzled with a peppery olive oil. The tea had come as such a pleasant surprise that I didn't mind lingering over it while awaiting the arrival of my blackberry tart.

I didn't have long to wait. The lunch rush died down as quickly as it had begun. In an hour, the coffeehouse was once again somnolent, with only a handful of customers popping in for takeout orders. When Dizz cleared our table and Adam's friends waved good-bye to him, I felt a rising sense of anticipation. I had to remind myself sternly that Badger, not blackberries, was my main priority as Carrie approached our table with my tart and a flask of hot water to top up my teapot.

"Enjoy your soup?" she asked, pulling a chair over to sit with us.

"Very much," I said. "Thanks for suggesting it."

"You'll like the tart, too," she said. "Berries picked fresh from the hedgerows this morning." She laid a finger alongside her nose. "I have countryside connections."

Like Adam, I didn't know if she was joking or not, but the blackberries were as plump and juicy as any I'd ever picked, the custard was as smooth as silk, and the crust was a minor masterpiece of buttery flakiness. I'd never expected to meet a baker as skilled as Finch's own Sally Cook, but Carrie Osborne, I thought, could give Sally a run for her money.

"Good?" Carrie said, raising her eyebrows.

"Heavenly," I mumbled through a forkful of perfection.

"I've told Lori about the leather chairs and your old gentlemen," said Adam. "She'd like to ask you a few questions about them."

"Why would a Yank take an interest in my boys?" Carrie asked, eyeing me narrowly. "Writing a book, are you?"

"No," I said, forcing myself to put my fork down. "I live in the countryside, in a very small village not too far from Oxford. I had a friend there—a village woman—who lived in Bloomsbury for a short time after the war. She was very fond of the Rose Café, which was, as you probably know—"

"Right here, on this spot," Carrie put in, nodding. "That's why my old boys come here. They're the last of the Rose Café crowd. There may be others out there, still in the land of the living, but they don't come here anymore. I know my regulars."

Having heard her grill Adam about his girlfriend, I didn't doubt it.

"My friend had a friend," I continued. "They used to meet at the Rose Café, but she lost track of him a long time ago, and she always regretted it. She asked me to find him and to give him a message. I hoped someone here might know him or know how I can contact him."

"A dying wish, was it?" Carrie asked, echoing Adam's earlier query.

"Yes," I said firmly. "It may sound odd, but my friend didn't know her friend's proper name. All I have to go on is his nickname."

"It doesn't sound odd to me," said Carrie. "All of my old dears have nicknames. If they weren't branded with them at boarding school, they picked them up in the RAF. There's Griff—Anthony Griffin-Hughes—a squadron leader by the tender age of nineteen. And Chocks—he was ground crew, a first-rate mechanic. And Ginger—he tells me his hair was as red as mine when he joined up. And Granddad—at twenty-three, the oldest man in his squadron. And Fish—he was plucked from the Channel by a trawler after he put his Spitfire into the drink. And Madge—"

"Madge?" Adam interrupted, looking perplexed.

"Short for Your Majesty," Carrie explained. "Old Madge came from old money." Her expression softened as she turned her head to gaze at the three leather chairs. "Madge is gone now, God rest his soul, along with Griff and Granddad. The only ones left are Chocks, Ginger, and Fish, and they're in their nineties." She sighed. "I don't suppose they'll be around much longer."

"But you'll look after them while you can," Adam said kindly.

"That I will," said Carrie, rousing herself. "It's the least I can do for my Battle of Britain boys."

"Have you ever heard them speak of someone called Badger?" I asked.

"I don't believe I have," said Carrie, frowning in concentration. "Doesn't mean they haven't spoken of him. I'm too busy to pay attention to everything my old boys say. I can run the name past them, if you like."

"Would you?" I said.

"They won't be in today," she warned, waving a hand through the air to indicate the rain dripping steadily from the striped awning. "Chocks roasted his hands when he pulled a pilot out of a burning Hurricane. Fish broke both kneecaps when his Spit went down. Ginger took a bullet in the shoulder from a passing Messerschmitt." She shook her head. "Old war wounds don't mix well with wet weather."

"I understand," I said, "but if you could mention Badger to them the next time they drop in, I'd be incredibly grateful. If they ask for a description, you can tell them that Badger had a dark beard, dark curly hair, strong hands, and a deep tan."

"He won't have dark hair anymore," Carrie commented, "but my boys might remember him from the old days."

"I hope they do," I said. I pulled a scrap of paper from my bag and scribbled my name and my phone number on it. "I'll leave my number with you, Carrie. If Chocks, Fish, or Ginger knows Badger or if they know anyone who knows Badger, please ring me. I'll be happy to meet them here or in their homes or wherever is most convenient for them."

"Dying wishes must be honored," Carrie said with a firm nod of approbation.

"I'd like to meet them for my own sake as much as my friend's," I said. "As you say, they may not be around much longer. I'd like to thank them face-to-face while they're still in the land of the living."

"They'll tell you not to be so soppy," said Carrie, "but they'll like it all the same." She took the scrap of paper from me and slipped it into her apron pocket. "Leave it to me, Lori. I'll put the word out." She pushed herself to her feet. "But first I'll give Dizz a hand with the washing up. I've enjoyed meeting you, Lori. Eat up the rest of your tart."

"Yes, ma'am," I said, but when her back was turned, I pushed the plate toward Adam and asked, "Would you finish it for me, please?"

"Why?" he said. "What's wrong?"

"Broken wrists, broken kneecaps, and bullet wounds," I said bleakly. "It doesn't seem right to eat dessert after hearing about what those men went through—what they're still going through."

"They'd disagree with you," said Adam. "If Ginger, Chocks, and Fish were here, they'd tell you to enjoy every bite. They'd say they fought the war so that you could eat dessert in peace."

"Is that what your granddad says to you?" I asked.

"All the time," he replied.

"Well," I said reluctantly, "if you insist . . ."

"I do," Adam said, getting to his feet, "because I'm ordering a cream bun, for myself, and I don't plan to share it with you!"

As he returned to the counter for his cream bun, I lifted a forkful of blackberry tart in a toast to the three empty chairs.

Eleven

dam was as good as his word. He didn't share so much as a crumb of his cream bun with me. I got even with him by buying a few to take home. Carrie's immortal buns were too rich for Bess, but they would, I was certain, be a big hit with my menfolk.

By the time we left the coffeehouse, the steady downpour had given way to intermittent showers. I opened my umbrella, Adam raised his hood, and we set out for the last stop on our Aunt Dimity–inspired walking tour.

Number 16 Northington Street turned out to be a major disappointment. I couldn't tell whether Aunt Dimity's borrowed flat had been in a charming Georgian row house or in a bland brown brick pile because every building on the block was covered from attic to cellar with scaffolding and draped in green safety netting. Even the chimney pots were shrouded in tarpaulins, presumably to protect them from the rain while they were being repaired or replaced.

"Gentrification," Adam observed. "A developer is turning affordable housing into upscale, upmarket flats for the upwardly mobile. It's happening all over London. If I wanted to be a millionaire, I'd invest in travertine flooring and complicated taps."

I tried bending over to peer under the safety netting, but it was like looking into a stalactite-filled cave.

"It's not much of an image to fix in my memory," I said, straightening.

"It's London as it was, is, and ever shall be," Adam intoned. "Like Great Ormond Street Hospital, London is always under construction. Your friend must have seen miles of scaffolding during the postwar building boom."

"True," I said. I almost added, "I'll ask her," but I swallowed the treacherous words before they could escape. "Well, Adam, we found the Rose Café, and we identified three members of the old Rose Café crowd who might lead me to Badger. I think we've done as much as we can do today."

"To Paddington?" he queried.

"To Paddington," I replied. "I should be home in plenty of time for dinner."

I could hardly believe how quickly we reached the tube station. With no sightseeing stops to delay us, we made it from Northington Street to Russell Square in ten minutes flat. The tube was less crowded than it had been in the morning, and I had to admit that it was nice to be out of the rain.

I allowed Adam to lead me to the correct platform in Paddington Station, and I didn't object when he offered to wait with me. I was coming down with a bad case of sensory overload, so I was grateful to have someone on hand to keep me from boarding the Outer Hebrides Express.

"Thank you, Adam," I said as my train pulled into the station. "I would have been lost without you—and I'm speaking literally. Shall we team up again the next time I'm in London?"

"I'd like that," said Adam. "Your husband has my contact information. And don't forget our day at the British Museum. If your sons like arms and armor, they'll love the Sutton Hoo exhibition. Once you've seen it, you'll realize that the early Anglo-Saxons weren't simple-minded barbarians."

"I never thought they were," I protested. "To be perfectly honest, I never thought about them at all," I continued, adding hastily, "but I'm willing to learn."

"You'll love it," Adam stated firmly.

"Until next time, then," I said, and boarded the train.

A train journey can offer a splendid opportunity for reflection. I'd planned to review the day's adventures while London's far-reaching tentacles slipped past me. I'd intended to contemplate the remarkable sights I'd seen and the stories I'd heard, but my overstuffed brain refused to cooperate. Instead of using my travel time to think deeply about my experiences, I fell asleep as my train left Paddington, and I stayed asleep until it reached Oxford.

Refreshed, I drove home without incident.

The cottage hadn't fallen down in my absence, and my family was gratifyingly pleased to see me. Will and Rob showed me the stories they'd written at school, which involved dinosaurs, race cars, and champion cricketers, and Bess informed me that she was considering a career as a timpanist. Bill had his doubts about my interpretation of her words—he doubted that they were words—but I understood her perfectly.

Bill's lentil stew filled the cottage with a savory aroma that reminded me of autumn leaves and bonfires. To my relief, it tasted even better than it smelled. While the boys set the table, their talented father stowed my box of cream buns in the refrigerator, made a green salad, and sliced a loaf of crusty brown bread.

Feeling pleasantly superfluous, I returned the garnet bracelet to Reginald's niche in the study, brought Bess upstairs with me, and swapped my big-city clothes for a soft flannel shirt, blue jeans, and sneakers.

We sat down to eat at our usual time, but our dinner table

conversation was highly unusual, in that it was more of a monologue than a discussion. I simply couldn't stop talking about my day in London. I didn't mention the Badger hunt in front of the boys, but I prattled on about everything else. My newfound enthusiasm for the metropolis must have been contagious because Will, Rob, and Bill listened intently rather than patiently.

"The next time you go to London," Will said when I finally ran out of steam, "can we come with you?"

"We want to see the little queen," said Rob. "And Sam the Cat."

"And the air raid shelter," added Will.

"You can't see the air raid shelter," I explained, "because it's underground."

"We could see Carrie's coffeehouse," Rob pointed out.

"And we could have a blackberry tart each," said Will.

"Carrie may not have blackberry tarts all the time," I warned, "but I'm sure she'll have something you'll like just as well."

"I wouldn't mind an eclair," Rob conceded.

"Or a jam doughnut," Will chimed in.

"Maybe *two* puddings each," Rob reconsidered, using the British word for dessert. He had, after all, been raised in England.

"I'll tell you what," I said. "Daddy and I will take you to London during your Christmas break." I looked at Bill. "The museums will be jam-packed, but the parks and the backstreets won't be too crowded, and they're just as interesting as museums. In some ways, they're more interesting."

"I'll ask Adam to design a walking tour for us," said Bill.

"Ask Adam to come along," Will suggested.

"We'd like to meet him," said Rob. "And see Sutton Hoo."

"Hoo!" Bess crowed from her high chair.

"Okay," I said, laughing. "We'll fit one museum into our schedule and we'll definitely ask Adam to join us there. I can give you a treat from Carrie's coffeehouse right now, though. Sit," I ordered as Bill started to get to his feet. "You made dinner. The boys will clear the table, and I'll get the dessert."

The cream buns were a big hit. Bess was shocked by my refusal to share mine with her, but she made do with a bowl of applesauce.

Will, Rob, and I spent the rest of the evening poring over the map of Bloomsbury Bill had printed for me as well as a detailed street map of London. When unfolded, the street map took up so much of the living room's floor space that Bill had to take Bess to the kitchen to keep her from crawling across Hyde Park or drooling on Buckingham Palace. The boys went to bed, still discussing ideas for our grand Christmas outing.

I carried Bess up to the nursery and rocked her to sleep. After settling her in her crib, I returned to the living room to find Super Dad sound asleep in his armchair, with Stanley curled into a contented black ball in his lap. I let them be and tiptoed up the hall to the study, where I closed the door behind me, lit the mantel lamps, and raised a finger to my lips.

"No loud parties tonight, Reginald," I cautioned. "Bill is whacked."

My pink flannel bunny signaled his understanding by remaining silent.

As I knelt to light a fire in the hearth, I noticed that it had been swept clean and laid with fresh logs. I tended to postpose hearth sweeping until the ash piles resembled a small mountain range, but my overachieving husband had evidently included the chore in his to-do list.

"That's just showing off," I muttered, striking a match with more force than was strictly necessary.

The tinder caught, the flames leaped, and the garnet bracelet in

Reginald's niche seemed to glitter with its own internal light. I took the blue journal from its shelf and sat with it in one of the tall leather armchairs that faced the hearth.

"Dimity?" I said as I opened the journal. "The Badger hunt is under way!"

I grinned as Aunt Dimity's familiar handwriting began to curl and loop across the blank page.

I don't understand, my dear. Did you go to London today?

"I did," I said proudly. "I haven't found Badger yet, but I found the Rose Café."

It's still there? On St. Megwen's Lane? I'm astounded.

"The building's still there," I confirmed, "but it's not the Rose Café anymore. According to Adam——"

Adam?

"Adam Rivington," I explained. "He works as a driver for Bill's firm, but Bill asked him to act as my guide today."

Was Bill afraid you'd get lost on your own?

"*I* was afraid I'd get lost on my own," I retorted. "But Adam made sure I didn't. He was born and raised in Bloomsbury, and he knows it inside out. He told me that the Rose Café has changed hands quite a few times over the years. At the moment, it's a coffeehouse."

Oh, dear. I'm sorry, Lori. I know how much you dislike coffee.

"It wasn't a problem," I said. "The owner serves tea as well, and believe me, she makes a decent cuppa. She bakes her own bread and pastries, too. I had a baguette sandwich and a blackberry tart I won't soon forget."

No mock whipped cream? No eggless fruitcake?

I peered at the page uncertainly.

"What's mock whipped cream?" I asked. "And how can you make a fruitcake without eggs?"

They're wartime recipes, my dear. Cream was strictly rationed, even in rural areas where cows were abundant, but my mother learned to make a whipped cream substitute that required four simple ingredients: milk, margarine, corn flour, and a tablespoon of sugar.

"Forgive me, Dimity," I said, "but it sounds revolting."

It was revolting. My mother made it once and decided we could do without whipped cream for the duration. The eggless fruitcake wasn't half bad, though, provided one could obtain the proper spices. You could try making it yourself. If you look in my old trunk, you'll find a slim volume titled Rational Recipes. *It was published in 1941 to help busy housewives cook nourishing meals under wartime restrictions.*

"It sounds like an interesting experiment," I said diplomatically, "but I think I'll stick with Sally Cook's five-egg fruitcake recipe."

A wise choice. Moist and delicious are better than not half bad. What does the coffeehouse look like?

"It's charming," I said. "Bright and airy and filled with mouthwatering fragrances."

Quite the opposite of what it was in my day. I'm afraid the Rose Café was rather dark and dank. Everyone there smelled of wet wool.

"Was it lit with candles?" I asked.

Certainly not. There was a small electric lamp on each table. Candles would have been a fire hazard, though I suppose the jury-rigged wiring wasn't much safer. But all of London was jury-rigged in those days. Its buildings were as war weary as its people.

"There's a fake fireplace there now," I said. "Not an electric-fire fake fireplace, but an expertly rendered trompe l'oeil painting. Carrie Osborne—the coffeehouse's proprietor—keeps three leather chairs in front of the painting. They're used exclusively by her three oldest customers—Chocks, Ginger, and Fish. Carrie calls them her

Battle of Britain boys because they served in the RAF during the war. After the war, they were regulars at the Rose Café."

Good heavens. I wonder if I crossed paths with them?

"I'm hoping they crossed paths with Badger," I said. "The rotten weather kept them at home today, but Carrie promised to mention Badger to them the next time they come to the coffeehouse. If the name rings a bell with any or all of them, she'll telephone me."

Palpable progress! On your first day out! How splendid! I must admit that I felt rather guilty after speaking with you last night. I felt as if I'd sent you on a wild goose chase, and I fully intended to release you from any obligation you might have felt to pursue it.

"It may still be a wild goose chase," I said frankly, "but I wish I'd been able to pursue it further."

Nonsense. You've established a line of inquiry——three lines of inquiry, to be precise.

"Chocks, Ginger, and Fish?" I said.

Who else? If we're lucky, they'll remember someone who knows Badger. If we're extraordinarily lucky, he'll be one of their oldest, dearest chums. We shall simply have to await developments. You have no reason to feel frustrated, Lori. You've done very well indeed.

"I enjoyed it," I said. "I wasn't looking forward to wandering around Bloomsbury with one of Bill's drivers, but I had a fantastic time."

Is Adam Rivington handsome?

I gave Reginald a meaningful look and suppressed an exasperated sigh. I had, in the past, on a few rare occasions, allowed myself to fall under the spell of a handsome man who was not my husband. I'd never fallen very far, and I'd long since put those days behind me, but Aunt Dimity was always ready to sound the handsome-man alarm.

"Adam's a nice-looking boy," I said, "but his looks have nothing to do with why I enjoyed his company. He opened my eyes to a London I'd never seen before, Dimity. The place is like a time machine—every step takes you into a different era. Adam and I traveled from 1775 to 1997 by crossing from one end of a park to another. We even caught a glimpse of the future, though it was covered in scaffolding . . ."

I repeated my dinner table monologue, describing Queen Square Gardens, the Great Ormond Street Hospital, Lamb's Conduit Street, St. Megwen's Lane, and number 16 Northington Street, and reprising Adam's running commentary on each. By the time I finished, my voice was growing hoarse.

"I don't know why I'm telling you about Bloomsbury," I concluded sheepishly. "You must be as familiar with it as Adam is."

My Bloomsbury was quite different from the Bloomsbury you experienced, Lori. It wasn't bombed as badly as some parts of London, but even so, it had rubble-filled streets, shattered windows, brick dust in the air, and endless queues outside every shop. As for Sam the Cat . . . he came along after my time, so I never had the pleasure of meeting him. Thank you for allowing me to see my old neighborhood through your eyes.

"I hope to see a lot more of it," I said. "The boys and I are planning a special family outing at Christmas—a walking tour of Bloomsbury."

You've certainly changed your tune about London, my dear.

"London is overcrowded, noisy, and exhausting," I said, "but there's magic around every corner." I smiled wryly. "I still need a native guide, though. I'm not brave enough to take on the big scary city single-handed."

Luckily, you have a native guide. Let's hope Adam Rivington's available when the Battle of Britain boys come through for us.

"If I hear from Carrie, I'll be in here like a shot to tell you about it," I said. "Unless I have to make a quick getaway."

Understood. What are your plans for tomorrow?

"James Hobson is giving a metal-detecting demonstration on the village green," I said. "I think the entire population of Finch will be there."

Including Sally Cook?

"She wouldn't miss it for the world," I said. "It'll be the main topic of conversation in Finch for the next six months."

Sally may wish to have a different conversation with you when she finds out that you've been gorging yourself on someone else's pastries. And she will find out. Will and Rob aren't known for their discretion.

"Oh, Lord," I moaned, sinking back in the chair. "She'll probably ban me from the tearoom."

I suggest feigning indifference to Carrie Osborne's culinary masterpieces and reminding Sally of how easily pleased little boys are when it comes to sweets.

"It's worth a try," I said. I covered my mouth with my hand as I was ambushed by a monstrous yawn. "Sorry, Dimity. I've been running on adrenaline since I came home, but I think my adrenaline supply just ran dry."

Of course it has. Time travel can be terribly fatiguing. I'm glad you're getting to know London better, Lori. It's an acquaintance worth cultivating.

"Adam's a good matchmaker," I said. "Good night, Dimity."

Good night, my dear. Sleep well.

I felt a quiet sense of satisfaction as I watched the curving lines of royal-blue ink fade from the page. I'd started the day with zero expectations of finding Badger and ended it with a flicker—three flickers—of hope. In between, I'd discovered a London I could grow to love.

"Don't look so worried, Reg," I said as I closed the journal. "I like London better than I did before, but I don't want to live there. Aunt Dimity's cottage will always be our home."

Reginald's black button eyes seemed to glimmer with relief as I returned the journal to its shelf, banked the fire, and switched off the mantel lamps.

"Look after Aunt Dimity's bracelet," I told him.

I touched a reassuring fingertip to his snout, then headed for the living room to coax Bill into coming upstairs with me.

I had no ulterior motives. We'd both earned a good night's sleep.

Twelve

The gray clouds shifted to a new location overnight, leaving a damp but sunlit world in their wake. Unless the weather changed its mind, which it did almost daily in England, it seemed willing to grant James Hobson the permission he needed to put on a show for the villagers.

When Bill volunteered to drive the boys to school, I didn't even try to talk him out of it. My tardy arrival at the moving van vigil had made me more determined than ever to show up at James's demonstration on time. I wasn't particularly interested in metal detecting, but I took a keen interest in Finch. As I'd told Aunt Dimity, James's hobby would be the talk of the village for the next six months. I wanted to be in on the conversation.

To avoid missing Carrie Osborne's call, I made doubly sure that my cell phone was fully charged before I put Bess and her all-terrain pram into the Range Rover. Though the clouds had moved out, the wind was still very much in residence, and it was a bit too brisk and breezy to take my baby girl for a stroll along the narrow, twisting lane that led to the village.

We cruised past Anscombe Manor, Bree Pym's redbrick house, my father-in-law's wrought-iron gates, and Ivy Cottage, then paused at the apex of the humpbacked bridge to take in the view of the village.

It was a sight that never failed to warm my heart. The village green lay before me, an elongated oval island of tussocky grass separated by a cobbled lane from honey-hued buildings that had stood the test of time for several centuries. The Celtic cross that served as our war memorial seemed to glow in the morning light. Every window box on every cottage was filled to overflowing with chrysanthemums, and wood smoke curled from every crooked chimney, enfolding the village in a golden-gray haze. St. George's stumpy, square bell tower played peekaboo with me through the waving boughs of the churchyard's towering cedars, and a colorful patchwork of fallen leaves spangled the Little Deeping River.

I sighed contentedly.

"Your first autumn," I said to Bess. "I hope all of them are as beautiful as this one—and less windy!"

James Hobson was already on the scene, with Mr. Barlow acting as his assistant. Mr. Barlow's participation was crucial to the success of any event in Finch, not only because he was a willing worker but because he held the keys to the old schoolhouse, where the community's folding chairs and tables were stored. I watched the two men carry a rectangular folding table from the schoolhouse and set it up in the center of the green.

"We can't seem to get our timing right," I told Bess. "We were late for the moving van vigil and now we're early for the demo. Shall we offer to give the men a hand?"

Bess was agreeable, so I bumped down the humpbacked bridge and drove past Sally Cook's tearoom, Bill's office, and the old schoolhouse to park in front of the vicarage, where there was more room for a car. I'd just finished placing Bess in her pram and tucking a blanket around her when Lilian Bunting opened her front door and came down the steps to say hello to Bess. The vicar's gray-haired, scholarly wife wore the tweed skirt suit she always wore when the temperature dipped, but she'd added brown leather gloves, a tweed fishing hat, and a hand-knitted wool scarf to her outfit, to protect herself from the nippy breezes.

"Good morning, Lilian," I said. "Will the vicar be joining us?"

"Teddy's at an ecclesiastical conference in Oxford," she replied. "I promised that I'd memorize James Hobson's presentation for him."

"If Mr. Bunting asks nicely, I'm sure James will give him a private lesson," I said. "On the other hand, he may not have to ask. James is *very* enthusiastic about his hobby."

"So I've heard," said Lilian. "May I push Bess?"

"Be my guest," I said, and relinquished the pram's handles.

We crossed to the folding table, where Mr. Barlow was placing bricks on piles of professionally printed brochures, presumably to keep them from blowing into the next county. While he greeted Bess and discussed the pamphlets with Lilian, I strolled over to speak with James, who was removing a curious device from the cargo area of his Fiat. The device bore a vague resemblance to a black metal broom handle with an L-shaped bend at the top and what appeared to be a black Frisbee at the bottom. I assumed it was his metal detector.

James Hobson was clearly dressed for fieldwork, in a wool turtle-neck, a quilted vest, multipocketed hiking trousers, and hiking boots. He'd accessorized his ensemble with a stocking cap, gloves, kneepads, and a utility belt. A rather large red-handled knife hung in a sheath from the utility belt, as did a trowel and a Day-Glo-orange instrument that looked like a fireplace lighter.

"Hello, Lori," he said as I approached. "Thanks for the blender. Felicity and I used it to make breakfast smoothies this morning."

"Yummy," I said. "Where is Felicity?"

"She's reorganizing our kitchen," James replied sotto voce. "The villagers have been very helpful, but—"

"But they arrange things the way *they* like them," I interjected, nodding. "Opal Taylor rearranged my kitchen cupboards during a Christmas party a few years ago. It took me a week to find the baked beans."

James began to laugh, then stopped short.

"Here they come," he said, peering over my shoulder. "I'd better get in position."

"Break a leg." I gave him a double thumbs-up and returned to Lilian and the pram while James carried his device to the table.

My neighbors were emerging from their homes and businesses to gather around the folding table. Christine and Dick Peacock left the pub to fend for itself, Sally and Henry Cook turned their backs on the tearoom, and Charles Bellingham and Grant Tavistock abandoned their clients' artwork to join in the fun. Peggy Taxman, who was less easygoing about her cash box than the others, locked the Emporium's door before taking her husband's arm and striding majestically toward the table.

The Handmaidens behaved like a synchronized skating team, leaving their cottages individually, then coalescing smoothly into a shoulder-to-shoulder quartet as they crossed the cobbled lane. I couldn't quite envision Opal Taylor, Elspeth Binney, Millicent Scroggins, and Selena Buxton in skimpy skating costumes, but I had to admire their moves.

"Do you know if Bree and Jack are coming?" I asked Lilian. Finch's youngest couple seldom missed a village event.

"They're in Oxford, too," said Lilian, "but unlike Teddy, they'll be there for the rest of the week. Jack's giving a series of lectures on environmental issues, and Bree went along to heckle him. Her words, not mine."

"It sounds like Bree," I said, laughing.

Everyone came over to chat with Bess. I lifted her and her blanket from the pram, gave her a teething ring to gnaw, and held her close to me for warmth. She smiled and drooled and peered interestedly at her admirers' red noses.

George Wetherhead, a painfully shy man who lived in the old schoolmaster's house, was the last of the villagers to appear, nodding bashfully to his neighbors and studiously avoiding Peggy Taxman. George, like everyone else, was bundled up against the wind, but he was the only member of the audience to refrain from talking. The lively conversations slowly rose in volume, as they always did, until Mr. Barlow stuck two fingers in his mouth and whistled shrilly.

"A bit of hush, if you please," he said severely. "That includes you, Sally Cook."

"Sorry," said Sally, who'd been discussing the price of malt vinegar with Christine Peacock.

"We've all met James Hobson," said Mr. Barlow, "and I'm sure we're grateful to him for coming out here on such a raw day to talk to us about his interesting hobby. Let's give him our full attention, shall we?" He glared at Sally, nodded cordially at James, and inserted himself into the audience.

There was a smattering of applause as our featured speaker took center stage.

"Thank you, Mr. Barlow," said James. "And thank you, everyone, for allowing me to talk to you about one of my favorite subjects. I put in an order for perfect weather, by the way, but the delivery was delayed."

The villagers chuckled and would have broken into speech if Mr. Barlow hadn't cleared his throat threateningly.

"If you become involved in metal detecting," James continued, "you'll soon discover that weather doesn't matter. You'll go out on the nastiest days—though possibly not on the snowiest—because your natural curiosity won't allow you to stay at home."

Lilian and I exchanged amused glances, and I knew that we were thinking the same thought: A hobby that rewarded curiosity was guaranteed to find followers in Finch.

"I brought some brochures that give a detailed explanation of how a metal detector works," James said, gesturing to the table. "They also spell out the rules and regulations that govern my hobby. Please feel free to take one with you at the end of the program."

An appreciative murmur ran through the assembled throng, but it was quickly stifled.

"You didn't come here to read pamphlets, though," James went on, smiling, "and you didn't really come here to listen to me. You came here to see a demonstration, so I won't try your patience any longer. Before I start, however, I must emphasize the first rule of metal detecting: Do not trespass. Obtain a landowner's permission, preferably in writing, before you set foot on private property. The village green is communal property, so you can scan it to your heart's content, but private property is off limits without the owner's permission. And now, on with the show!"

The villagers shifted their positions and craned their necks to get a better view of the bent-broom-handle device as James lifted it from the table.

"Here we have a basic metal detector," he said. "It has four parts: the shaft, the stabilizer, the control box, and the search coil. The shaft is self-explanatory. The stabilizer"—he strapped his forearm into a plastic cradle at the top of the shaft—"keeps the unit steady as you sweep the detector back and forth over the ground. The control box"—he pointed to a small black plastic box affixed to the bottom of the shaft's L-shaped curve—"contains the detector's microprocessor, speaker, and batteries. The search coil"—he pointed to the Frisbee at the bottom of the shaft—"is the part that senses metal." He looked every inch the schoolteacher as he lifted his gaze to survey his informal classroom. "All clear?"

My neighbors and I behaved like typical students and nodded, whether it was clear to us or not.

"When the search coil detects a metal object underground," James continued, "it sends an electronic signal up to the control box. The control box then emits an audible signal, to let you know that you've found something. Any questions?"

"What does the audible signal sound like?" asked Charles Bellingham.

"I'd describe it as the mournful wail of a brokenhearted robot," said James, "but I'll let you decide for yourself."

He pressed a button on the control box and swept the coil from side to side a few inches above the ground in front of him. Nothing happened. He looked up and shrugged, then walked slowly forward, moving the coil back and forth in a hypnotic rhythm. Bess and I followed the coil's movement intently, then flinched along with everyone else when the control box gave a mournful wail.

"Sounds as though we've found something," said James.

The wail grew louder and softer as he continued to move the detector over one particular spot in the tufty grass.

"The louder the signal, the closer you are to an object," he explained.

He passed the detector to Mr. Barlow, knelt on the damp ground, and pulled the red-handled knife from its sheath. The blade had one straight edge and one deeply notched serrated edge.

"My digger," said James. "I use it to cut through turf so I can replace the plug neatly when I'm finished. Always replace the turf. If you don't, there will be an outbreak of twisted ankles, and Finch will begin to look like a gopher hotel."

The villagers chuckled distractedly, and I could only manage a tense smile. My heart began to beat faster as the suspense built. It suddenly seemed as if anything were possible. James might uncover gold doubloons or a glittering tiara or the Treasure of the Sierra Madre, though the last find was the least likely, since it was fictional.

James carefully removed the square plug of moist, grass-covered soil he'd cut from the green, then pulled the fire-lighter-like instrument from his utility belt.

"My pinpointer," he explained. "It's a miniature metal detector. It zeros in on an object so I won't have to dig around blindly."

He moved the pinpointer over the plug of dirt, then stuck it inside the hole. Bess and I flinched again as a high-pitched beep rent the air. James returned the pinpointer to his belt, reached into the hole, and clasped something in his fingers. I could almost feel my neighbors holding their breath as he withdrew his hand and held his find high in the air for all to see.

It was a round brooch made of pearls inset in gold to mimic a daisy's petals.

Dick Peacock gave a shout of laughter. "It's the same brooch!" he exclaimed. "The same tatty brooch you showed us the other day in your back garden!"

The laughter spread as the others caught on to James's trick.

"I thought the turf came away too easily," said Henry Cook, smiling ruefully. "You'd cut it already, hadn't you?"

"I cut it first thing this morning," said Mr. Barlow, stepping forward to stand beside James. "And I buried the brooch. James and I reckoned you wouldn't take much notice if I was mucking about on the green, seeing as I look after it."

"You'd make a fine magician's assistant," said Lilian Bunting.

James replaced the plug of soil and grass, returned his digger to its sheath, and got to his feet.

"Mr. Barlow has been an invaluable ally," he said. "I hope the rest of you will forgive our little deception. If my demonstration had taken as long as a real hunt, we might have been here all day."

Peggy Taxman, who'd been uncharacteristically silent throughout the program, gave a disparaging sniff.

"Seems like a lot of nonsense to me," she boomed. "Grown men playing in the dirt. Whatever will you think of next? Toy soldiers? Skipping ropes? Come, Jasper," she bellowed to her husband. "We have less childish things to do."

She wheeled around and sailed imperiously back to the Emporium, with Jasper trailing meekly at her heels.

"Don't bother your head about Peggy," Sally Cook said to James. "Her nose is out of joint because no one asked her to take charge of the demonstration."

"Does Mrs. Taxman know anything about metal detecting?" James asked, looking baffled.

"She does now," said Elspeth Binney, "but she didn't before. It wouldn't have stopped her from taking charge, though."

"She *always* takes charge," said Selena Buxton.

"She thinks it's her *right* to take charge," said Millicent Scroggins.

"And we let her," said Lilian, with a hint of reproof in her tone, "because someone has to take charge, and most of us don't want to."

"True enough," said Mr. Barlow. "Peggy may be bossy, but she gets things done. Have you finished with your talk, James?"

James, who had been following the conversation closely, looked blank for a moment, then nodded.

"The demonstration is over," he announced. "Thanks for coming.

Don't forget to take a brochure home with you. If you have any questions, or if you'd like to have a go with my metal detector, please feel free to knock on my door."

He received a rousing round of applause that wasn't as loud as it should have been because nearly every member of his satisfied audience was wearing gloves.

"Who's for hot cocoa?" Sally asked the group at large.

The group responded by snatching brochures from the table and moving as one toward the tearoom.

"I hope you'll join us, James," said Henry. "My wife makes an excellent cup of cocoa."

"I'll pack up my things and fetch Felicity," said James. "She loves cocoa. And she can't find ours," he added when the others were out of earshot. "Are you coming to the tearoom, too, Lori?"

"I wish I could," I said, "but duty calls. Bess needs a diaper change, a snack, and a nap, so I'll drink my hot cocoa at home. Bravo, James. I think you'll be hearing quite a few knocks on your door."

"I hope so," he said. "Metal detecting is a peaceful pastime, with brief spikes of excitement that keep me coming back for more."

"You could be describing Finch," I said, smiling.

As it turned out, I had it backward. There was plenty of excitement in store for Finch, but peace would be hard to come by.

Thirteen

The perfect weather James Hobson had ordered arrived the following morning. The wind faded, the temperature rose, and the sun smiled down on my little corner of England. London was not so fortunate. The rain that had driven Adam and me into Carrie's Coffees had decided to extend its stay in the city. Carrie Osborne had touched base with me the previous evening, but her call had merely confirmed what she'd already told me: Her Battle of Britain boys would remain at home until the wet weather passed.

"You could ask Carrie if she has their addresses," Bill suggested over breakfast.

"They're old men nursing war wounds," I reminded him. "If they're feeling too lousy to go to their favorite coffeehouse, I'm not going to disturb them in their own homes."

"Why do the old men have war wounds?" Will asked.

"They were injured in battle a long time ago," I told him, "and their injuries still ache when it's rainy."

"Why do their injuries ache when it's rainy?" asked Rob.

"I think it has something to do with the change in air pressure," I replied, and since it was far too early in the morning to explain the concept of air pressure to a pair of inquisitive nine-year-olds, I continued, "Daddy knows much more about it than I do. He'll explain it to you when you get home from school."

Bill gave me a "thanks a lot" look and went back to eating his porridge.

After waving him off to work, dropping the boys off at school, and looking in vain for chores Bill hadn't done, Bess and I enjoyed a midmorning snack, then drove to Finch to deliver a box of baby clothes to the vicarage for the next jumble sale. We were instantly diverted from our mission by the sight that met our eyes as we topped the humpbacked bridge.

Mr. Barlow was using James Hobson's metal detector to scan the village green, while a knot of villagers followed his every move. Dick Peacock, Henry Cook, and the Handmaidens looked as if they were watching a Lilliputian tennis match as Mr. Barlow swept the device back and forth over the ground. I'd never thought of metal detecting as a spectator sport, but it had clearly become one in Finch.

Mr. Barlow wore his own utility belt and knee pads, but he'd borrowed James's red-handled digger as well as the pinpointer. To judge by his rapt expression, I had little doubt that he would have his own equipment the next time I saw him.

The action was taking place on a narrow swath of green between the Emporium and the tearoom, so I parked the Rover in front of the tearoom, put Bess in her pram, and joined Mr. Barlow's retinue. I was given a neighborly welcome, and Bess received her usual chorus of accolades. While Dick, Henry, and the Handmaidens passed her around, I asked Mr. Barlow if he'd found anything.

"Six tenpenny nails, a horseshoe, and a handful of coins," he replied, patting a pocket on his utility belt.

"An impressive haul," I said. "What kinds of coins?"

"Mostly modern," he said. "Post-decimalization, that is. I did find a 1965 halfpenny, though. You don't see many of them around anymore."

"I have a milk bottle filled with old halfpennies," Dick said dampingly.

"You don't see them in circulation, is what I meant," said Mr. Barlow.

"They're not *in* circulation," Dick pointed out. "That's why you don't see them around anymore."

"Never mind," said Mr. Barlow with a long-suffering sigh.

I suspected that his next foray into metal detecting would take place in a less conspicuous location.

"We've been talking, Lori," Elspeth Binney said.

"Yes, you have," Mr. Barlow muttered grumpily.

He continued his slow march while his entourage—and Bess—stayed behind with me.

"We think we should take a page out of James Hobson's book," Elspeth went on, "and create a little museum of our own, right here in Finch."

"Where?" I asked.

"In the schoolhouse," said Millicent Scroggins, with the triumphant air of someone who'd solved a challenging riddle. "We could display our finds in a glass case in the schoolhouse."

"*Our* finds?" queried Mr. Barlow over his shoulder.

"I'm sure *most* of us will regard it as a duty as well as a privilege to donate our finds to the village museum," Elspeth said pointedly. "We'll give full credit to the donors," she added in a slightly raised voice, looking hopefully at the back of Mr. Barlow's head.

"We're studying calligraphy with Mr. Shuttleworth," Selena Buxton informed me, referring to the Handmaidens' art teacher. "We could make beautiful handwritten labels for the items in the glass case."

"We'd record the donor's name as well as where and when the donated item was discovered," said Opal Taylor. "It would be just like James's museum room, only with more than one donor." She, too, raised her voice as she addressed Mr. Barlow's back. "I'm sure *everyone* in the village will be eager to participate in such a worthy project."

"Sounds like a great idea," I said. "Do you have a display case?"

"Not yet," Millicent admitted.

"There's a glass case in the back room of the Emporium," said Henry Cook. "Maybe Peggy would lend it to us for the museum."

There was a brief silence, as if everyone present had recalled Peggy Taxman's disparaging comments about "grown men playing in the dirt."

"Or we could buy one secondhand," Henry Cook amended hurriedly, realizing his mistake.

"With whose money?" called the ever-practical Mr. Barlow.

"We could take up a collection," Millicent Scroggins proposed. "Or we could hold bake sales. Or—"

"Maybe we should see what kind of things people find," Dick interrupted, "before we start raising money for a museum. If it's just a load of old nails and a handful of coins I can find in my own till, I don't see the point of—"

He, too, was interrupted, but not by a human voice. Every head swiveled in Mr. Barlow's direction as the detector's mournful wail cut through the chatter.

"Wait!" Henry shouted at Mr. Barlow. "I promised Sally I'd tell her when the thing went off again."

Henry ran into the tearoom, and the Handmaidens ran toward Mr. Barlow. After passing Bess to me, Dick Peacock scurried over to gaze, enraptured, at a spot a few inches in front of Mr. Barlow's work boots. Mr. Barlow laid aside the detector, knelt on the ground, and pulled the red-handled digger from its sheath.

Having received a surfeit of adoration, Bess was happy to return to the pram and munch on the shark-shaped teether her brothers had picked out for her. I was still fastening her safety harness when Henry and Sally trotted out of the tearoom and sped past us, hand in hand. Bess and I reached the circle of observers in time to see Mr. Barlow pull the digger out of the soil and slide it back into its sheath.

"Probably another ruddy nail," he grumbled as he pulled the square plug of dirt from the ground. He pointed the pinpointer at the plug of dirt, and to his evident surprise, the miniature metal detector beeped. With the delicacy of a man who knew every blade of grass on the village green personally, he dug his finger and thumb into the spot the pinpointer had indicated and removed a small, mud-covered object. It didn't look like a nail.

"It's a ring," Mr. Barlow announced, brushing the wet soil from his find.

The rest of us responded with a sharp communal intake of breath, except for Bess, who continued to chew placidly on her shark.

"A lost ring," breathed Elspeth, who was a romantic at heart. "How tragic."

"It could've been thrown away in a fit of pique," said Opal, who was less of a romantic.

"Maybe she threw it at her boyfriend's head," said Millicent, "because she saw him kissing another girl."

"How do you know it's a woman's ring?" Dick demanded. "Could be a man's."

"It's a wedding ring," Mr. Barlow informed us, getting to his feet. "A gold wedding band. There's an inscription inside it."

"Wonderful!" cried Elspeth, clasping her hands to her chest. "If it's a name, perhaps we can restore the lost ring to its rightful owner."

"If she wants it back," said Opal.

"It may not be a *she*," Dick insisted.

"Too big to be a woman's ring," said Mr. Barlow.

"I told you so," said Dick, preening.

"Unless it belonged to a big woman," Mr. Barlow added, taking some of the wind out of Dick's sails. He squinted at the gold ring, then shook his head. "Can't read the inscription. Looks foreign." He held the ring out to me. "You have a go, Lori. You're better at foreign languages than I am."

I didn't know what had given him that idea, but I took the ring from him and examined it closely.

"I think it's Spanish," I said, and attempted to read the words aloud. "*Te amaré para—*" I broke off and looked uneasily at Sally.

"*Siempre.*" Sally finished the sentence for me in a voice that could have frozen molten steel. "*Te amaré para siempre.*" She turned a gimlet eye on her wilting husband. "You can translate the inscription into English for us, can't you, Henry?"

But Henry didn't have to translate the inscription for us because we'd heard him translate it once before. Everyone in Finch knew that, having met and fallen in love in Mexico, Sally and Henry had decided to have their wedding rings engraved in Spanish. Henry had read the inscription aloud at their wedding ceremony, then repeated it in English as he'd slipped Sally's ring onto her finger. It was a moment none of us would ever forget.

" 'I will love you forever,' " Sally said frostily. "Isn't that what it means, Henry?"

"Yes, dear," he croaked.

"Henry?" said Sally, tilting her head toward the ring I was holding. "Is that your wedding ring?"

Henry gulped.

"If it is," Sally continued remorselessly, "then what's that *thing* you're wearing on your ring finger?"

"I can explain," he said, hiding his left hand behind his back.

Sally folded her arms and said, "I sincerely hope you can."

"Do you remember when you asked me to pick up a jar of macadamia nuts at the Emporium?" Henry asked as beads of sweat began to glisten on his forehead.

"Macadamia nuts?" Sally peered at him as if he'd lost his mind. "Henry, that was *ten months* ago, when I made the macadamia nut cake for my granddaughter's birthday."

"Yes, I know." Henry held his hands up in a pacifying gesture, caught himself, and thrust his left hand behind his back again. "But here's the thing: The ring was on my finger when I left the tearoom, but it wasn't there when I came back from the Emporium. I looked everywhere for it, Sal, but I couldn't find it, and I couldn't ask if anyone else had found it because I couldn't let anyone know I'd lost it. I knew how much it meant to you, Sal, so I went back to the jeweler and had another ring made in a smaller size so it wouldn't slip off so easily."

"Wait a minute," said Sally. A distant look came into her eyes, as if a memory were clicking into place. "That would be about the time you cut your finger with the bread knife, wouldn't it? The finger you covered up with the sticking plaster?"

"I couldn't think of any other way to keep you from seeing my finger," said Henry. "It took a week to get the new ring from the jeweler. I promise you, Sal, it was the worst week of my life."

Sally didn't appear to be sympathetic. Her nostrils flared as she took a deep breath and said through tightened lips, "You've worn a counterfeit wedding ring for the past *ten months*, Henry Cook?"

"It's a very nice ring," Henry said pleadingly. "It's eighteen-karat gold, just like the first one. And it's not as if our marriage is counterfeit, is it, Sal? It's—it's just a ring."

The Handmaidens groaned, I winced, and Dick looked away, as if he couldn't bear to watch a man dig his own grave.

"It's *just a ring*?" Sally repeated in a voice shrill enough to shatter the tearoom's windows. "It may be 'just a ring' to you, Henry Cook, but it's ten months of barefaced lies to me!"

She wheeled around and made for the tearoom. Henry ran after her and managed to slip inside mere seconds before she slammed the door. A plump hand appeared in a window to flip the OPEN sign to CLOSED.

And all was silence.

"Um," I said awkwardly. "What should I do with Henry's ring?"

"I don't think Sally'll let you put it in the museum," said Mr. Barlow, with a hearty guffaw.

"It's no laughing matter," Elspeth scolded. "Henry should have told Sally the truth instead of pulling the wool over her eyes with his little charade."

"She would have hit the roof either way," said Dick. "I don't blame him for putting it off as long as he could."

"You don't blame a man for lying to his wife for nearly a year?" Opal said, looking outraged.

"Not if it keeps peace in the family," Dick responded.

"But it's a false peace," Selena objected.

"Better than no peace at all," said Dick.

Mr. Barlow quietly replaced the plug of grassy soil, tamped it into place, and picked up the metal detector.

"I'm packing it in for the day," he said. "I can't stand the noise."

Dick and the Handmaidens stared at him as he walked home.

"Was he referring to us?" Opal asked indignantly.

"I don't think he was talking about the metal detector," said Elspeth.

"We were making a bit of a racket," Dick acknowledged equitably.

"Ah, well, it's lunchtime. I'd best get back to the pub or Christine'll think I've abandoned her. See you later, ladies. 'Bye, Bess."

Sated by the morning's entertainment, the Handmaidens made their farewells to Bess and turned automatically toward the tearoom. When the CLOSED sign brought them up short, they executed a neat about-face and headed for the pub instead. I was sure that they would continue the debate about marital deception over their shepherd's pies and their fizzy lemonades, but I was also sure that Dick would change his tune in front of his wife.

I pushed the pram toward the Rover, then swung around when someone called my name. James Hobson waved to me from the pub's doorstep, then strode purposefully in my direction. He looked disturbed and slightly bewildered as he came to a halt in front of me.

"Lori," he said, "what on earth is going on?"

Fourteen

ince it looked as though my conversation with James might be a lengthy one, I pulled Bess into my arms yet again.

"What happened?" he said. "I was having a swift half at the pub when Dick Peacock and—"

"The ladies," I put in, to save him the trouble of remembering the Handmaidens' names.

"When Dick Peacock and the ladies," he continued, with a grateful nod, "came storming in with some story about Mr. Barlow using my metal detector to unearth an appalling secret that would ruin a marriage and tear the village apart."

"Yep," I said. "That about sums it up."

James blinked at me for a moment, then observed, "You don't seem concerned."

"I'm not concerned," I said, "and you shouldn't be, either. You'll soon learn to take most of what our neighbors say with a truckload of salt."

Bess said hello to James. He gave her a preoccupied glance, then did a double take.

"Is your daughter chewing on a shark?" he asked.

"She is," I said. "It was a gift from Will and Rob."

"Better than a shark chewing on your daughter, I suppose." He smiled, but quickly became serious again. "Then there's no truth to the story I heard in the pub?"

"There's a kernel of truth," I replied, "in the shape of a wedding ring. . . ."

I told him about Mr. Barlow's unfortunate discovery, its impact on Sally and Henry Cook, and the argument it had spawned between Dick Peacock and the Handmaidens. When I finished, James looked more distressed than ever.

"The poor Cooks," he said. "It must have been a painful revelation."

"It's a tempest in a teapot," I assured him. "Sally and Henry will kiss and make up, and the great debate about whether husbands are allowed to lie to their wives under special circumstances will go on until the end of time—or until another hot topic comes along to replace it. Spats are pretty common in Finch. It's a way of letting off steam."

"Spats can lead to feuds, though," James said. "I've seen it happen." He glanced anxiously at the tearoom, then went on. "I was out detecting near my seaside village when I found a pocket watch. It had belonged to a local landowner who'd died the year before, and it had been a bone of contention in the family ever since, with one side accusing the other of hiding it before the will was read."

"You proved that the pocket watch had been lost," I said. "They must have been relieved to know that no one had hidden it."

"You'd think so, wouldn't you?" said James. "In fact, my discovery only made things worse. The family had just begun to settle down when I turned up. It was like throwing fuel on a fire. The watch reignited all the old resentments, and the feud became more heated than ever. The watch was awarded to eldest son, but he had to go to court to get it. I wanted to sink through the floor every time he consulted it, which he did, ostentatiously, whenever his cousins were around. As far as I know, the two sides of the family still aren't speaking to each other."

"You can't blame yourself for their foolishness," I said.

"I know," said James, "but I should have told the story of the pocket watch during the demonstration on Wednesday. It should have been the first thing on my agenda. I should have warned the villagers to be careful when they dig up the past. Because it's not always pretty."

"The villagers can handle it," I said. "Quarrels are soon mended in Finch. Sally will give Henry what-for for a while, but they won't let a lost ring or a few little white lies come between them. Those two were made for each other. You'll see."

"Their dirty linen was washed in a very public manner," said James. "It must have been humiliating for them."

"We've all had our dirty linen washed, dried, and folded in public at one time or another in Finch," I said. "It can't be avoided in such a small village, but we've survived. If you ask me, Sally enjoyed her moment in the limelight. She'll be out and about again before you know it."

"I hope so," James said earnestly, "because she's the next person in my rota."

"Your rota?" I said.

"As you predicted, I had quite a few knocks on my door after the demonstration," said James. "Everyone who'd been there wanted to borrow my metal detector, so I made up a rota. Mr. Barlow was at the top of the list, of course."

"And Sally is next?" I said.

"She was supposed to have her turn with the detector this afternoon," said James, gazing worriedly at the tearoom, "but I'm not sure she'll be up for it now."

"Don't give her place away too soon," I cautioned. "Sally won't like it if the next person in the rota gets the jump on her. If I were you, I'd carry on as if nothing had happened. I can just about guarantee that Sally will."

"In that case," said James, "I'd best collect the detector from Mr. Barlow. I hear he found some interesting nails."

"I'm sure he'll be happy to show them to you," I said. "And I'm afraid I have to be going. Bess needs her lunch."

"Sorry, Bess," he said, patting her arm. "I didn't mean to hold you up. Thanks for clarifying the situation for me, Lori. Enjoy your lunch, Bess. I hope you haven't spoiled your appetite with that shark."

James took off for Mr. Barlow's house, Bess went back into the pram, and I wheeled her into Wysteria Lodge, the lovely old building that served as Bill's place of work. I hadn't counted on having a picnic lunch with my husband, but I always packed extra provisions for Bess in the diaper bag, and Bill and I could improvise.

Bill was delighted to see us, not least because he was dying to know what had caused the ruckus on the village green. Although my husband pretended to avoid gossip, he never tired of hearing it from me. After running across to the pub to fetch an oversized ploughman's lunch for us to share, he sat back and listened while I filled him in on Mr. Barlow's sensational debut as a metal detectorist.

"Metal detecting is a hobby custom-made for Finch," he said when he finished laughing. "It's just another form of snooping."

Bill and I dug into our cheddar cheese, smoked ham, pickled onions, green salad, and crusty bread, undeterred by the sight of Bess feeding herself mashed butternut squash and puréed chicken. When she was finished, I cleaned her and her immediate surroundings, handed her over to her father, and crossed to the window to survey the village green.

"I knew it!" I exclaimed. "Sally Cook and James Hobson are out there right now with his metal detector. I knew Sally wouldn't give up her place in the rota."

"I'll bet James stuck around to deliver his pocket watch speech," said Bill, "should the need arise."

"You're probably right," I said, concentrating on Sally. "Oh, Bill, I think she's found something!"

"Go," he urged. "I'll look after Bess."

"Thanks," I said, opening the door.

"And you can explain air pressure to the boys when they come home from school," he added slyly.

"No problem," I said. "If I know our sons, they'll have forgotten all about it by then."

I glanced to my left as I left Wysteria Lodge, saw that the tearoom's CLOSED sign had been flipped to OPEN, and smiled. Sally was too canny a businesswoman to let private quarrels interfere with her bottom line.

I crossed the cobbled lane at a trot, then slowed to a walk as I approached Sally, who'd elected to scan a narrow section of green behind the war memorial. If she'd hoped to avoid drawing a crowd, she'd succeeded. James was the only one following her progress.

"Everything okay, Sally?" I asked when I was within earshot.

She favored me with a complacent smile.

"Everything's fine," she said. "Henry's promised never to lie to me again."

Knowing Sally as I did, I raised an eyebrow as I said, "And . . . ?"

"And he's agreed to clean the kitchen in the tearoom for the next month," she said smugly, "while I have a lie-down." She bent once more to her task. "Have I found something, James?"

Whatever James's intentions had been, Sally had evidently kept him around to do the dirty work. While he went through the usual routine with the digger and the pinpointer, Lilian Bunting emerged from the vicarage and strolled over to see what we were doing.

"It looks as though I've arrived at an exciting moment," she said after we'd exchanged greetings.

"Let's hope it's not *too* exciting," I murmured.

James pulled a small object out of the hole and sat back on his heels to examine it.

"What is it, James?" Sally asked.

"It's a coin," he replied.

"An old one?" she asked hopefully.

"It's not particularly old," said James, getting to his feet, "but it's unexpected." He passed the coin to Sally. "It's an Italian coin. A 1951 one-lira piece."

If he'd expected to astonish us, he must have been disappointed.

"Ah," said Lilian, nodding.

"Piero," said Sally.

"Must be," I said.

"Who is Piero?" James asked.

"The late Piero Alessandro Sciaparelli was an Italian prisoner-of-war," Lilian explained. "After the war he married a local girl and went on to sire one of the most powerful farming families in the county. There's no way to prove it, of course, but it's likely that Sally's lira once belonged to Piero."

"His family will want it," said Sally, pocketing the one-lira coin. "I'll make sure it gets to them."

"You should record the time and date of your find," I told her, "in case the Sciaparellis decide to donate Piero's lira to our museum."

Three pairs of uncomprehending eyes turned to stare at me.

"What museum?" Sally asked suspiciously.

"Not the kind with a tearoom," I said quickly. "Just a glass case in the schoolhouse where Finch's metal detectorists can display their finds. Elspeth, Opal, Millicent, and Selena came up with the idea."

"It's a splendid one," said Lilian. "Perhaps Mrs. Sciaparelli would donate a photograph of her father-in-law to go along with the lira."

"I'll ask her," said Sally. "But for now, I'd like to get on with my detecting."

There was a new spring in James's step as he ambled along beside Sally, as if he were relieved that her find had produced concord rather than discord.

Our foursome more than doubled in size when Mr. Barlow, Dick Peacock, and the Handmaidens, having finished their respective lunches, succumbed to the lure of the metal detector and joined us. Lilian paused to speak with the Handmaidens about the proposed museum while the men and I followed James and Sally, but the ladies scrambled to catch up with us when the device wailed again.

James dropped to his knees and went to work with the digger. He left the pinpointer in his utility belt, however, because he didn't need it. He simply reached into the hole he'd created and pulled out a rusty hammer.

"That's my hammer!" Mr. Barlow exclaimed.

Sally sighed and moved on. She was clearly on the lookout for bigger game.

Mr. Barlow took the hammer from James and studied it closely.

"That's my hammer, all right," he said, nodding.

"The hammer you accused me of stealing?" Dick inquired waspishly.

"I never accused you of stealing it," Mr. Barlow retorted. "I just wondered when you planned to return it, is all. Seems a reasonable thing to wonder, seeing as you borrowed the ruddy thing five years ago."

"You as good as called me a thief," Dick persisted.

"No, I didn't," Mr. Barlow said stoutly. "Must be your guilty conscience talking."

"I don't have a guilty conscience," Dick snapped, "because I'm not a thief."

"What would you call a man who borrows things and doesn't return them?" Mr. Barlow shot back.

James plugged the hole in a somewhat slapdash manner and stood.

"Gentlemen," he began, but before he could deliver his pocket watch speech, Sally cut him off.

"Stop your bickering, you two!" she hollered. "I've found something else!"

Fifteen

The men's raised voices had masked the metal detector's wail, but Sally's shout rang out loud and clear. Mr. Barlow and Dick Peacock put their argument on hold and joined the rest of us as we clustered around another seemingly innocuous patch of grass.

James was already at work with the digger. As he utilized the pinpointer and probed the soil with his fingers, I felt the same thrill of anticipation I'd felt during his demonstration. The small oblong object he extracted from the hole was grimier than his tatty brooch had been, but its anonymity only increased my sense of infinite possibilities.

"A trick of the trade," James said, pulling a small squirt bottle from his utility belt. "Water reveals what mud conceals."

He stood, and his rapt audience leaned in as he washed away the soil clinging to Sally's most recent discovery. As the mellow autumn sunlight touched the object's glittering surface, I was struck by a dizzying wave of déjà vu. In an instant, I was back in my attic, gazing in horror at the gap behind Aunt Dimity's leather trunk, while a row of glittering bloodred eyes peered at me from the shadows.

"Aunt Dimity's bracelet," I said under my breath.

"Pardon?" said Lilian.

"Nothing," I said absently, and leaned in further.

I couldn't tell what the oblong object was, but I could see that it was gold colored and inset with tiny garnetlike gems in a pattern that looked startlingly familiar.

"W-what is it?" I asked unsteadily.

"A hair clip," Sally answered, sounding bored to death. "A spring-loaded hair clip."

I stared at her, taken aback by the speed of her reply.

"A hair clip?" I said. "Are you sure?"

"Of course I'm sure," said Sally. "I must have seen it a hundred times. It's Peggy Taxman's. She won it at the fair in Upper Deeping years ago, when she was still Peggy Kitchen. You could win all sorts of cheap baubles at the fair. Peggy won most of hers at the coconut shies. No surprise there. She had arms on her like a stevedore."

"It was a traveling fair," said Mr. Barlow, as if Sally's words had stirred a distant memory. "Came to Upper Deeping once a year, in the spring. Madame Karela's Fair, it was called."

"Best bull's-eyes on the planet," said Dick, smacking his lips. "And the best candy floss."

"I liked the rides," said Opal. "The roundabout, the swing boats, the dodgems—"

"Don't forget the helter-skelter," Millicent put in with a demure titter. "The boys always tried to look up our skirts when we slid down the helter-skelter."

"I didn't," said Mr. Barlow. "I was too busy winning my spurs at the Wild West shooting gallery."

"I won a giant gorilla at the shooting gallery," said Selena. "Don't look so surprised, Mr. Barlow. I was quite a good shot. I knew how to compensate for the misaligned sights."

"I *knew* they tampered with the sights!" Mr. Barlow expostulated, looking chagrined.

A pleasant hum filled the air as my neighbors shared stories about Madame Karela's traveling fair. James seemed to relax as a flood of nostalgia overtook the hammer controversy.

"A fortune-teller told me I'd meet a tall, dark stranger," said Sally. "She meant Henry, naturally."

"She must have seen a long way into the future," Millicent commented, giving Sally a skeptical glance.

"What do you mean by that?" Sally demanded.

"I mean that you and Henry met two years ago," Millicent replied, "but the fair hasn't been to Upper Deeping in decades."

"Fortune-tellers prey on the simple-minded," said Dick. "It's a well-known fact."

Sally bristled, and James, sensing another brouhaha brewing, held the hair clip out to her.

"It's not worth much, Mrs. Cook, but it's a pretty thing," he said. "Some might say that the decoration was inspired by ancient Celtic jewelry, but the use of gold and red combined with the symmetrical, interlacing pattern of abstract zoomorphic forms reminds me of the Anglo-Saxon artifacts on display at the British Museum."

He might as well have spoken in Anglo-Saxon. The villagers greeted his remarks with looks of polite incomprehension, then nodded amiably at him and resumed their reminiscences. I, on the other hand, heard an alarm bell ring in the back of my mind.

Aunt Dimity's bracelet was no cheap fairground prize. It seemed absurd to think that it could be a priceless Anglo-Saxon artifact, but I couldn't deny that James had described its characteristics with uncanny precision. If I closed my eyes, I could see the intricate, interlacing pattern of garnets gleaming in the gold setting. In retrospect, I could even see the "abstract zoomorphic forms" James had mentioned, writhing like stylized snakes across the bracelet's surface.

"James," I said, as the alarm bell continued to ring, "are you referring to the Sutton Hoo ship burial exhibition?"

"I am," he replied, looking pleased. "Have you seen it?"

"Not yet," I said.

"I've seen it," said Lilian, "and I agree with you, James. Whoever designed Peggy Taxman's hair clip must have been inspired, albeit remotely, by Anglo-Saxon design."

"Did the Anglo-Saxons make jewelry?" I asked.

"Anglo-Saxon hoards and burial sites almost always contain jewelry," said James. "Their craftsmen made pendants, rings, bracelets, brooches . . ." He smirked slightly as he held the hair clip at arm's length. "As far as I'm aware, however, they did not make spring-loaded hair clips."

Lilian chuckled, and I forced a smile.

"What would happen," I said, keeping my voice light, "if we discovered an Anglo-Saxon hoard?"

"You'll find a detailed answer in the brochures I brought along to the demonstration," said James, "but the simple answer is: You'd have to report your find to the proper authorities or risk receiving a severe penalty. Treasure found on English soil belongs to the Crown, you see. If you pocketed an ancient artifact made of gold or silver, you'd be nothing more than a common thief."

Mr. Barlow's voice broke through my tangled thoughts.

"Someone'll have to return the hair clip to Peggy," he said.

"I'll take it to her," Elspeth said bravely. "She might be willing to donate her glass case to our museum if she has something to display in it."

"Good luck," said Mr. Barlow, without sounding the least bit hopeful.

As Elspeth sallied forth on what the rest of us regarded as a suicide mission, Sally handed the metal detector to James.

"Done for the day?" he inquired.

"I'd better be," she said, "or there won't be anything left for the next person to find. Thank you, James. I've enjoyed my little poke-about."

"Don't forget to bring Piero's lira to Mrs. Sciaparelli," said Lilian.

"Piero's lira?" Millicent said alertly.

"The first item I detected this afternoon," Sally informed her. "Come to the tearoom, and I'll show it to you."

Our metal-detecting party dispersed. Mr. Barlow, Dick Peacock, and the remaining Handmaidens followed Sally to the reopened tearoom. James, Lilian, and I, having witnessed the discovery of Piero's lira, went our separate ways, James to Ivy Cottage, Lilian to the vicarage, and I, my thoughts racing, to my husband's office.

I entered Wysteria Lodge to find Bess asleep in her pram and Bill on a conference call with a pair of quarrelsome clients in Andorra. I checked Bess's diaper automatically, then sat on the leather sofa Bill used primarily for power naps and fidgeted restlessly until he ended the call.

"What's wrong?" he asked, studying my pensive expression. "Did Sally find my *real* wedding ring buried in the village green?"

"I almost wish she had," I said, and rose resolutely to my feet. "I need to see the Sutton Hoo exhibition at the British Museum, Bill, and I need to see it now. Would you please bring it up on your computer?"

"No problem," he said, looking intrigued.

I crossed to stand behind him while he tapped a few keys on his desktop, then watched in dismay as he scrolled through the striking images that popped up on the screen.

"Do those Anglo-Saxon trinkets remind you of anything?" I asked.

His eyes widened as comprehension dawned.

"They remind me of the bracelet you found in the attic," he said. "The bracelet Badger gave to Aunt Dimity. Similar materials, colors, decorations . . ." He craned his neck to look up at me. "You're not suggesting that Aunt Dimity's bracelet came from an Anglo-Saxon burial mound, are you?"

"I may be suggesting just that," I said, and before he could make fun of me for going off the deep end, I added firmly, "Hear me out."

I walked around to the front of the desk, sat in the chair reserved for clients, and began to assemble the thoughts that had triggered my alarm bell.

"Dimity told me that Badger looked like a man who did outdoor work," I said. "Her exact words were: 'He was fit and trim and very brown, and he had a gardener's strong, rough hands.'"

Bill rested his forearms on the desk and nodded for me to go on.

"Dimity was deeply impressed by Badger's intelligence," I continued. "She didn't think he could be an ordinary jobbing gardener because, and I quote, 'He had the accent and the vocabulary of a well-educated young man.'"

"If he hadn't been well educated," Bill reasoned, "he wouldn't have been able to converse knowledgeably about so many subjects."

"That's right," I said. "He talked about all kinds of things with Dimity—art, music, literature, architecture. He helped her to broaden her cultural horizons, and he couldn't have done that unless his own cultural horizons were pretty broad to begin with."

"Makes sense," said Bill. "Go on."

"Badger was a regular at the Rose Café," I said, "so he must have lived or worked or lived *and* worked in Bloomsbury. What's the biggest attraction in Bloomsbury?"

Bill glanced at his computer screen, then looked at me.

"The British Museum," he said.

"The repository of the world's greatest collection of Anglo-Saxon artifacts," I said as emphatically as I could without waking Bess. "What if Badger wasn't a gardener, Bill? What if he was an *archaeologist*?"

Bill pursed his lips thoughtfully.

"Archaeologists tend to work outdoors," he acknowledged. "I imagine they have strong hands, and they'd have to be well educated. The British Museum sponsors excavations, and Badger would be an apt nickname for a man who's involved in excavations."

"An archaeologist would oversee the stuff that came out of his excavations, wouldn't he?" I said. "He'd make sure it was being processed properly, and he'd probably have a say in how it was displayed. So he'd be in and out of the museum all the time."

"I suppose so," said Bill.

"What if Badger worked for the British Museum?" I said urgently. "What if . . ." I took a steadying breath, then went on in a stage whisper, as if I were afraid of being overheard by the museum police. "What if Badger *stole* Aunt Dimity's bracelet from the British Museum?"

"It's a big leap," Bill said slowly, "but young men in love have been known to do crazier things."

"The bracelet could be the tip of the iceberg," I said. "Who knows how many irreplaceable treasures Badger took home with him?"

"I suspect someone at the museum would have noticed if he'd emptied a storage room into his briefcase," Bill said dryly.

"Okay," I said, backing down. "Let's stick with the bracelet. If it was found on English soil, it belongs to the Crown. Taking it from the British Museum would be like picking the queen's pocket!"

"I doubt that Her Majesty would have him drawn and quartered," said Bill.

"He could end up in jail, though," I said earnestly. I looked down, then shook my head. "To tell you the truth, I don't much care about what happens to Badger."

"I know," Bill said gently. "You care about Dimity."

"She respected and admired Badger," I said. "In her own way, she loved him. She still thinks of him as the kind, wise man who gave her a sense of direction when she was rudderless. By tarnishing his name, I'll be tarnishing one of her most precious memories." I clasped my hands together tightly and leaned forward on the desk. "If I'm right, then the man who helped Aunt Dimity to find her purpose in life was nothing more than a common thief."

There was a pause during which my words seemed to linger in the air. Bess made a snuffling noise, Bill gazed into the middle distance, and I wished more fervently than ever that I'd left the garnet bracelet in the attic.

"Are you going to share your suspicions with Dimity?" Bill asked.

"No," I said. "Not until I have something more substantial to tell her. That's why I have to speak with Adam."

"Adam Rivington?" said Bill, looking confused. "My driver?"

"Your driver," I said, "is studying Anglo-Saxon archaeology."

"Is he?" said Bill.

"Typical," I said scornfully. "You don't know the first thing about Adam, do you?"

"I know that he's honest, clean, polite, punctual, levelheaded, and able to find his way around London," Bill replied. "What else should I know?"

"It's lucky that one of us takes an interest in people," I said, rolling my eyes. "For your information, four generations of Adam's family have lived in Bloomsbury. His great-grandfather witnessed the zeppelin raids, and his grandfather was an air raid warden during the Blitz. Furthermore, he takes his coffee black, he doesn't like to share his desserts, and he has a girlfriend named Helena."

"I'll burn it into my memory," said Bill. "Especially the part about desserts. I'm not sure how it relates to the subject at hand, but—"

"I haven't gotten to the relevant part yet," I interrupted. "Because

I take an interest in people, I also learned that Adam's parents work at the British Museum and that he hopes to work there after he gets his postgraduate degree. He knows a lot about the museum's collection of Anglo-Saxon treasures. He may know if something went missing from the collection a long time ago. With his family connections, he may even know of thefts that were hushed up. It's worth finding out."

"You won't share your suspicions with *him*, will you?" Bill asked.

"Of course not," I said. "Adam offered to give the boys and me a guided tour of the Sutton Hoo exhibition. I'll ask him to give me a preview tour—or you'll ask him for me—so I can decide whether Will and Rob will find it as riveting as he does. While he's pointing out his favorite pieces, I'll slip in a few questions about thefts and robberies and the pilfering of national treasures."

"He'll think you're planning a heist," said Bill.

"I'll be subtle," I assured him. I sat back in my chair and frowned. "If I could find Badger, I'd ask him outright if he stole the bracelet."

"An unusual conversation starter," Bill observed.

"One I may never use," I retorted. "Until Badger turns up—if he ever does—I'll have to rely on Adam Rivington. He's the only Anglo-Saxon expert I know."

"I'll call Adam right now and convey your wishes to him," said Bill. "Can you get to the British Museum on your own?"

"Piece of cake," I said. "You don't mind another day of Daddy duty, do you?"

"Piece of cake," he echoed airily.

As he reached for the phone, Bess stirred. I went to crouch beside her as she clenched and unclenched her tiny fingers, smacked her rosy lips, and opened her velvety brown eyes. It was a sight I never tired of seeing.

"Done," Bill said a moment later. "Adam will meet you at ten o'clock tomorrow morning at the British Museum's south entrance."

I had no idea which entrance was the British Museum's south entrance, but I would have eaten dirt before I admitted as much to my husband. If he could run our household without my help, I told myself, I could find the south entrance without his.

"Excellent," I said as I checked Bess's diaper again.

"Adam refused to accept his usual fee," Bill said.

"Pay him anyway," I said, straightening. "He'd like to show me the exhibition out of the goodness of his heart, but he's working his way through school. He needs the money."

"I'll see to it that he gets paid," Bill promised.

"Thanks," I said. "Now, come and kiss your daughter. She and I have to drop off a box of clothes at the vicarage, get dinner started, and fetch her brothers."

"Good thing you had a nap," Bill said to Bess as he bent over the pram.

I smiled as he nuzzled Bess's cheek and giggled when he rose to nuzzle mine, but I left Wysteria Lodge feeling as though I had the weight of the world on my shoulders.

Though I tried very hard to think levelheadedly about Badger and his potentially ill-gotten gains, I couldn't help wondering what I would do if Adam confirmed my suspicions about Aunt Dimity's bracelet.

"How can I tell her?" I asked Bess as I put her in her car seat. "How can I possibly tell Aunt Dimity that Badger is a crook?"

Sixteen

inch's glorious warm spell came with me to London the following morning. I arrived at Paddington Station to find its platforms dry and its vast glass-and-wrought-iron roof flooded with soft sunlight.

I left my umbrella in my shoulder bag, tucked snugly beside Badger's bracelet, unbuttoned my voluminous raincoat, and allowed myself to be carried along on a tide of travelers to the nearest cab stand, where I joined the fast-moving queue. I scarcely had time to check my watch before I was whisked away to the British Museum in a classic London taxi driven by a friendly, talkative gentleman who knew exactly where the south entrance was.

"Piece of cake," I murmured smugly.

As it turned out, the south entrance was the only entrance my family and I had ever used. The imposing Greek Revival colonnade, the pediment depicting humankind's rise from ignorance to enlightenment, and the Union Jack fluttering from the white flagpole atop the pediment were pretty hard to forget. As I paid the cabdriver, I harbored uncharitable thoughts toward Bill for failing to inform me that I would recognize the south entrance as soon as I saw it.

I spotted Adam leaning against one of the colonnade's towering columns and ran up the wide stairs to greet him. His response was so muted that I pulled him aside to find out what was up with him. I detected clear signs of strain in his cornflower-blue eyes.

"Adam," I said, "if you have to attend a lecture or work on a paper, we can easily reschedule today's outing."

"Thanks, but I'd rather go ahead with it," he said. "I'm hoping it'll distract me from . . ." He bowed his head and sighed sorrowfully.

"From what?" I asked.

"From Helena," he replied.

My eyebrows rose. "Your girlfriend?"

"My ex-girlfriend," he stated grimly. "Helena traded me in for a bloke who doesn't have to work for a living."

"Good riddance," I said without thinking and immediately regretted my words. "Forgive me, Adam. I'm truly sorry about Helena. Breakups are always tough."

"Do you know what the worst part of it is?" he asked, scuffing the ground with his boot. "The worst part is that I'll have to tell Carrie Osborne that she was right about Helena."

"If that's the worst part," I said, "maybe it was time for a breakup."

I could have kicked myself for making yet another thoughtless remark, but Adam responded with a rueful smile.

"Helena's change of heart was a blow but not a surprise," he admitted. "I've seen it coming for a while. I just wish Carrie hadn't seen it first. Ah, well . . ." He lifted his chin, threw back his shoulders, and turned toward the nearest door. "Come on, Lori. Let me show you one of the most magnificent—"

He broke off as my cell phone rang. I pulled it from my shoulder bag, glanced at the name on the small screen, and looked apologetically at Adam.

"Speak of the devil," I said, and raised the phone to my ear. "Hello, Carrie?"

"Lori!" she boomed. "Glad I caught you. Chocks, Ginger, and Fish are here, and they've settled in for the day. How quickly can you get to London?"

"I'm already here," I told her. "I'll be with you shortly. Thanks for the heads-up, Carrie."

"Dying wishes must be honored," she said. "I'll see you soon."

I dropped the cell phone in my shoulder bag and turned to Adam.

"I'm afraid Sutton Hoo will have to wait," I said.

"Are the Battle of Britain boys at the coffeehouse?" he asked.

"They are," I said. "Would you mind becoming my Bloomsbury guide again? You know how to get to Carrie's Coffees from here and I don't."

"We can be there in ten minutes," he assured me.

"Are you ready to face Carrie?" I asked.

"She probably knows about Helena already," he replied philosophically. "Bloomsbury is like a village. News travels fast among the locals."

"I know what you mean," I said feelingly, and followed him as he raced down the stairs.

I had no time to gawk at the buildings, gardens, and statues we passed on our way to Carrie's Coffees. I was too busy keeping up with Adam as he dodged in and out of foot traffic and dashed across streets without the aid of stoplights. By the time we reached the coffeehouse, I was winded but exhilarated.

The prospect of meeting three Battle of Britain veterans was thrilling all by itself. If one or more of my three lines of inquiry panned out, however, I'd also stand a very good chance of bringing my Badger hunt to a successful conclusion. If fortune continued to smile upon me, Aunt Dimity's long-lost admirer would be able to convince me that he'd acquired her bracelet legally.

Adam seemed to brace himself as we entered the coffeehouse, but Carrie greeted him with an understanding nod.

"I heard about Helena," she said. "Here's hoping for better luck next time!"

"Thanks," he said gratefully. He gave me a look of mingled disbelief and relief as he hung his jacket and my raincoat on the pegs near the door.

"Give me a minute, Lori," Carrie went on, "and I'll introduce you to the chaps."

The coffeehouse was more crowded than it had been during my previous visit, but I had no trouble picking out Carrie's boys. Not only were they sitting in the leather chairs reserved for them, they were far and away the oldest customers in the place. While I waited for Carrie to finish taking an order, I realized that I could identify the three men without her help.

Chocks, the mechanic who'd roasted his hands pulling a pilot from a burning Hurricane, sat to the left of the faux fireplace. He cradled his teacup in hands that looked as though they'd melted, then solidified in a mottled, puckered patchwork of skin grafts.

Fish, I was certain, sat across from Chocks. The kneecaps he'd broken when he'd ditched his Spitfire in the English Channel would account for the wheelchair parked against the wall behind his chair.

Ginger had his back to me, but the awkward way in which he lifted a scone from the plate on the low table in front of him suggested that the bullet he'd taken in the shoulder from a passing Messerschmitt had left him with a limited range of motion.

One thing was certain: The Battle of Britain boys hadn't been boys for a very long time. Their thinning hair was as white as snow, their faces were deeply creased, and their suits hung loosely from their diminished frames, but their eyes were full of life when Carrie brought Adam and me over to meet them.

"Pull up a chair, young lady," Ginger said after Carrie returned to the front counter. "You, too, young man."

Adam and I borrowed chairs from neighboring tables and placed them on either side of the trompe l'oeil fireplace. Adam sat next to Chocks and I seated myself beside Fish, but the men directed their initial comments at Adam.

"Hear you're having a spot of woman trouble, young man," said Ginger.

"If a woman's giving you trouble," said Chocks, "she's more trouble than she's worth."

"Best to move on," Fish advised.

"Oh, I will," said Adam, "but maybe not today."

The three old friends chuckled sympathetically, and Chocks patted Adam's knee with a clawlike hand. I thought of the enormous sacrifices he and his brothers-in-arms had made and wondered if the rest of Carrie's customers would be willing to do the same. Most of them, I told myself, looked as if they wouldn't have the courage to dress in nondesigner clothing.

"Penny for your thoughts, young lady," said Ginger.

His words brought me out of my reverie.

"I'm not sure my thoughts are worth a penny," I told him, "but since you asked . . ." I let my gaze rove over the young men and women sipping their espressos and savoring their quiches. "If Britain went to war today, I'm not sure this lot would be up to it."

"They're braver than you think," said Ginger. "If their backs were to the wall, as ours were, they'd do their bit. I know what Carrie's told you about us—she tells everyone the same nonsense—but don't mistake my chums and me for heroes. We're ordinary blokes, just like them"—he hooked a thumb over his shoulder to indicate the café's stylish patrons—"but you'd be surprised by what ordinary blokes can do when they're pushed hard enough."

"We were gobsmacked by what we did," said Chocks, and he laughed again with his friends, who nodded their agreement.

"Carrie tells us you're looking for one of the old crowd," said Fish, after the laughter faded. "A chap who used to come to the Rose Café."

"That's right," I said. "He had dark, curly hair and a dark beard, and he called himself Badger."

"I remember the beard," said Chocks. "Not many chaps wore beards round here in those days. He stood out."

"I remember the beard, too," said Fish, "and the pretty girl he met here."

"We all remember the pretty girl," said Chocks.

"Why do you remember the girl?" I asked. "It was an awfully long time ago."

"She was an awfully pretty girl," said Fish, grinning. "And she came here every day for weeks on end, asking about the bearded chap. Seems they'd had a tiff."

"She wanted to know where the bearded fellow lived," said Ginger. "She went from table to table, asking everyone in the café. It's not the sort of thing a chap forgets."

"The pretty girl was my friend," I said. "Before she died, she asked me to find the bearded fellow."

"Why?" Ginger asked bluntly.

"She wanted me to give him a message," I explained.

"She left it a bit late," Ginger commented.

"Better late than never," said Chocks.

"Did your friend ever tell you why things didn't work out between her and . . . Badger, did you call him?" Ginger asked. "A blind man could see he was mad about her, and she seemed to like him well enough."

"She did like him," I said. "She liked him very much, but she'd lost her fiancé in the war, and—"

"Ah," Fish interrupted, nodding. "Couldn't move on, eh?"

"No, I'm afraid she couldn't," I said. "I don't suppose you've heard about Badger since then, have you?"

"We haven't heard about him," Chocks replied, "but we've caught glimpses of him from time to time."

My heart seemed to skip a beat, and I leaned forward in my chair. To my utter amazement, my three lines of inquiry seemed to be on the verge of panning out big-time.

"Do you know where he lives?" I asked, on the edge of my seat in more ways than one.

The three men shook their heads.

"Sorry," said Chocks.

"Not a clue," said Fish.

"When Carrie told us about you," said Ginger, "we had a think about this Badger chap. We came to the conclusion that we didn't know the first thing about him." He looked from Chocks to Fish, then turned to me with a maddeningly mischievous smirk. "But we know someone who does."

"Who?" I asked, restraining the urge to stamp my foot.

"Her name is Sarah Hanover," said Ginger. "She's the great-granddaughter of Nigel Hanover, the chap who owned the Rose Café. I rang her yesterday, and I learned a few things that surprised me."

"Carrie rang her after you arrived," Chocks said to me, "and asked her to come along."

"Here she is now," Fish announced, looking toward the door.

My heart began to pound as the answer to Aunt Dimity's prayers entered the coffeehouse, said hello to Carrie, and strode purposefully toward the Battle of Britain boys.

Seventeen

arah Hanover looked as if she might be in her midtwenties. She was a fresh-faced, pretty girl, with almond-shaped blue eyes, dark lashes, and a sprinkling of freckles across the bridge of her nose. She wore her long brown hair in a ponytail pulled back from straight bangs, and though she was petite, she was pleasantly curvy.

Instead of the standard youth uniform of top, jeans, and sneakers, she wore a short, tailored black wool jacket over a fitted dress patterned with brightly colored swirls. Black tights and ballet flats completed a look that was sophisticated but not in the least intimidating.

As she wound her way between the coffeehouse's tables, I heard Adam catch his breath and turned to look at him. His lips were parted, and his blue eyes were fixed unblinkingly on the approaching damsel. When she reached us, he jumped to his feet.

"Please, take my chair," he said. "I'll get another."

"Thank you," said Sarah. Her smile produced a fetching pair of dimples as she took Adam's place next to Chocks.

Adam managed to trip over his feet twice while retrieving the extra chair, but he was composed enough to place it carefully between Fish and Ginger, a strategic location that would allow him to feast his eyes on the new arrival without being too obvious about it. My inner matchmaker noted hopefully that she wore no rings on either hand.

Chocks, Ginger, and Fish exchanged knowing glances. Their

amused smiles spoke volumes, but they were too kind to tease a freshly smitten young man in front of the young woman who'd smitten him. They greeted Sarah Hanover like an old friend and introduced her to Adam and to me.

Carrie, too, displayed remarkable self-restraint. She'd observed Adam from the moment he'd jumped to his feet, but when she brought us a tray loaded with miniature scones, tiny custard tarts, an enticing selection of petits fours, two pots of tea, and enough cups and saucers to go around, she placed it on the low table without even looking at him.

"Lovely dress," she said to Sarah. "Another one of yours?"

"Yes," Sarah replied with a becoming blush. "I found the jacket at the Oxfam shop on Goodge Street, but I made the dress myself."

"Such a talented girl," said Carrie. "And so thrifty!"

She nodded to the rest of us matter-of-factly and went back to work, but I had a sneaking suspicion that I wasn't the only matchmaker in the coffeehouse.

"Awfully good of you to join us, Sarah," said Ginger.

"Yes," I chimed in. "It's very good of you, Sarah. Is it true that you know Badger?"

"I haven't met him," she said, "but I've known the story of Badger and Dimity since I was a child."

I almost gasped. I wasn't used to hearing Aunt Dimity's name spoken aloud in public, much less by a stranger, but I covered my startled reaction by pouring myself a cup of tea.

"It was a story passed down through my family," Sarah was saying, "a love story with an unexpected ending."

"I talked it over with you yesterday," said Ginger. "But you take it from the beginning, Sarah, so Lori can see the whole picture."

"That's the plan," she said and the dimples made another appearance as she smiled at me. "My great-grandfather, Nigel Hanover, owned Carrie's Coffees before, during, and after the war, when it was known as the Rose Café."

I couldn't tell her that a dead woman had mentioned Mr. Hanover's name to me recently, so I confined myself to an interested nod.

"To Great-Granddad, the Rose Café was a kind of theater," she went on, "and his customers were the players. When he sold the business and retired, he loved to talk about the comedies and the tragedies he'd witnessed. But the story he told most often—the story my grandfather told to me—concerned a young man called Badger and a young woman named Dimity."

"Is Badger the chap's real name?" asked Fish.

"Let the girl talk," Ginger scolded.

"Sorry," said Fish, and he motioned for Sarah to continue.

"My great-grandfather was on the spot when Badger fell head over heels in love at first sight with Dimity," said Sarah. "Great-Granddad called it a *coup de foudre*—a thunderbolt. Badger had always been a rather shy man, but his shyness fell away when he caught sight of Dimity. Something about her allowed him to come out of his shell."

"He lit up like a Christmas tree whenever she was around," said Fish, apparently unable to contain himself.

"That he did," Chocks agreed, nodding.

"Great-Granddad had seen many couples meet at his café," Sarah said, "but he'd never seen a pair more suited to each other. Badger would show up early whenever they were due to meet, so he could lay claim to 'their' table, and he made sure a cup of tea was waiting for her when she arrived, so she wouldn't have to join the queue. They'd talk for hours about everything under the sun, and when their cups were empty, Badger would tell Dimity to stay put while he fetched fresh cups of tea for both of them."

"Sounds like a real gentleman," said Fish.

"He was a real gentleman," said Sarah. "Great-Granddad was absolutely convinced that he would see an engagement ring on Dimity's finger before the month was out." She paused. "But he didn't."

"What happened?" Fish asked.

"Great-Granddad didn't know," Sarah answered. "They seemed to be getting along famously, when suddenly and for no apparent reason, Badger fled the café, never to return."

I detected Nigel Hanover's love of drama in his great-granddaughter's quaint phrasing and smiled inwardly.

"After Badger left," she went on, "Dimity returned to the Rose Café every day for several weeks. She hoped that he, too, would return, but he never did. She asked my great-grandfather if he knew where she could find Badger, but Badger's whereabouts were as much a mystery to him as they were to her. After a time, she stopped coming to the café, but my great-grandfather never ceased to wonder why such a promising relationship had ended so catastrophically."

Sarah chose that crucial moment to pop an entire petit four into her mouth with unabashed gusto. I suspected her of employing a touch of theatrical timing to hold our attention, but Chocks seemed to think that she was torturing us unnecessarily.

"Come along, Sarah," he said peremptorily. "The story can't end there."

"It doesn't," she said after a mighty swallow. "Many years later, shortly before Great-Granddad died, he bumped into Badger in Russell Square. Badger seemed to have no problem chatting about old times at the café, so Great-Granddad felt free to ask the question he longed to ask: Why had Badger walked away from Dimity?"

"What did Badger say?" Fish asked when Sarah paused again.

"He said he'd misread Dimity's intentions," Sarah answered. "He said she'd given him a gift, a silly gift, which he'd taken much too seriously."

The image of a badger flashed across my mind as I recalled the stuffed toy Aunt Dimity had purchased for Badger at a street market.

"When he gave her a far more meaningful gift," Sarah continued, "he realized his mistake. He understood all at once that, no matter what he did, Dimity would never love him, and he felt as if the sky had fallen in on him."

"Poor chap," Chocks murmured.

"After that," said Sarah, "he couldn't bear to see her, couldn't bear to be near her, so he left the café and avoided it from then on."

"Understandable," said Ginger. "No future in it."

"Then he laughed," said Sarah.

"He laughed?" I said, taken aback.

"He laughed," Sarah repeated firmly. "Badger told my great-grandfather that if Dimity hadn't broken his heart, he wouldn't have thrown himself into his work. However painful it had been at the time, her rejection had spurred him into becoming one of the foremost men in his field."

"What is his field?" I asked.

"Before he and my great-grandfather parted," said Sarah, "Badger introduced himself formally." She twisted her hands in her lap and regarded us with a barely controlled quiver of excitement. "Badger's real name is . . . *Stephen Waterford.*"

The Battle of Britain boys and I were unmoved by the revelation, but it seemed to galvanize Adam.

"*The* Stephen Waterford?" he asked, sitting bolt upright. "The Egyptologist?"

"That's right," said Sarah. She looked at him delightedly, as if she were glad that one of us understood the name's significance.

"I've read all his books," Adam marveled.

"So have I." Sarah's ponytail danced as she bobbed her head enthusiastically. "He's brilliant, isn't he?"

"Inspiring," Adam agreed.

The two locked eyes for a moment, then Sarah turned to me, looking a bit flustered.

"Stephen Waterford also gave my great-grandfather his card," she said. "When Carrie told me that you were searching for him, Lori, I went through Great-Granddad's biscuit tin, and—"

"His what?" Fish interrupted.

"Great-Granddad used a biscuit tin to illustrate his stories," Sarah explained. "It's filled with all sorts of odds and ends that meant something to him—matchbooks, a handkerchief, a clothes peg, a Royal Automobile Club badge. I went through his biscuit tin, and I found Stephen Waterford's card."

"The information on it must be out of date by now," said Ginger.

"It's not," said Sarah. "I rang Stephen yesterday—"

"Did you call him by his Christian name?" Adam asked in awestruck tones.

"He insisted on it," Sarah replied, with a disbelieving giggle.

"Yes, yes, we're all very impressed," Ginger said patiently, "but we'd also like to hear what this Stephen fellow said to you."

Sarah pulled herself together.

"I told Stephen what Carrie had told me," she said. "I told him that an American woman who lived in a small village not far from Oxford wished to deliver a deathbed message to him from a village woman he'd met at the Rose Café. I could tell that he was surprised, but he wasn't put off. In fact, he'd very much like to meet you." She pulled a folded piece of paper from her jacket pocket and handed it to me. "Here's his address. He lives in Wilmington Square."

I looked to Adam for guidance.

"It's not ten minutes from here," he said.

"Ten of your minutes or ten of mine?" I asked wryly. "My minutes are slower than yours."

"Let's say fifteen minutes, then," he amended, grinning.

"I'm afraid you won't be able to visit him today," Sarah said hastily. "He was admitted to hospital this morning for some tests."

Ginger snorted dismissively.

"I never have tests, myself," he said. "I don't trust them."

"No more do I," said Chocks.

"Doctors," Fish said scornfully. "I'd have been dead fifty years ago if I'd listened to doctors."

"Yes, well, Stephen *does* listen to doctors," Sarah said. "He'll be home on Sunday, Lori. He said he'd set aside the whole of Monday for you."

A scheme began to take shape in my crafty matchmaker's mind. I waved at Adam to get his attention, then asked him if he would be free on Monday.

"Free as a bird," he said.

"Adam's my navigator," I explained to Sarah. "He keeps me from getting lost when I'm in London. If you can spare the time, would you consider coming to Wilmington Square with us? I think Badger, er, Stephen, will be more comfortable if you're there."

"I can spare the time," said Sarah. "And not just because I admire Stephen's work as an Egyptologist. I'd like to meet the man Great-Granddad knew, the man whose love story had such an unexpected ending." She looked from me to Adam. "Shall we meet here on Monday at ten o'clock?"

"Ten o'clock it is," said Adam, sounding as if he'd never heard of a more perfect plan.

"And now, if you'll excuse me, I must go," Sarah said, standing. "I work part time at the British Museum. My hours are flexible, but if I'll be away on Monday, I should probably put in a few extra hours today."

"I'll walk you out," said Adam.

The old gentlemen and I watched the pair thread their way through the tables and out into the half courtyard, where they stood, chatting animatedly.

"Looks like the lad's moving on today after all," said Fish.

"That one won't give him any trouble," said Chocks.

"Good luck to them," said Ginger.

"I'd better be going, too," I said. "Would you three mind if I stopped by to visit with you again?"

"We'd be hurt if you didn't," said Ginger. "We're counting on you to tell us what this Stephen chap is like."

"When the weather's fine, you'll find us here," said Chocks.

"We creak too much when the weather isn't fine," said Fish.

"I'll be back with the full story," I promised. I glanced toward the line of customers at the front counter. "I'd like to say good-bye to Carrie, but it looks as though she has her hands full. Would you say good-bye to her for me and give her my thanks?"

"Leave it with us," said Ginger.

"Carrie has it right, you know," I said, as I shook hands with each of them. "You can protest all you want, but you're heroes in my book. Thanks for helping me today, and thanks for doing your bit back then. The world's a better place because of you, and I, for one, won't let you forget it."

The Battle of Britain boys dismissed my comments vehemently, but when I turned to look at them on my way out of the coffeehouse, they didn't seem in any way displeased.

I took a cab back to Paddington. It was safer than following Adam, whose dazed expression and absentminded remarks indicated that he was happily ensconced on Cloud Nine.

Bill and Bess were out when I got home. A note on the kitchen table informed me that they'd gone to the Cotswold Farm Park to visit the goats and that they'd pick the boys up from school on their way back.

The ingredients Bill had laid out on the table indicated that we were to have spaghetti with meat sauce for dinner. I made sure we had a wedge of Parmesan on hand, then went to the study, switched on the mantel lamps, and said hello to Reginald.

"I'm back from London," I told him. "No sightseeing, unless you count the British Museum's south entrance, but it was a good day—a *great* day—nonetheless." I took the gold and garnet bracelet from my shoulder bag and ran a finger across its intricately inlaid surface, wondering how Stephen Waterford, the renowned Egyptologist, had managed to lay his hands on a piece of Anglo-Saxon jewelry. "Monday should be even more interesting."

Reginald's black button eyes gleamed inquisitively. I twiddled his ears, placed the bracelet in his niche, and took the blue journal with me to a tall leather armchair.

"Dimity?" I said triumphantly as I opened the journal. "I have very nearly achieved the impossible."

Aunt Dimity's graceful handwriting began at once to loop and curl across the page.

Are you referring to the impossible task I so inconsiderately asked you to achieve? Did the Battle of Britain boys come through for you?

"With flying colors," I said. "They couldn't tell me much about

Badger, but they introduced me to someone who could. You won't believe it, Dimity, but I've been chatting with Mr. Hanover's great-granddaughter."

Mr. Hanover? The man who owned the Rose Café?

"The one and only," I said. "His great-granddaughter's name is Sarah Hanover, and she grew up hearing about you and Badger."

What in heaven's name did she hear about us?

I recounted Nigel Hanover's story of star-crossed lovers and the chance encounter in Russell Square that had provided him with the story's unexpected conclusion.

"Mr. Hanover didn't know the whole story because Badger didn't know it," I said, "but he learned enough from Badger to quench his curiosity."

How I wish I'd told Badger about Bobby MacLaren! It would have saved him so much heartache.

"Mr. Hanover didn't get the impression that Badger regretted the breakup," I said. "Badger admitted that in the long run, he was grateful for it. He ran away from you to concentrate on his career, and he made a success of it. Sarah told me Badger's real name, Dimity, and it's a fairly well-known one."

I'll always think of him as Badger, but go ahead: Tell me his real name.

"He's Stephen Waterford," I said.

The Egyptologist?

"Y-yes," I faltered, caught off guard. "How on earth do you know who Stephen Waterford is? I'd never heard of him until today."

Stephen Waterford made a number of quite remarkable discoveries in the Middle East. I read about them in the Times. *The articles were accompanied by photographs of a clean-shaven man with closely cropped hair. He looked nothing like the man who'd shared his table with me at the Rose Café.*

"The café wasn't lit very well," I reminded her. "And there's a reason beards are used in disguises. They change the way a person looks."

Even so, I should have detected some resemblance. It simply never crossed my mind that my well-educated gardener might be an eminent archaeologist. I can't tell you how pleased I am.

"I have news that will please you even more," I said. "I'm meeting Stephen Waterford at his home on Monday."

Oh, well done, Lori! Very well done, indeed! You'll tell him about Bobby? You'll tell him why I never married? You'll tell him how much his friendship meant to me and how grateful I was for his advice and guidance? You'll show him that I kept the bracelet until my dying day?

"I will," I promised. I hesitated, but couldn't keep myself from asking, "Did you ever visit the Sutton Hoo exhibition at the British Museum?"

I'm afraid I never got past the Greek, Roman, and Egyptian collections on the ground floor. Why do you ask?

"Adam Rivington wants to show the Sutton Hoo collection to Will and Rob," I said. "He thinks they'll find it interesting."

Everything at the British Museum is interesting.

The garnet bracelet drew my gaze, and I wondered yet again how Badger had acquired it. He hadn't always been a highly respected Egyptologist. He'd been young once, and as Bill had said, young men in love had been known to do crazier things. Would Badger's youthful indiscretion come back to haunt him because of a clumsy accident in my attic?

I looked from the bracelet to the blue journal. I'd seldom known Aunt Dimity to be so elated, but her elation would be short-lived if I cluttered the moment with nebulous accusations of wrongdoing. After a brief hesitation, I steered the conversation away from Anglo-Saxon treasures.

"I almost forgot to tell you about Adam and Sarah," I said, and went on to describe how well the two had hit it off. "There must be some Rose Café magic lingering in Carrie's coffeehouse," I concluded, "because Adam fell for Sarah as instantaneously as Badger fell for you."

Let's hope Adam's road to happiness is more straightforward than Badger's was.

"I'm working on it." I heard the crunch of tires in our graveled driveway and looked toward the diamond-paned windows above the old oak desk. "The family's home, Dimity. I haven't seen them since breakfast, so would you mind if I . . . ?"

I won't keep you from them any longer than it takes for me to tell you how very, very grateful I am to you for pursuing my wild goose chase.

"Don't be silly," I said. "It was a piece of cake."

As the curving lines of royal-blue ink faded from the page, I hoped with all my heart that Aunt Dimity's wild goose chase would end happily.

Eighteen

Saturday dawned fresh and fair. After a leisurely breakfast, Bill drove Will and Rob to Anscombe Manor for their weekly riding lessons, and I drove Bess to Finch to pick up a gallon of milk at the Emporium.

The village green appeared to be devoid of metal detectorists when Bess and I crossed the humpbacked bridge. I wondered if the villagers had lost interest in James Hobson's hobby until I remembered that Saturday was sale day in Upper Deeping. Nothing, not even the joy of unearthing lost wedding rings, would keep my neighbors at home when there were bargains to be found in the nearby market town.

I parked the Range Rover in front of the Emporium, lifted Bess from her car seat, and took a deep breath before entering the shop. I always took a deep breath before I dealt with Peggy Taxman because she tended to knock the wind out of me.

Jasper Taxman was shelving bags of potato chips when the sleigh bells dangling from the Emporium's front door announced our arrival, and Peggy was in her usual place behind the old-fashioned mechanical cash register. Her pointy, rhinestone-studded eyeglasses seemed to flash dangerously when she caught sight of me.

"If you've come here to beg for my glass case," she thundered, "you can save your breath!"

Peggy Taxman rarely spoke softly. Her deafening pronouncements made me wince, but Bess thought they were hilarious. The moment Peggy opened her mouth, Bess began to laugh.

Peggy was too full of righteous indignation to acknowledge her biggest fan.

"I've got better things to do with my display case than to fill it with a load of old rubbish," she bellowed.

"I wasn't going to——" I began, but I got no further.

"Elspeth Binney came marching in here as bold as brass on Thursday to ask me for it," Peggy boomed scathingly. "Thought I might like to put my old hair clip in it, the one Sally Cook dug up. Can you imagine? Putting a mucky old hair clip that isn't worth tuppence on display for all the world to see? *And putting my name with it?* It's foolishness, that's what it is!"

"I think Elspeth meant——" I subsided again as Peggy overrode me.

"It's that man's fault," she bellowed. "That so-called clever clogs, James Hobson. It's no wonder his cliff-top village is falling into the sea. The place never stood a chance with him chopping away at the cliffs! Him and his talk about digging up history. Pah! Some things are best left buried!"

I checked Bess's diaper, straightened the ribbons on the pale pink cap Millicent Scroggins had crocheted for her, and allowed Peggy's diatribe to wash over me.

"Lilian Bunting is out there right now, wasting her time with that infernal contraption of his," she shouted. "A vicar's wife! Playing in the dirt! Have you ever heard of such a thing? I expect more dignified behavior from a woman in her position, and you can be sure I'll tell the vicar so after church tomorrow morning!"

"Lilian's using James's metal detector?" I said while Peggy paused for breath.

"I saw her with my own eyes," Peggy roared. "That Hobson fellow took himself off somewhere, but they're still out there, Lilian Bunting and Mr. Barlow, ruining the turf behind the war memorial.

Looking for another hair clip, I'll wager. Well, you can tell them from me that I only ever lost one!"

"I'll do that," I said, and after nodding to Jasper, I turned on my heel and left the Emporium.

If Lilian and Mr. Barlow had been behind the war memorial when I'd driven over the humpbacked bridge, it stood to reason that I wouldn't have been able to see them. Now that I knew where they were, however, I felt an irresistible urge to join them. I pulled the pram from the Rover and set it up as quickly as I could with only one free hand at my disposal. When everything was locked into place, including Bess, I strolled up the cobbled lane to search for the searchers.

The first person we encountered, however, was Elspeth Binney. Most uncharacteristically, she was on her own. I couldn't recall the last time I'd seen one Handmaiden without the other three.

"Good morning, Elspeth," I said. "Why aren't you in Upper Deeping with Millicent, Opal, and Selena? It's sale day, isn't it?"

"I'm afraid my association with the women you've mentioned is over," she replied stiffly.

"Since when?" I said, startled.

"Since yesterday," she answered. "I'm not an intolerant person, Lori, but there are some outrages that cannot be tolerated."

"What happened yesterday?" I asked, and for a moment I came close to regretting my trip to London.

"My *dear friends*," she said, her voice laden with sarcasm, "showed their true colors."

"I'm sorry, Elspeth, but you'll have to be more specific," I said. "I wasn't in Finch yesterday, and I haven't caught up on the news since I've been back."

As I'd hoped, Elspeth couldn't resist an invitation to describe the intolerable outrage that had caused her to sever ties with her three closest friends.

"It was Opal's turn with the metal detector," she began. "I came along to support her, as a friend should. Opal elected to scan the part of the green we'd used for our *en plein air* painting party in September. *En plein air*," she explained, "means to paint outdoors."

"I remember the painting party," I said. "If I recall correctly, you . . . lost something, didn't you?"

"I lost my palette knife," she said. "It was on my easel when we went to the tearoom for lunch, but it wasn't there when we returned. Since I didn't have another palette knife, I couldn't complete my painting of the old schoolhouse."

"Did Opal find your palette knife yesterday?" I asked, in an effort to move the story along.

"She did," Elspeth said in frigid tones.

"But you weren't glad to have it back?" I hazarded.

"I was extremely glad to have it back," said Elspeth, "but I wasn't glad to hear the remarks made to me after I said, in all innocence, that my painting of the schoolhouse would have won the blue ribbon at the art show, had I been able to complete it. I wasn't boasting, Lori. Mr. Shuttleworth has frequently admired my work with the palette knife."

"I'm sure he has," I said soothingly.

"My so-called friends disputed my claim," she continued. "Millicent said that I had as much chance of winning a blue ribbon at the art show as she had of winning the London Marathon."

"She *didn't*," I said, frowning sympathetically.

"She *did*," Elspeth retorted. "Opal said that my painting looked as though it had been done by a *bricklayer* using a *trowel*."

"What did Selena say?" I asked avidly.

Elspeth seemed to choke on her own ire, but after a brief pause, she gallantly soldiered on.

"Selena," she replied, "said that the universe had done the art world a favor when it took away my palette knife."

"How rude," I said, while a wicked part of me admired Selena's wit. "Did James Hobson hear all this?"

"No," said Elspeth. "He'd gone off to speak with the vicar. I suppose I should be grateful that I wasn't humiliated in front of our new neighbor."

I was grateful that James hadn't witnessed another metal-detecting brouhaha. The taunts, hurt feelings, and division that had followed the palette knife's recovery would have reminded him all too clearly of the pocket watch incident.

"I don't know what I've done to deserve such abuse," Elspeth went on, her voice quavering with indignation.

"I'm sure you haven't done anything," I said, jiggling the pram to let Bess know that I hadn't forgotten about her. "I'll bet they were just joking around and it got out of hand."

"Hurling insults at a friend may be your idea of humor, Lori," she said loftily, "but it isn't mine."

"Have they apologized?" I asked.

"As if I'd accept their apologies," Elspeth said with a sniff. "No, Lori, I shall never forgive them. Some things are patently unforgivable."

For the first time since Elspeth had begun speaking, I felt a real sense of concern. The Handmaidens were known for their spats, but they'd never had a serious falling out. Until now.

"Will you continue to take lessons from Mr. Shuttleworth?" I inquired.

"Of course I shall," Elspeth said. "But I shall take them on a different day, to avoid ignorant and baseless critiques of my knife work."

"Good idea," I said, hoping that a cooling-off period would smooth her ruffled feathers. "They'll miss you, you know. They'll come to realize how foolish they were to let a palette knife come between them and one of the most considerate, loyal, and talented friends they've ever had."

"It'll be their loss, then," she snapped. "And they'll have no one to blame but themselves." She looked down at Bess, but instead of beaming at her, she seemed to become even more angry. "If that's one of Millicent's crocheted caps, I'd check it for barbed wire."

With another sniff, she bade me good day and marched across the green. I watched worriedly as she entered the tearoom without her boon companions.

"It may be a long cooling-off period," I murmured to Bess, and resumed my walk to the war memorial.

Nineteen

Lilian Bunting was scanning a swath of ground closer to the war memorial than the one that had produced Peggy's glittering hair clip, and she was moving the detector more slowly and methodically than Sally Cook had.

"Maybe Mrs. Bunting will discover the lost treasure of Finch beneath the village green," I said to Bess. "I don't know if Finch has a lost treasure, mind you, but if it does, wouldn't it be exciting to be on the spot when someone discovers it?"

Bess agreed that it would be the thrill of a lifetime.

I doubted that Lilian Bunting was on a mission to recover missing hair clips, but I wasn't surprised that she was taking a turn with the metal detector. She was a gifted amateur historian with a special interest in village history. Mr. Barlow might rank a handful of tenpenny nails low on the index of desirable finds, but Lilian wouldn't. She'd regard them as hard evidence of a flourishing building trade in Finch.

"If Mrs. Bunting finds *anything*," I murmured to Bess, "she'll cherish it."

Mr. Barlow stood beside Lilian, his bowed head moving from side to side as he followed the detector's rhythmic motion. He wore knee pads over his twill trousers, and he'd tucked James Hobson's red-handled digger as well as the pinpointer into his utility belt. The grass stains on his knee pads suggested that he'd already done some digging.

"Where's James?" I called when Bess and I were within hailing distance.

"He and Felicity are visiting their grandchildren in Upper Deeping," Lilian replied. "Mr. Barlow kindly offered to act as my mentor in his place."

I parked the pram next to the war memorial, released Bess's harness, and sat her on the leaf-strewn grass with her teething shark. She promptly threw the shark aside and crawled through the rustling leaves to play with Mr. Barlow's shoelaces. I dutifully retrieved the shark and dropped it in the pram, then strolled over to stand beside Lilian.

"Has Elspeth been telling you about the unfortunate incident that occurred yesterday?" she asked.

"Chapter and verse," I said, nodding. "She's very upset."

"She has every right to be," said Lilian. "Her friends should be ashamed of themselves."

"Maybe they are," I said. "It wouldn't help, though. Elspeth's not in a forgiving mood."

"She'll get over it," said Mr. Barlow. "She always does."

"I hope you're right," I said. "She'll be awfully lonely without Millicent, Opal, and Selena." I nodded at the metal detector. "Any luck?"

"Lots!" Lilian replied, brightening.

Mr. Barlow tilted his head noncommittally.

"Before I show you my finds," said Lilian, "let me show you my little project."

She passed the detector to Mr. Barlow—who wisely held it out of Bess's reach—then took a folded sheet of paper from the pocket of her tweed jacket, unfolded it, and handed it to me.

"I've made a rudimentary map of the green," she explained, "and I've marked the spots where various items have been discovered." She drew her finger across the map as she continued, "Here are the places where Mr. Barlow found his nails and his coins, and here's where he discovered Henry Cook's wedding ring. Here's where Opal Taylor found Elspeth's palette knife—but perhaps the less said about that the better," she added, and hurried on. "Sally Cook found Piero Sciaparelli's lira here and Mr. Barlow's hammer—"

Mr. Barlow grunted irritably.

"—here," Lilian went on without missing a beat. "I've used the letters of the alphabet to mark the spots. The letters correspond to a separate list I've made of the dates and the approximate times of the finds as well as the detectorists' names and a description of each item."

"It's wonderful," I said. "Absolutely wonderful."

"It's merely a working copy," she said modestly. "I intend to make a more accurate map of the green for future use. It will be a work in progress for quite some time, I expect, but when it's finished, I think it will look well above the display case."

"If we ever lay our hands on one," Mr. Barlow muttered.

"I've added a few letters of my own this morning," Lilian said, pointing to a cluster of letters behind the circle she'd drawn to represent the war memorial. "K through M are mine."

"Show and tell?" I requested.

While Lilian refolded her map and slipped it into her pocket, Mr. Barlow opened a pouch on his utility belt and pulled from it three rusty horseshoe nails and a silver coin.

"Mr. Barlow tells me that the horseshoe nails were hand-forged," said Lilian. "Horseshoe nails are notoriously difficult to date, but I think it would be fair to say that they were made before the local blacksmith shut up shop in 1952."

"And the coin?" I queried.

"It's a 1965 English florin," Lilian informed me.

"We called it a two-bob bit," said Mr. Barlow.

"As you can see, it has the head of our present queen on the obverse," said Lilian, "and the Tudor rose on the reverse, surrounded by shamrocks, thistles, and leeks, the symbols of the United Kingdom."

"Another good coin lost to ruddy decimalization," said Mr. Barlow.

"Your finds will be a fine addition to the museum," I said to Lilian. "Are you done for the day?"

"Not at all," she replied. "We were about to uncover another mysterious object when you and Bess arrived."

Bess had finished dribbling on Mr. Barlow's shoes and taken off for parts unknown. I trotted after her, scooped her up, and held her while Lilian took charge of the metal detector. She moved it confidently over the patch of grass at her feet, and it immediately emitted its mournful wail.

"There, I think, Mr. Barlow," she said unnecessarily.

Mr. Barlow was already on his knees. He cut out a neat square of turf and scanned it with the pinpointer, but the grassy plug was apparently metal free. The pinpointer responded, however, when he dipped it into the hole.

"There's something in there, all right," he said.

He dug carefully with his hands until he uncovered a ragged bit of ribbon that appeared to be attached to a medal of some sort. He sat back on his heels and, having learned James Hobson's trick of the trade, withdrew a small squirt bottle from another pouch on his belt.

Mr. Barlow shielded the ragged ribbon in his fist while he rinsed the medal with water, then got to his feet and held it in his cupped palm for Lilian and me to see. The medal was bronze colored, with a raised image of a winged female figure on one side. Though the ribbon had deteriorated badly, I could still make out the vestiges of its vertical rainbow stripes.

"It's a Wilfred," Mr. Barlow announced.

"What's a Wilfred?" I asked.

"It's a sardonic nickname British soldiers gave to the Victory Medal they received at the end of the First World War," Lilian explained, leaning in to look more closely at her find. "Three campaign medals were issued at the end of the Great War. Returning soldiers named them after characters in a comic strip that was popular at the time: Pip, Squeak, and Wilfred."

"My uncle had all three," said Mr. Barlow, "but this"—he nodded at the medal resting in his palm—"is a Wilfred. It should have a name impressed on it. Let me see. . . ." He pulled a magnifying glass from yet another pouch on his belt and used it to examine the Victory Medal's serrated rim.

"I hope the name is still legible," said Lilian. "It would be a privilege to return the medal to the soldier's family. Can you see a name, Mr. Barlow? Mr. Barlow?" she repeated more sharply. "Is something wrong?"

Mr. Barlow had turned his head to one side, pursed his lips, and closed his eyes, as if reading the name on the medal had shaken him. He groaned softly, then slipped the magnifying glass back into its pouch and handed the medal to Lilian.

"It's Dave Dillehaye's," he said. "Poor bloke must've buried it here, next to the memorial."

"Who is Dave Dillehaye?" I asked.

"I've seen the surname on a headstone in the churchyard," said Lilian, "but it isn't preceded by Dave or David. And there's no one by that name listed on the war memorial."

"I need to sit," Mr. Barlow said heavily.

He headed for the wooden bench in front of the memorial. Lilian laid the metal detector on the ground and scurried to catch up with him. Bess and I followed in their wake.

"Come to the vicarage," Lilian urged Mr. Barlow as he lowered himself onto the bench. "Let me make a cup of tea for you. You've clearly had a shock."

"I'll be fine in a minute," he said. "It's a sad story, is all. Saddest one I know. I heard it from Mr. Whitelaw. He was the parish sexton before me."

"Teddy and I never had the pleasure of meeting Mr. Whitelaw," said Lilian. "We came to St. George's after he'd passed away."

"Mr. Whitelaw had the story from Mr. Meacham, the sexton he replaced." Mr. Barlow rubbed the back of his neck, then let his hands rest limply in his lap. "Seems that Dave Dillehaye was the only child of a couple who'd come to Finch to work as farm laborers. They lived in a ramshackle cottage on the edge of the village, and no one had much to do with them because they weren't from around here. Dave quit school early and worked alongside his mum and dad until he went off to war."

"He must have survived," said Lilian, giving the Victory Medal a puzzled glance.

"He came back in one piece," Mr. Barlow allowed grudgingly, "but he was broken inside—inside his head, I mean. Post-traumatic stress, they call it nowadays. Back then, it was called shell shock, and Dave never got over it. He lived with his parents until they died, then stayed on alone in their cottage."

Bess stretched her arms out to Mr. Barlow, and he took her from me, holding her to his shoulder and patting her back as he spoke, as if he found comfort in comforting her.

"A neighbor looked in on Dave not too long after his mum died," Mr. Barlow said wearily. "Found him hanging from a rafter in his bedroom. The vicar refused to bury him in the churchyard with his mum and dad, but Mr. Meacham put him as close to them as he could."

"Are you saying that there's a grave beyond the churchyard's boundaries?" Lilian asked, looking nonplussed.

"I can take you to it, if you like," said Mr. Barlow.

"Please do," said Lilian.

Mr. Barlow showed no signs of wanting to be rid of Bess, so I pushed the pram after him as he led Lilian and me to St. George's churchyard. He turned left when he reached the lych-gate, followed the churchyard's low stone wall around the corner, and stopped a few yards short of the next corner. The weed-covered spot where he stopped was indistinguishable from the rest of the rough pasture that bordered the wall.

"Dave's buried here." Mr. Barlow jutted his chin at the ground, then pointed to a weathered headstone just inside the wall. "His mum and dad are over there."

He passed Bess to me, bent low, and separated the weeds to reveal a stumpy, square block of lichen-covered stone.

"Vicar wouldn't let him have a proper headstone," said Mr. Barlow, "but Mr. Meacham put the block there anyway and carved Dave's dates in it." He touched the stone, then straightened. "The villagers wouldn't put his name on the war memorial, on account of the way he died. But Mr. Meacham reckoned that Dave gave his life for his country, same as those who were shot dead on the battlefield. And I reckon he was right."

For a moment there was no sound, save for the whisper of wind in the cedars. Lilian bowed her head, and Mr. Barlow gazed grimly at the weed-covered grave. Bess, as if sensing the somber mood that had settled over the grown-ups, nestled her head against my neck and remained quiet. I thought of the Battle of Britain boys and their visible scars and said a silent prayer for those whose war wounds could not be seen.

"Were Mr. Dillehaye's next of kin notified of his death?" Lilian asked.

"He put down his mum and his dad as his next of kin on his enlistment papers," said Mr. Barlow, "and they were already dead. The police looked into it, but they couldn't find anyone else. So he was buried here"—he shook his head—"like this."

"Mr. Barlow," said Lilian, "why didn't you tell Teddy or me about Mr. Dillehaye's grave?"

"Nothing much you or the vicar can do about it," Mr. Barlow said reasonably. "Didn't want to upset you."

Lilian's lips compressed into a thin line as she stared at the lichen-covered block of stone. She took the map from her pocket and folded it reverently over the Victory Medal. She tucked the little packet into her pocket, then swung her leg back and gave the wall a vicious kick. Mr. Barlow and I fell back a step in surprise.

Lilian paused to watch a gentle shower of stone flakes tumble from the wall, then rounded on Mr. Barlow.

"I *am* upset," she said. "I'm upset with *you*, Mr. Barlow." She kicked the wall again, releasing a few more flakes. "You are our sexton. The upkeep of church property is your responsibility, yet you've allowed this section of wall to fall into disrepair. Look at it. A sharp breeze would knock it over."

Mr. Barlow and I turned our attention to the section of wall Lilian had kicked. It seemed perfectly sound to me.

"The wall will have to be relaid, Mr. Barlow," Lilian stated authoritatively. "It will have to be torn down and reconstructed from the ground up. Since the wall must be rebuilt, it may as well be moved. I'm sure I can persuade the Hodges to donate a sliver of their farm to St. George's. I see no reason why the wall can't be moved five or even ten feet from its present position."

Mr. Barlow's gaze shifted from Lilian to the wall, then came to rest on the grave. A small smile played about his lips, but when he looked at Lilian again, he was all business.

"It's a big job," he said. "I'll have to hire a crew to help me."

"Hire one," snapped Lilian. "Teddy and I will pay the men's wages."

"No, you won't," I said, stepping forward. "Bill and I will pay the crew. We'll cover whatever expenses are involved." Lilian opened her mouth to protest, but I raised my hand to silence her. "When our time comes, we'll want to be buried in St. George's church-yard, Lilian. I imagine the rest of our family will want to be buried here, too. It's in our interest to make sure there's enough room for all of us."

A look of understanding passed between us. I didn't have to ex-plain to Lilian that my desire to finance the wall's realignment had nothing to do with my family and everything to do with reuniting a family that had been cruelly separated in death. She acquiesced to my wishes with a brief nod, then turned to Mr. Barlow.

"How soon can you finish the new wall?" she asked.

"With the right crew?" He shrugged. "A month, if the weather cooperates. Six weeks or more if it doesn't."

"I suggest you make a start," said Lilian. "It's never too late to rectify a wrong, Mr. Barlow, and I would like to rectify this partic-ular wrong as expeditiously as possible. When you've finished relay-ing the wall, Teddy will bless Mr. Dillehaye's grave and hold a service of remembrance in his honor."

"Right you are, Mrs. Bunting," said Mr. Barlow.

"I'll see to it that Mr. Dillehaye's name is added to our war memorial," said Lilian. "In the meantime, I'll have a little chat with Mrs. Taxman. I shall not rest until Mr. Dillehaye's Victory Medal is displayed *properly*."

Sparks seemed to fly from her eyes as she spoke, and her jaw was set as she strode away from us.

"I'm guessing we'll get the glass case," said Mr. Barlow.

"It'll be in the old schoolhouse by nightfall," I agreed, nodding.

"And before too long, Dave'll be with his mum and dad," said Mr. Barlow, "where the poor chap should've been all along."

If nothing else came of Finch's foray into metal detecting, I thought, the righting of this wrong would be enough to satisfy me. I squatted beside the grave to lay a hand on Dave Dillehaye's marker, then put Bess in her pram and headed for home.

The gallon of milk could wait. I had no intention of intruding on Lilian Bunting's showdown with Peggy Taxman. I was a Finch-trained snoop, but I wasn't crazy.

Twenty

It came as no surprise to Mr. Barlow or to me when the vicar announced from the pulpit on Sunday morning that Mrs. Taxman had generously donated a fine antique glass cabinet to the village museum.

Hardly anyone else was surprised, either. News traveled at the speed of light in Finch, and the news of Lilian's triumph over the formidable Peggy Taxman had been a headline grabber. Everyone agreed, though not within Peggy's hearing, that we owed the vicar's wife a debt of gratitude.

The vicar went on to welcome James and Felicity to the parish and to assure them that the vicarage door would always be open to them. He then managed to surprise me greatly by delivering James's pocket watch speech.

As he described the family feud James had unintentionally reignited, I recalled that James had visited the vicarage on the day of the palette knife incident. When he exchanged a meaningful look with Felicity, I couldn't help but think that he'd gone there to explain the dangers of metal detecting to the vicar.

"It would be a great pity," the vicar concluded, "if we allowed our discoveries to damage the bonds of affection that hold our village together. Let us not emulate a family fractured by a petty dispute over a pocket watch. Let us not be dismayed by a few unpleasant revelations. Let us explore our past fearlessly, secure in the knowledge that its gifts will outweigh its gaffes. Let us continue to be the strong, loving family we have always been."

The villagers took the vicar's words to heart, in part, I suspected, because they wished to show themselves to be superior to the silly people James Hobson had known before he'd moved to Finch. When we gathered in the churchyard after the service, it was as if nothing unsettling had ever happened. Sally and Henry had clearly put the wedding ring crisis behind them, and Mr. Barlow spoke to Dick Peacock without scowling. Best of all, Elspeth accepted an invitation to join Opal, Millicent, and Selena for brunch at Opal's cottage.

Peggy, meanwhile, attempted to turn defeat into victory with an unaccustomed but welcome show of humility. She dismissed James Hobson's thanks for the cabinet donation with a gracious wave of her hand, saying that, as a member of the community, it was her duty to support community projects.

Sally Cook reacted to Peggy's magnanimous statement by clucking her tongue and pulling me aside to inform me that it would be some time before the "fine antique glass cabinet" found its way to the schoolhouse because it was scratched, stained, and crammed with broken knickknacks.

"It'll take a week for her to empty it," said Sally, "and a month for Jasper to refinish it."

I was certain that, with Sally to nudge it along, the truth about Peggy's gift would enter the public domain before lunchtime. I was equally certain that the villagers would be as tickled as I was to hear that the cabinet Peggy had refused to fill with old rubbish was already filled with it.

Bill, Will, Rob, Bess, and I spent the rest of the day with my father-in-law and his new wife at Fairworth House. After a sumptuous brunch, Amelia accompanied the boys on a long walk through the grounds while Willis, Sr., stayed indoors with Bess, following her as she crawled from room to room and gazing adoringly at her when she lost her lunch on his exquisite Aubusson carpet. He was, as has been previously noted, besotted.

We left for home shortly after dinner, in part because it was a school night but also because I had a big day ahead of me. If all went according to plan, I would finally meet the elusive Badger.

I wanted to be wide awake when I achieved the impossible.

Adam was there to meet me when my train pulled into Paddington Station on Monday morning. Although I could have found my way to Carrie's Coffees without his help, I'd asked him to meet me because I couldn't pass up the chance to speak with him privately. I was extremely curious to know what, if anything, had transpired between him and Sarah Hanover since I'd last seen them.

I thought I'd have to get the ball rolling with a delicate inquiry or two, but Adam took the ball and ran with it without my prompting.

"What did you think of Sarah Hanover?" he asked, and before I could answer, he said, "I thought she was amazing, coming forward as she did and telling you what she knew and setting up your meeting with Stephen. She works in the British Museum bookshop. That's how she came to know about Stephen's work—his books fill an entire shelf. I met her there on Saturday and took her to lunch at the Court Café, and she mentioned a film she wanted to see, so I said, 'Why don't we see it tonight?' and we went to dinner afterward and for a walk along the river after dinner—"

I interrupted the flow to remind him to change trains at Piccadilly, but once we were on our way, it continued unabated.

"Sarah's from Ipswich," he informed me, "and she's studying

design. Well, you can tell it just by looking at her, can't you? She has a great sense of style, and she loves to sew, and she's filled a whole sketchbook with drawings of artifacts from the Sutton Hoo ship burial because she reckons the Anglo-Saxons knew a thing or two about beautiful design. We went to see the exhibition on Sunday, and she seemed to be quite interested in the things I pointed out. . . ."

He went on and on until we spotted Sarah Hanover waiting for us outside Carrie's Coffees, when he became completely tongue-tied. After saying hello to her, I waved to Carrie Osborne through the café window. She pointed at Sarah, then gave me a broad wink accompanied by a crisp okay sign. I could not have agreed with her more.

Nor could I blame Adam for losing the power of speech. Sarah was as cute as a button. She'd pinned her braided hair over her head in a close-fitting, wispy halo and paired her thrift store jacket with what I assumed to be another one of her creations. The skirt of her colorful peasant dress seemed to flutter joyously as we set out for Wilmington Square.

"I rang Stephen a few minutes ago," she informed us, "to let him know that we were on our way."

It took me a moment to recall that Stephen was Badger, but after a brief pause, I said, "Good thinking, Sarah. Thanks."

"He's quite looking forward to meeting you, Lori," she said.

"The feeling's mutual," I told her, running my hand over the spot where the garnet bracelet rested in my shoulder bag.

Like Adam, Sarah was a fast walker, but when I began to fall behind, she put a hand on his arm to slow him down. He responded to her touch instantly, and I was given a reprieve. I was not, however, given any information about the places we passed on the way to Wilmington Square. Adam was far too distracted to act as my tour guide, and I didn't mind in the least.

Wilmington Square was lined mainly with Georgian and postwar pseudo-Georgian town houses. They were pleasingly uniform in color—brown brick upper stories with white stucco ground-floor facades—and they overlooked a small park that was called, unsurprisingly, Wilmington Square Gardens. The park's black boundary railings enclosed an assortment of trees, shrubs, and flower beds that looked rather forlorn without their leaves, buds, and blossoms.

My companions and I didn't enter the gardens, but as we strolled alongside the railings, I caught glimpses of a somewhat shabby open-sided pavilion and a pair of decrepit water fountains. Though the square's buildings appeared to be in fine shape, its centerpiece hadn't been maintained half so well as the one Adam had shown me in Queen Square.

"Wilmington Square Gardens," Adam said to me out of the blue, as if he'd suddenly heard the clarion call of duty, "has streets on three sides and a pedestrian walkway on the fourth. The walkway is there because the square's builder—a man named John Wilson—ran out of money. He couldn't afford to construct another street, so he put in a walkway instead. And here it is."

We passed through an opening in the park railings, climbed a short flight of stone steps, and found ourselves on a wide sidewalk bordered on one side by the park and on the other by a long row of tidy three-story Georgian town houses.

"A happy accident, I'd say," I commented admiringly. "The people who live on the walkway can look into the park directly, as if it were their front yard."

"I wonder what they do when they have furniture delivered?" said Sarah. "There's no room for a lorry."

"There's room round the back," said Adam. "The tradesmen's entrance." He turned to me. "Most of the town houses were converted into flats at one time or another, but the ones that weren't are worth a fortune. You won't find poor people living in them."

"Stephen lives with his son," said Sarah. "As his son is a barrister, I expect he can afford to live wherever he likes."

It was the first I'd heard of Badger's son, but I found the news oddly reassuring. If Badger had married and started a family, it meant that he hadn't wasted his life pining for the girl in the Rose Café. Though I was certain that Aunt Dimity would be pleased for him, I wasn't quite as certain that Badger's son would be pleased to meet me. I hoped he'd be well out of earshot when I delivered a host of messages from a woman his father had once loved.

"Rather humble digs for a barrister, I would have thought," said Adam.

"Perhaps he's a humble barrister," Sarah suggested.

"There's no such thing," said Adam, and they both laughed.

"Hey, guys," I scolded, "go easy on the lawyer jokes. My husband's an attorney, and he happens to be a very humble man." I thought of the study's spotless hearth and added judiciously, "Most of the time."

"Your husband is the exception that proves the rule," Adam stated firmly.

"He's pretty exceptional," I agreed.

"We're here," Sarah announced, coming to a halt.

If it hadn't been for the numbers on the doors and the drapes in the windows, the town houses overlooking the park would have been difficult to tell apart. Each had one set of stairs leading down to a basement entrance and another set leading up to a shallow porch framing the elevated ground-floor entrance. The four-panel front doors were bracketed by white pilasters and surmounted by half-moon fanlights, and although each town house's door was painted a different color, the colors seemed to come from the same dark palette. Badger's was dark blue.

It was only when Adam smoothed his hair nervously and Sarah patted her braids that I remembered how excited they were about meeting the famed Egyptologist Stephen Waterford. I expected Sarah to charge up the stairs ahead of us and ring the doorbell, but she remained glued to the pavement, as if she'd been struck by stage fright. Adam, too, hesitated, and before I could take matters into my own hands, the door was opened by a strapping man with a headful of salt-and-pepper curls.

The man stepped onto the porch, closed the door behind him, and joined us at the bottom of the stairs. He appeared to be in his fifties, and he was dressed casually but expensively in a pale gray cashmere cardigan, a soft white cotton shirt, beautifully tailored charcoal-gray trousers, and gleaming black leather wing tips.

"Good morning," he said in a bluff, genial voice. "You must be Sarah Hanover, Lori Shepherd, and Adam Rivington. Have I got that right?"

"Yes," I said. "I'm Lori."

"Pleased to meet you. I'm Steve Waterford," he said. "Named after my father—Stephen to my colleagues, but Steve when I'm at home, to avoid confusion. Glad I caught you." He glanced up at the ground-floor window and lowered his voice to a confidential murmur. "I wanted to have a word with you about Father."

"If he's ill, we can—" I began, but Steve cut me off.

"No, no, he's remarkably healthy for a man of his age," he said. "His mind is still razor sharp, too, but he does tire easily. Three of you at once might be a bit much, if you see what I mean."

"It's your show, Lori," said Adam, manfully concealing his disappointment. "Sarah and I will make ourselves scarce."

"It's not that he doesn't wish to meet you," Steve said anxiously.

"We understand," said Sarah in flattened tones.

"Wait," I intervened. "Would it be okay if my friends came in just for a minute? Just to say hello?"

Someone rapped loudly on the ground-floor window. I looked up to see a wrinkled hand make a beckoning gesture. Steve glanced at the hand and smiled.

"Apparently it would be okay," he said. "But just for a minute and just to say hello, I beg you. Father is sometimes too hospitable for his own good."

Adam and Sarah nodded solemnly, straightened their jackets, and followed Steve and me up the stairs and through the dark blue door.

Twenty-one

S teve Waterford escorted us to a sunny, pleasantly disordered sitting room at the front of the house. Framed etchings of desert scenes hung on the biscuit-colored walls, and books seemed to be everywhere, piled on small tables, stacked on the parquet floor, and packed into the built-in shelves that flanked the white marble fireplace in which a coal fire was burning steadily.

The room had two windows, each taller than I was and considerably wider, offering unobstructed views of the park. A bird's-eye maple desk sat between the windows, and a pair of slipcovered, overstuffed armchairs faced the hearth. An arched opening in the wall opposite the windows led to the room next door, which appeared to be a bedroom, though it was similarly littered with books.

An elderly man stood beside the desk, facing us, his hands resting one atop the other on the worn silver handle of a malacca cane. He wore a pale blue shirt and loose-fitting black trousers, and though the room seemed overheated to me, he'd donned sheepskin bedroom slippers and a navy blue cable-knit cardigan. A tousled crop of white ringlets framed his lean, clean-shaven face. His gaze was as keen as a hawk's, and his voice was deep and mellow, with none of the reediness I associated with old age.

"You must be Sarah Hanover," he said, scrutinizing my companion. "You have your great-grandfather's eyes as well as his nose. And you," he went on, surveying Adam, "must be Sarah's young man. She tells me you're an Anglo-Saxon scholar."

Adam, who'd turned beet-red when he'd heard himself described as *Sarah's young man*, could only nod.

"Fascinating period," the old man observed. "Not my bailiwick, of course, but I'd like to hear what you have to say about it. We shall have to postpone our tête-à-tête, however, because I wish to speak privately with"—his hawklike gaze came to rest on me—"the third member of your party. I'm Stephen Waterford, by the way, though Ms. Shepherd knows me by a different name."

I felt a strange sense of recognition as his eyes met mine, as if Aunt Dimity had brought him to life for me before he and I had ever stood face-to-face. The years seemed to fall away as he held my gaze, and I saw in him the young man who'd sat at a rickety table in a badly lit café and opened Aunt Dimity's mind to the beauty that would revive her war-weary soul. The vision lasted for no more than a breath, but when he turned away, the world seemed to spin for a moment as I left the past behind and returned to the present.

As if he understood what was expected of him, Stephen extended his right hand. After Sarah and Adam dashed forward to shake it, he addressed his son.

"Steve? Would you be a good fellow and give these youngsters a cup of tea and a biscuit? I believe they might be persuaded to consume them in the library."

"Your son won't need to persuade us, sir," Adam assured him, looking as though he would happily spend the next five years exploring the great man's library.

"May we handle your books?" Sarah asked.

"I'd be baffled if you didn't," Stephen replied. "Books are meant to be handled. You'll find a few odds and ends in the library that may interest you as well. Please feel free to handle them, too. I'll ring you when Ms. Shepherd is ready to leave."

"Thank you, sir," said Sarah, and she came very close to dropping a curtsy.

"It's an honor, sir," said Adam, with a neat head bow.

"The honor is mine," Stephen said courteously, returning the bow.

Steve collected my raincoat, then ushered Adam and Sarah out of the room. When they'd gone, Stephen motioned for me to sit beside him before the hearth.

"Silly children," he said as he eased himself gingerly into his chair. "They act as though I'm a national treasure. A month of fieldwork would disabuse them of the notion. Once they'd seen me covered in sand, sweat, and blackflies, they'd realize that I put my trousers on one leg at a time, the same as everyone else."

"Not everyone else has made remarkable discoveries and written books about them," I pointed out.

"You flatter me, Ms. Shepherd," he said.

"Please," I said, "call me Lori."

"I will," he responded, "if you'll call me Badger."

"I'd love to," I said, relieved. "I keep forgetting that your real name is Stephen."

"My father gave me my soubriquet," he said. "If I had any brains, I'd have done the same for Steve. As it is, we've spent the past eight months opening each other's mail."

"Did you move in with your son eight months ago?" I asked. Though I was eager to gather details to share with Aunt Dimity, I would have used just about any excuse to postpone the moment when I would have to ask Badger how he'd come by the garnet bracelet.

"Other way round," he replied. "Steve and his wife left their country house eight months ago to move in with me. My wife died, you see, and they were worried about leaving the old man on his own. They could have packed me off to a nursing home, but they came here instead. They created a bed-sitting-room for me on the ground floor, took over the upper stories, and installed Mr. and Mrs. Callender in the basement flat. Mrs. Callender looks after me when Steve and his wife are away. She is, to use a time-honored cliché, a gem."

"Sounds ideal," I said.

"Nothing on this earth is ideal," said Badger, "but we rub along well enough. Steve and Penny moved to the country to raise their kiddies, but the chicks left the nest long ago. After years of commuting, they were only too glad to shed their great barn of a house and move back to town. It's all worked out rather well, apart from my wife's death, of course."

"Of course," I said. "I'm sorry."

"Thank you," he said with a dignified nod. He frowned suddenly. "How on earth did we start talking about my living arrangements?" He pursed his lips, then nodded. "Ah, yes, Steve's name and how much simpler life would be if I'd called him Tutankhamen."

"Simpler for you, maybe," I said, laughing, "but I think little Tut's classmates would have given him a hard time."

"You're probably right," he agreed, smiling.

"Why did your father call you Badger?" I asked.

"Therein lies a tale," he said, leaning back in his chair. "But before I tell it, I think you should tell me how you came to know Dimity Westwood."

"Yes, of course," I said, discomposed. "I should have told you about Dimity and me right away."

"I distracted you," said Badger. "Forgive me. I will not do so again. Please, proceed."

I gave him as much of the truth as I could and steered it onto safer ground when it veered into the improbable. I said that I'd gotten to know Dimity Westwood through my mother. I explained that, after my mother died, her best friend and I had grown even closer. I then took a small but familiar detour from the path of total honesty and told him that, before she'd passed away, Dimity had asked me to find a man called Badger and to give him a message she'd wished she'd given him in the Rose Café.

Having successfully negotiated the trickiest bit of my story, I went on to tell him how Adam had taken me to Carrie's Coffees, how Carrie had introduced me to Chocks, Ginger, and Fish, how the Battle of Britain boys had led me to Sarah Hanover, and how Sarah had made the final connection needed to bring me to Wilmington Square. I then paused to make sure that Badger was all right.

"An admirably succinct account of what could have been a convoluted tale," he said. "Well done."

"Uh, thanks," I said, feeling as though I'd passed an exam without knowing I'd taken it.

"Now for the conclusion," he said. "Go ahead. Deliver Dimity's message. My heart won't stop beating, I promise you. As my son is fond of telling people, I'm remarkably healthy for a man my age."

I took a deep breath and told him about Dimity's unwavering love for the doomed fighter pilot, Bobby MacLaren. I told Badger that she'd never married. I told him how much his friendship had meant to her and how grateful she'd been to him for his advice and his guidance. Finally, I withdrew the gold and garnet bracelet from my shoulder bag and held it out to him in the palm of my hand.

"Dimity kept your gift until her dying day," I said. "The bracelet reminded her of a turning point in her life, a turning point you made possible. But it also reminded her of the regret she felt for the unhappiness she'd caused you."

Badger took the bracelet from me and tilted it back and forth in his hand. The garnets glittered in the firelight like ruddy tears.

"It's not a bracelet, you know," he said softly. "It's an armlet." He tapped his biceps. "Meant to be worn here."

I nodded, recalling that when I'd first seen the armlet, I'd thought it was too large to be a bracelet.

"I intended to tell Dimity that it was an armlet, but . . ." He shook his head. "I was a fool. I was the architect of my own unhappiness. I expected too much of her, and I couldn't bear the disappointment when she failed to meet my absurd expectations."

"What did you expect of her?" I asked.

"I expected Dimity to recognize me," he said, smiling wryly. "I knew her the moment she walked into the Rose Café, but my face meant nothing to her."

"Why would she recognize you?" I asked. "Had your photograph been in the newspapers?"

"No." He closed his hand over the bracelet. "I'd been in her village."

I gaped at him, thunderstruck.

"You've been to *Finch*?" I exclaimed.

"Oh, yes," he replied. "I spent two weeks there one summer, between the wars. My father and I camped in the meadow behind Dimity's cottage."

"I *live* in Dimity's cottage," I told him, my mind reeling. "She left it to me when she died. My husband and I have lived there for over a decade. Our children are growing up there."

"Then you'll be familiar with the meadow," he said. "I'll wager it floods in the spring."

"The lower part of it does," I said, "the part closest to the brook."

"It's a lovely place to camp in the summer," he said. "Protected from the north wind by the oak grove, carpeted with wildflowers, and provided by nature with a ready supply of fresh water."

"It's a very nice meadow," I agreed. "My sons play cricket in it, and we have picnics in it, and I think my friend Emma has identified every wildflower that grows in it, but what I'd really like to know is: What brought you and your father to Finch?"

"A desire to delve into history," Badger replied. "My father was an amateur archaeologist. He taught Latin at a London prep school, but in his spare time he immersed himself in the past. He dreamed of making a groundbreaking discovery—a Roman villa, an Iron Age hill fort, a medieval monastery—and he identified places where he thought such a site might exist. My summer holidays were spent traveling with him to those places and helping him to dig exploratory trenches. Hence, the name Badger."

I smiled and urged him silently to go on.

"My father knew that there had once been a Roman villa near Finch," he continued, "in a place called Hillfont Abbey. Are you familiar with it?"

"I am," I said. "I've seen the remains of the Roman well in Hillfont's main courtyard."

"My father hoped to find further traces of the villa," Badger informed me, "so off we went to Finch. Mr. and Mrs. Westwood were only too happy to let us pitch our tent in their meadow. I think they felt sorry for us because we lived in London, where fresh air was in short supply."

"Didn't your father explain to them why you were there?" I asked.

"My father never told anyone what we were doing," said Badger. "He'd read about looters plundering archaeological sites, so he conducted his surveys and dug his test trenches quietly and unobtrusively. It's common practice among archaeologists, but it made life rather difficult for a young boy in love." The wry smile reappeared. "And I was quite desperately in love."

"With Dimity?" I asked.

"Naturally," he replied. "I saw her every day. She rode a black bicycle with a silver bell and a willow basket, and she seemed to me to be the most beautiful girl on earth. I was at an impressionable age, to be sure, but when I saw her years later, I still thought her beautiful." He paused, as if to savor the memory, then went on. "My father cautioned me against speaking with her, and she was far too busy to speak with me, but she would give me a friendly wave whenever she noticed me. On those days, I walked on air." He pulled his cardigan more closely around him and peered at the hearth. "Would you be so kind as to throw more coals on the fire, Lori? I find that I don't cope with the cold as well now as I did when I camped under the stars with my father."

I scooped a shovelful of coals from the scuttle beside the hearth, slid them carefully onto the glowing embers, used the bellows to ignite them, and returned to my chair.

"Did your father make any groundbreaking discoveries?" I asked.

"Just one," said Badger, "but he didn't make it until after I'd joined up. While I was dodging tanks in North Africa, he discovered an Anglo-Saxon hoard."

I was glad that Adam had gone to the library. I was fairly sure his head would have exploded if he'd heard Badger say that his father had found an Anglo-Saxon hoard. I, on the other hand, was too ignorant to be more than vaguely impressed by the discovery.

"To tell you the truth," I said, "I'm not really clear on what a hoard is."

"It's a collection of objects hidden in the ground or elsewhere," Badger explained. "Hoards can contain coins, weapons, armor, gems—anything of value. Current theory holds that hoards were used as a kind of safe deposit box, to be emptied as needed. Hoarders sometimes failed to retrieve their possessions, however, which is why hoards continue to turn up, intact and untouched."

"Your father must have been ecstatic when he found his hoard," I said.

"He believed it to be the largest and most valuable hoard ever found in the British Isles," said Badger. "Since he lacked the financial resources to conduct a proper excavation, he took one artifact from the site"—he opened his clasped hand to reveal the glittering armlet—"to show to those who would understand its significance."

"Your father took the armlet from the hoard?" I asked quickly. "Not you?"

"Since I was in North Africa at the time," said Badger, "it would have been rather difficult for me to remove anything from the hoard."

"Yes, of course, how stupid of me," I babbled, but my heart was singing. If Badger's father had removed the armlet from the hoard, then Badger was in the clear. He hadn't stolen the armlet from the British Museum or from anywhere else. His father might be considered a thief, but Badger couldn't be accused of breaking the law. A great rush of relief flooded through me as I realized that I would never have to share my suspicions with Aunt Dimity.

"As I was saying," Badger went on, "my father hoped to persuade an individual or an institution to provide him with the funds he required to excavate, record, and protect the hoard."

"Was he successful?" I asked, refocusing my attention on the matter at hand.

"Quite the opposite," Badger replied. "No one responded to his telephone calls or to his letters, and his unannounced visits ended before they began. His discovery was ill timed, you see. There was a war on. People had more important things to do than to listen to crackpot claims about buried treasure."

"He must have been incredibly frustrated," I said.

"He was, but not for long," said Badger. "On the sixteenth of June, 1944, a V-1 rocket obliterated our house. Mother was out at the time, but Father was in his study, writing yet another letter. The rocket destroyed his notebooks, his maps, his life's work, so perhaps it's just as well that it killed him, too."

"I'm so sorry," I said. "It must have been terrible to lose your father when you were so far away."

"It was terrible," he acknowledged, "but it wasn't wholly unexpected. If the Blitz taught us anything, it was that one didn't have to be on the front line to die in battle. Anyone could be killed at any time, anywhere."

"A harsh lesson," I said.

"Wars tend to deliver harsh lessons," he observed dryly. "My father would have been pleased to know that the armlet survived. It was rescued from the rubble by a scrupulously honest fireman, who handed it over to my mother. When I came home, she gave it to me."

"And you gave it to Dimity," I murmured. "You must have loved her very much."

"It was a young man's grand romantic gesture," he said, "a prelude to the moment when I would reveal myself to Dimity as the boy who'd camped in her parents' meadow. I knew at once that it was pointless. I'd seen the look before, in other eyes, the undying devotion to the dead. One grew accustomed to it after the war, but when I saw it in Dimity's eyes, I felt as if I'd been dealt a double blow. By failing to remember me, she'd erased me from her past. By failing to accept my love, she'd ruined my future—or so I thought. Like a young idiot, I stormed out of the café, too caught up in my own misery to consider hers."

"Idiocy is the hallmark of youth," I observed.

"It is indeed," he agreed. "I couldn't bring myself to throw away the gift she'd given me, though. It was a soft toy, a badger. I don't know why I kept it, but I did. I still have it."

He nodded at the bird's-eye maple desk. I looked over my shoulder and saw the pointed, black-and-white face of a badger poking out from a jumble of books, papers, penholders, and notepads.

"Maybe the badger reminded you of a turning point in your life," I suggested. "If Dimity hadn't let you down, you might not have gone on to achieve such a high level of excellence in your field."

"When one door closes, another opens," he said, "if one tugs on it hard enough. And I did work very hard after the Rose Café debacle."

"Dimity tried to find you after you stormed out of the café," I told him, "but no one knew where you were. Where did you go?"

"Cambridge," he said. "I gathered an armload of degrees and took them with me to Egypt, where I spent the next twenty-five years of my life. I met my wife there, and our children were born there."

"Children?" I said curiously.

"Steve isn't my only child," he said. "I have two other sons and a daughter, and they've all turned out rather splendidly." He laughed. "When I left the Rose Café, I was convinced that true happiness would be forever beyond my reach. How wrong I was! And how foolish I was to run away from someone who could have been a lifelong friend."

"Dimity didn't blame you," I said. "She understood."

"Did she?" he said thoughtfully. "I'm not surprised. She was a remarkable woman."

We sat in silence for a time, and I added more coals to the fire. Badger's energy didn't seem to be flagging, so I thought his son wouldn't mind if I asked a question that was nagging at me.

"Did you ever try to find your father's hoard?" I asked.

"No," he replied.

I nodded. "I suppose it would have been close to impossible, after his papers had been destroyed."

"As a matter of fact, the rocket didn't destroy all of his papers," Badger informed me. "I still had the letters he'd written to me while I was fighting in North Africa. In his last letter, he used a coded clue to direct me to the hoard's location."

"Were you able to decode the clue?" I asked.

"Oh, yes," said Badger. "At the time, I was the only one who *could* decode it."

"If you understood the clue," I said, "why didn't you look for the hoard?"

"It took me a while to settle back into civilian life," he said. "Then came Cambridge, followed by Egypt, fieldwork, marriage, children, research, writing, lectures, interviews, and more fieldwork. I simply didn't have enough time to complete my father's work as well as my own. And as I told Adam, the Anglo-Saxon period isn't my bailiwick."

"You could have told an Anglo-Saxon scholar about it," I said.

"I could have," Badger agreed. "I could have told those who'd ignored my father that he had, in fact, made a marvelous discovery. I could have handed the hoard over to those who'd turned him away and insulted him, but I chose not to." He gave me a sidelong look and a twinkling smile. "I'm afraid I haven't yet outgrown my petulant streak."

I began to return his smile, but frowned instead as I recalled something he'd said only moments earlier.

"What did you mean by 'at the time'?" I asked. "You said that you were the only person who could decode your father's clue *at the time*. Were you implying that someone else was able decode it later on?"

"Well spotted, Lori," he said approvingly. "There is only one person other than myself capable of understanding my father's clue, and she happens to be sitting beside me."

"Who?" I said, eyeing him doubtfully. "Me?"

"Yes, you," he said. "In his last letter, my father told me that he'd found the hoard in the place where I'd first lost my heart." He bent his head toward me and raised an eyebrow. "I don't need to elaborate, do I?"

I blinked stupidly at him for a moment, then caught my breath.

"No," I said, grinning incredulously. "Are you serious? Are you telling me that there's an Anglo-Saxon hoard in *my meadow*?"

"I am serious," said Badger. "There's an Anglo-Saxon hoard in your meadow. I'm afraid Father didn't specify which part of the meadow, but the hoard's in there, somewhere."

"Good grief," I said, leaning my head on my hand. "What am I supposed to do about it?"

Badger held the armlet out to me.

"Put this back," he said.

"Put it back with the hoard?" I shrank away from his outstretched hand. "I can't, Badger. It's all you have left of your father."

"Nonsense," he said, letting his hand drop. "My father lives on in my children, grandchildren, and great-grandchildren, and the memories I have of him are more precious to me by far than any trinket. Please, Lori, put the armlet back where it belongs. It was my father's intention to return it to the hoard. I'd be grateful to you if you would carry out his wishes."

"What if I can't find the hoard?" I asked.

"You found me," he pointed out. "Surely you can find something that's buried in your own backyard."

"But what if I *do* find it?" I asked a bit desperately. "What then?"

"It's entirely up to you," he said. "You knew Dimity. Ask yourself what she'd do. You won't go far wrong by following her example."

Badger held the armlet out to me again. I hesitated, then took it from him, tucked it into my shoulder bag, and stood.

"If I have a hoard to find, I'd better get going," I said, peering through the windows. "Night comes early in October."

"Do you intend to start your search today?" Badger asked, sounding amused.

"I don't have gold fever," I assured him, "but I do find it hard to believe that an Anglo-Saxon treasure trove has been sitting right under my nose ever since my husband and I moved into Dimity's cottage. I guess I won't believe it until I see it."

"How do you intend to search for it?" he asked. "It would be a pity to dig holes all over your lovely meadow."

"Don't worry," I told him. "I have a less destructive plan. But I'll need daylight to put it into action."

"I'll ring Sarah." Badger pulled a cell phone from his pocket and made the call, then rose slowly to his feet with the aid of his malacca cane. "I have one more question for you, Lori. Dimity Westwood died more than a decade ago. Have you really spent the past ten years and a bit looking for me?"

"Not exactly," I said, clearing my throat nervously. "You know how it is, Badger. New country, new village, new house, new friends, a pair of twins, a baby girl, a—"

"Say no more," Badger interrupted. "I understand completely." He reached out to shake my hand. "Thank you, Lori. For everything. I hope we meet again."

"Of course we'll meet again," I said. "I'll have to fill you in on what I find."

"I hope I'm still around to hear your report," he said.

"You will be," I stated firmly. "In case you haven't noticed, you're in remarkably good health for a man your age."

Badger was still chuckling a moment later, when Steve, Adam, and Sarah entered the room. Steve surveyed his father anxiously, but Adam and Sarah looked as if they'd been handed the keys to heaven. They couldn't thank Badger enough for giving them free rein in his library, but when they began to burble on about the scarabs, urns, and statues it contained, Steve shot them a warning look, and they fell silent. Badger invited them to visit him again, and Steve walked with us to the front door.

"I don't know what you said to my father," he told me, "but it's done him a world of good. I haven't seen him looking so well since before my mother died."

I thanked him for looking after Adam and Sarah, waved good-bye to Badger, who was watching us from one of his windows, and ran down to the walkway, where my companions were waiting to invite me to lunch.

"Would you mind very much if I took a rain check?" I asked. "I, uh, have something to do before dark."

"We'll take you to Paddington, then," Adam offered.

"No need," I told him. "If you'll take me to the nearest tube station, I'll find my own way from there."

As we set out, I realized with a start that I'd lost my fear of getting lost in London. Aunt Dimity, I thought, would be proud of me. And Bill would be gobsmacked.

Twenty-two

$\mathcal{F}$ caught the express train to Oxford. To quell the hunger pangs that were creeping up on me, I bought a cheese and tomato sandwich in the buffet car, but I telephoned James Hobson before I ate it. When I asked him if I could borrow his metal detector, he astounded me with the news that Peggy Taxman had disrupted his rota, commandeered his metal detector, and spent much of the day scanning the village green, ably assisted by Jasper.

"I'm not surprised by the disrupting and the commandeering," I explained, "but I didn't expect Peggy, of all people, to take up metal detecting."

"She's gone at it full bore," said James. "She seems intent on collecting more items than anyone else in the village."

"Ah, yes, that sounds about right," I said. "Peggy doesn't like to be second best at anything."

"I could lend you my spare detector," he suggested. "It operates in much the same way as the one I used at the demonstration."

"That would be great," I said.

"Will you share the green with Mrs. Taxman?" James inquired.

"Peggy's not very good at sharing," I replied, "so I'll scan my own property."

I detected a quizzical note in his voice as he said, "I was beginning to think you weren't interested in my hobby, Lori."

"I was just waiting my turn," I told him brightly.

A second telephone call confirmed that Bill had taken Bess with him to his office and that he intended to drive from there to Upper Deeping to pick up Will and Rob after school. If all went well, I told myself as I unwrapped my sandwich, I would have two uninterrupted hours to find the hoard.

All went well. The train arrived in Oxford ahead of schedule, Bill's car didn't break down on the way to Ivy Cottage, and James handed over his spare metal detector and utility belt without delay. I swapped my long raincoat for a short jacket when I got home, but I didn't bother to change the rest of my clothes. I simply strapped the utility belt around my waist before I trotted outside to study the meadow that sloped gradually from the rear wall of my back garden to the brook Badger and his father had found so useful.

The wildflowers Badger had admired were long gone, and the trees in the oak grove had shed their leaves, but the brook was still flowing freely. The cheerful little stream was content to remain within its banks for most of the year, but as Badger had reminded me, it tended to inundate the lower part of the meadow in the spring. As soon as the thought of flooding entered my mind, the penny dropped.

"He was giving me a clue," I said aloud, clapping a hand to my forehead. "Badger was telling me to concentrate on the upper part of the meadow because no Anglo-Saxon in his right mind would store his valuables in a safe deposit box that might be carried away in the spring floods."

I switched on the metal detector and began to scan the meadow's uppermost reaches. I was nearing the edge of the oak grove when I hit pay dirt. The detector's mournful wail sounded deafeningly and continuously as I moved the coil head over a slightly sunken, circular patch of dried grasses. Visions of coins, weapons, armor, and glittering gems danced in my head as I leaned the detector against a tree. My hands trembled with excitement as I pulled the digger from its sheath and dropped to my knees, but I couldn't bring myself to cut through the soil.

I sat on my heels and took a calming breath. Badger's father had considered his find important enough to back away from it until he could excavate it properly. If I dug it up willy-nilly, I told myself, I'd be no better than a looter. By disturbing the site, I might destroy clues about the hoard's origins. One clumsy jab with the digger might damage an artifact that had survived intact for centuries. If, as James Hobson claimed, every object told a story, I might silence an entrancing tale forever. The craftsman who'd fashioned the gold and garnet armlet seemed to whisper in my ear, urging caution.

I decided to listen to him. I got to my feet, slid the digger into its sheath, and picked up the metal detector. I took a long look at the sunken, circular patch of dried grasses, then turned around and headed for the study.

It was time to heed Badger's advice. I would ask Aunt Dimity how she'd deal with buried treasure.

Reginald regarded me expectantly when I entered the study. I knelt to light a fire in the hearth, then straightened to run a fingertip along his hand-sewn whiskers.

"It's not a bracelet," I explained to him as I placed the armlet in his niche. "It's an Anglo-Saxon armlet, and it came from our meadow. But don't tell anyone. Not yet. Not until I figure out what to do next."

Reginald remained resolutely silent. I took the blue journal from its shelf and seated myself in one of the tall leather armchairs that faced the fire.

"Dimity?" I said as I opened the journal. "Do you remember a father and son who camped in your parents' meadow between the wars?"

Aunt Dimity took a long time to respond, but when she did, her handwriting flowed swiftly across the page, as if, in answering my question, she'd answered a few of her own.

Badger was the boy from London who camped in our meadow one summer. He thought I'd remember him when we met again in the Rose Café, and he was devastated when I didn't.

"People who want to be recognized shouldn't grow beards," I muttered.

Did he serve in the navy, Lori? Beards were quite popular in the navy.

"Badger spent the war dodging tanks in North Africa," I said, "so I'm pretty sure he wasn't in the navy."

A North African posting would explain his deep tan. I suppose he let his beard grow out to celebrate his return to civilian life.

"He's clean-shaven now," I said, "but his hair is longer than it was when he posed for the photographs you saw in the *Times*."

Is it still curly?

"It's as curly as mine," I said, "but it's not dark anymore. It's pure white. He's still handsome, he still has a great sense of humor, and he's"—I smiled inwardly—"remarkably healthy for a man his age."

Did you tell him about Bobby?

"I delivered each of your messages," I said, "and I told him you understood why he'd behaved so badly."

He didn't behave badly, Lori. He behaved brokenheartedly.

"He thinks he behaved badly," I stated firmly, "but I told him not to worry about it because most of us behave like idiots when we're young."

Did you really? How did he react to your forthright pronouncement?

"He agreed with me," I replied. "He said he'd been a fool to run away from someone who could have been a lifelong friend."

Did he tell you where he went?

I recounted everything Badger had told me about Cambridge, Egypt, his late wife, and his four splendid children. I described Wilmington Square, the town house, and the comfortable bed-sitting-room Badger's son and daughter-in-law had created for him on the ground floor.

"I didn't see the rest of the town house," I concluded, "but I'm sure I'll hear a detailed description of the library the next time I get together with Adam and Sarah."

Do you intend to get together with them again? In London?

"Definitely," I said. "But that's another story. For now, let's stick with Badger. I haven't quite finished telling you about him." I glanced fondly at Reginald, then looked down at the journal. "Badger kept the badger you gave him, Dimity. I saw it on his desk. He pointed it out to me."

He kept it all this time? I'm as surprised as I am delighted. It's nothing compared to the gift he gave me, but it was a small, a very small, token of my friendship. I'm glad he didn't throw it away.

"He is, too," I said. "But speaking of the gift he gave you . . ." I put my feet on the ottoman and launched into Badger's tale of the armlet and the Anglo-Saxon hoard. I was about to explain my role in the tale when Aunt Dimity's handwriting sped across the page.

My mother wrote to tell me that our visitor from London had returned without his son. He gave her the impression that he'd returned for nothing more than a much-needed break from the war-ravaged city. My mother had no idea that he was an amateur archaeologist or that he intended to excavate our meadow. I'm terribly sorry that his life ended so tragically and I'm sorry that his life's work was destroyed, but I must confess that I'm not one bit sorry that circumstances prevented him from digging a dirty great hole in our meadow.

"Well, Dimity," I said awkwardly, "it's funny that you should mention digging a hole in the meadow, because when I got back from London just now, I borrowed James Hobson's spare metal detector and . . ." I hesitated, then said in a rush, "I'm just about completely sure that I found the hoard, Dimity."

Will you dig it up?

"I'm not qualified to dig it up," I said. "Buried treasure belongs to the Crown. By rights, I should report it to the British Museum or to some other respectable institution. I should let a trained archaeologist, or maybe a team of trained archaeologists, conduct the excavation. The hoard should be disinterred, recorded, transported, researched, and displayed by people who know a whole lot more about such things than I do. I should step aside and let the professionals take over."

What's stopping you?

I gazed into the fire and asked myself the same question. An answer came to me when I realized that the only sound I could hear was the crackle of burning logs.

"I like a quiet life," I said slowly. "The thought of strangers trampling my wildflowers turns my stomach. I don't want people driving by the cottage to take pictures of the place where the famous hoard was found, and I certainly don't want to be known as the woman who found it."

Why not?

"It wouldn't be fair," I said. "I could talk about Badger's father until I was blue in the face, but he'd never get the recognition he deserves. The focus would be on Badger because he's so well known and on me because I happen to have a neighbor who's a metal detectorist." I shook my head. "I don't deserve the praise, and I don't want the five minutes of fame that would come along with finding 'the largest and most valuable hoard ever found in the British Isles.'"

Does Badger expect you to excavate his father's find?

"He asked me to put the armlet back where it came from," I said, "and he told me to ask myself what you would do."

You don't need my help to make a decision.

"Badger still has a high opinion of your judgment," I said, "as do I. So I'm asking you, Dimity: What do you think I should I do about my groundbreaking discovery?"

You have to break ground to make a groundbreaking discovery, Lori, and you haven't yet turned a spadeful of earth. Until you do, you can't know what's buried in the meadow. James Hobson's spare metal detector might have reacted to a pile of toy trucks Will and Rob buried just for the fun of it.

"It sounds like something they'd do," I acknowledged, smiling.

Someone will come along one day and rediscover the hoard. In the meantime, I'd advise you to act as its guardian.

"What should I do with the armlet?" I asked.

You should give it a decent burial. Dig its grave near the spot that gave the metal detector fits, drop the armlet in it, cover it over, and move on.

The anxiety I'd carried with me into the study suddenly vanished, to be replaced by a heady feeling of relief. I'd boxed myself into a corner, and Aunt Dimity had shown me the way out. As the hoard's guardian, I wouldn't have to sacrifice my family's privacy for the greater good, nor would I have to fight a losing battle to give credit where credit was due. A guardian would have a much quieter life than a groundbreaker.

"I'll do it," I said decisively. "I'll bury the armlet before Bill finishes the school run."

You'll tell him about it, won't you?

"I'll tell him the whole story," I said, "and I'll tell Badger as well, but I won't tell anyone else. Bill and I will keep an eye on the boys, in case they decide to play gravedigger; we won't throw metal-detecting parties; and we'll never, ever let Adam Rivington pitch a tent in our meadow."

I believe you'll be an exemplary guardian, Lori.

"I will be," I said. "I already have a motto. In the immortal, ear-splitting words of Peggy Taxman . . ." I tilted my head back and bellowed, " 'Some things are best left buried!' "

I heard a scrabble of claws in the living room as Stanley leaped from Bill's armchair and ran for cover. I called out an apology and a promise of tuna for dinner, then glanced at the ormolu clock on the mantel.

"I'd better get the burial under way," I said. "Bill and the children will be home in about forty minutes, at which point my quiet life will cease to be quiet. I'll be back later, though, to bring you up to date on what's happening in Finch."

Before you go, my dear, please allow me to tell you how grateful I am to you for finding Badger. You've polished a tarnished memory until it gleams. From now on, when I look back on the moments I shared with him, I'll feel nothing but happiness. Thank you.

"The gratitude goes both ways, Dimity," I said. "If you hadn't sent me on a wild goose chase, I wouldn't have met Adam, Sarah, Carrie, Chocks, Ginger, Fish, and one of the foremost archaeologists of our time. My new friends mean more to me than any hoard." I glanced at the clock again. "And now I really do have to run."

Go! But come back soon. I can hardly wait to hear the latest news!

I smiled as the curving lines of royal-blue ink faded from the page, then returned the journal to its shelf and took the armlet from Reginald's niche. I held it in the firelight one last time and wondered who had made it, worn it, buried it. As I slipped it into my pocket, I could almost hear a chorus of whispers thanking me for leaving it in peace.

Twenty-three

Finch's history museum was unveiled on a fine Sunday afternoon in mid-November. The folding tables in the old schoolhouse groaned under the weight of the food the villagers had prepared, and everyone had dressed up for the occasion. I'd been unable to dissuade Will and Rob from wearing riding gear, but I had at least persuaded them to don the formal attire they wore at gymkhanas instead of the grubby garb they wore while cleaning the stables.

Thankfully, Bess was too young to make her own sartorial decisions. I thought she looked adorable in the festive red velvet ensemble I'd chosen for her, and her adoring fans seemed to think so, too. Willis, Sr., took her from Bill's arms as soon as we walked into the schoolhouse and proudly showed her off to his friends and neighbors, while Amelia recorded the grandfather-granddaughter moment with yet another series of captivating sketches.

Peggy Taxman's antique cabinet occupied a prominent position in the center of the schoolhouse's north wall. The cabinet was at least six feet tall and four feet wide—much larger than I'd imagined it— but I couldn't tell whether it was Victorian or Edwardian or Early Troglodyte because it was shrouded in one of Mr. Barlow's paint-spattered drop cloths. I suspected that Jasper's refinishing work had met Peggy's exacting standards, however, because she looked as serene as a millpond.

Though the cabinet and its contents were concealed by the drop cloth, the Handmaidens' ink-stained fingers bore witness to their calligraphic endeavors, and a laminated version of Lilian's minutely marked map of the village green was being passed from hand to hand, to great acclaim.

I was discussing Lilian's map with Grant Tavistock and Charles Bellingham when Sally Cook collared me. Will and Rob, who clearly had no future in diplomacy, had evidently informed her that the cream buns I'd brought back from London were the best they'd ever tasted. I appeased Sally by employing Aunt Dimity's strategy of downplaying Carrie Osborne's baking skills and playing up my sons' indiscriminate fondness for all forms of pastry. The boys atoned for their blunder by appearing at my elbow with powdered sugar mustaches and chocolaty fingers.

"Well done, Lori," said Grant, after Sally, Will, and Rob had departed.

"Handled like a pro," Charles agreed. "Were the London cream buns better than Sally's?"

"My lips are sealed," I said, "but I'll give you an address where you can find them."

Grant and Charles were feeling rather pleased with themselves, having discovered a hammered farthing from the reign of Edward I in their back garden. They'd dutifully reported it to the proper authorities, who'd returned it after recording it for posterity.

Bree Pym had also scored a major coup with James Hobson's metal detector, but she hadn't had to report it to anyone. While scanning her front garden, she'd unearthed a trowel that had once belonged to her great-grandaunts. Bree, like Grant and Charles, had donated her find to the museum, along with a photo of Ruth and Louise Pym and some dried flowers from the garden they'd created.

At the appointed hour, Lilian Bunting asked for everyone's

attention. My family group was scattered far and wide, but Bill managed to tear himself away from the sausage rolls Christine Peacock had brought to the festivities and join me. The vicar, who had been similarly engaged, brushed crumbs from his fingers, made his way to the shrouded cabinet, and gave a short homily on the importance of preserving the past.

He expressed his gratitude to Peggy Taxman for presenting her display case to the village, and he singled out the donors without whom the display case would be an empty shell. He acknowledged the Handmaidens' artistic contributions, and he concluded by thanking his wife for her map and for the research she'd done to enhance our understanding of the objects within the cabinet.

After a brief round of applause, I expected Peggy Taxman to sweep past the vicar and yank the drop cloth from the display case. Instead, the vicar asked James Hobson to step forward. James seemed genuinely taken aback by the request, but after Felicity gave him an encouraging shove, he smiled sheepishly and went to stand beside the vicar.

"James," said the vicar, "I know I speak on behalf of the entire village when I say that you have done us a great service by introducing us to your fascinating hobby. You have shown us that metal detecting can be used, not for personal gain, but for the enlightenment of a community. It is with great pleasure and sincere gratitude that I invite you to, er, remove the drop cloth from our history museum."

"M-me?" James faltered, glancing furtively at Peggy Taxman. "Are you sure you don't mean—"

"He means you, James," Peggy boomed. "Get on with it!"

The hearty round of applause that followed was directed solely at Peggy. The good people of Finch knew a generous gesture when they saw one, and Peggy's willingness to allow a newcomer to take the lead in a once-in-a-lifetime village event redefined the boundaries of generosity.

I was proud of Peggy for giving James the spotlight he deserved, but I was also relieved that she hadn't stepped into it. If she'd assumed her usual role, she would almost certainly have subjected us to a lengthy and full-throated panegyric about a hobby she'd once dismissed as "playing in the dirt." James, by contrast, waited until the applause died down to make the shortest speech ever heard in Finch.

"Without further ado . . ." He left the sentence hanging as he reached up and plucked the drop cloth from the cabinet. The tumultuous applause he received suggested that I wasn't the only one who was aware of our lucky escape.

A crowd of villagers converged on the cabinet, but I could see enough of it to realize that, although it was handsome, it was no more antique than I was. The plain cherrywood frame, the mirrored rear wall, the massive glass panels, and the interior lighting hinted at a relatively recent date of manufacture.

"Antique, my foot," I whispered to Bill.

"Haven't you heard?" he murmured in return.

"Heard what?" I asked, pulling my allegedly gossip-proof husband away from prying ears.

"Christine Peacock told me that Peggy's old display case was riddled with woodworm," Bill explained. "It came apart in Jasper's hands."

"Disaster," I said, wincing.

"To save face," Bill continued, "Peggy bought a brand-new curio cabinet at the discount furniture shop in Upper Deeping." He looked around to make sure no one else was listening before he added delightedly, "Rumor has it that she persuaded them to cut the price in half."

"The woman knows how to haggle," I acknowledged.

"Christine saw Peggy and Jasper unload the flat pack from the trunk of their car," said Bill. "She says it took Jasper a week to assemble the parts."

"Poor Jasper," I said, trying not to laugh.

"What are you two whispering about?" inquired Lilian, strolling over to us.

"Woodworm and flat packs," I replied.

Lilian disguised an unseemly snort of laughter with a cough.

"I never thought I'd say it," she said quietly, "but thank God for woodworm. Peggy's original donation was dark, musty, and horridly Victorian. I much prefer the new one. The shelves are adjustable, the glass door slides sideways for easy access, and the light switch is mounted on the back, so we won't have to open the case every time we turn the lights on and off."

"Thank God for woodworm," Bill and I chorused.

"It's no good looking at it from over here, though," said Lilian. "The crowd's thinned a bit. You should be able to see the displays now. I'd like to know what you think of them. Your honest opinion, mind. I'm impervious to flattery."

Bill and I walked with her to take a closer look at Finch's history museum. A small placard on top of the cabinet credited the Handmaidens' calligraphy and Lilian's research, while a modest brass plaque mounted on the base cited Peggy's major contribution. Since I'd expected Peggy to emblazon her name across the schoolhouse wall in lurid pink neon, the brass plaque came as a pleasant surprise.

Each object or group of objects was accompanied by a simple white place card upon which the Handmaidens had inscribed the donor's name in a script reminiscent of Aunt Dimity's fine copperplate, though they'd elected to use black ink instead of royal blue.

While the place cards were both handsome and legible, Lilian's painstaking research gave the little collection of odds and ends an unexpected depth.

Mr. Barlow's horseshoe and Lilian's hand-forged horseshoe nails were grouped together in front of a sepia photograph of the old smithy. Sally Cook's lira was paired with a group photograph of Piero Sciaparelli's numerous descendants. Peggy's hair clip glittered prettily before a black-and-white photo of a Ferris wheel at Madame Karela's traveling fair, and Elspeth Binney's palette knife was accompanied by a color photo of all four Handmaidens dressed in their pastel painters' smocks.

Henry Cook's counterfeit wedding ring stood in for the real one Mr. Barlow had discovered. It lay before a color photograph of Sally and Henry grinning at the camera while he held his left hand, fingers splayed, over his heart. Mr. Barlow's rusty hammer and his tenpenny nails were displayed with a photo of him putting up shelves in the vicarage.

Grant's and Charles's hammered farthing was dwarfed by a postcard portrait of Edward I, and Bree's dried flowers had been lovingly arranged around the trowel and the photo of her great-grandaunts.

Lilian had selected photographs of world events to go along with the modern English coins the villagers had unearthed. Her 1965 florin, for example, had been placed before a photograph of Sir Winston Churchill's state funeral. As expected, Peggy had donated more items to the museum than anyone else, and though most of her finds fell into the *extremely* modern coin category, Lilian had diligently dug up photographs to accompany them.

Not content merely to illustrate the displays, Lilian had also written captions for them. All of the captions contained basic information—

the place and date of an object's discovery as well as a brief description of it—but a few contained much more. Lilian had taken the time to write detailed and occasionally humorous narratives about the fair, the smithy, Mr. Barlow's hammer, Henry Cook's wedding ring, Elspeth Binney's palette knife, Bree Pym's great-grandaunts, and Piero Sciaparelli's prisoner-of-war camp.

Lilian had clearly saved her best efforts for the top shelf. She'd lined it with black velvet, placed Dave Dillehaye's bronze-colored Victory Medal on a faded Union Jack, and surrounded the faded flag with photographs from the First World War.

It wasn't easy to look at the shattered limbs, the blood-soaked bandages, the filth, the rats, and the ragged corpses—and I was glad that the images were too high up for my sons to see—but the photographs brought home the horrors that had pushed Dave and others like him past endurance. His caption was much longer than the others' because it included his honorable service record, the shameful story of his original burial, and Lilian's plans to give the story a new and kinder ending.

Tears stung my eyes as I finished reading about Dave, and when I turned to Lilian, I had to swallow hard before I could speak.

"Is it all right?" she asked.

"It's a long way beyond all right," I replied, wiping my eyes. "The scholars at the British Museum couldn't have done better."

Lilian flushed with pleasure as Bill added his praise to mine. While they discussed the displays, I gazed in silence from one object to the next. None of the villagers had unearthed the tiaras and the gold doubloons I'd envisioned during James's metal-detecting demonstration, and they knew nothing of the Anglo-Saxon hoard, but they'd discovered buried treasure nonetheless.

My neighbors' mundane finds served as portals to the past. The hoard might outshine the rusted, worn, and broken treasures the villagers had rescued from oblivion, but it was part of the same story, the story of an ordinary place where ordinary people had always lived extraordinary lives.

Epilogue

*F*t was a cold and snowy night in mid-December. Bill was dozing in his favorite armchair, and Stanley was dozing in his lap. Will and Rob had gone to bed, and Bess was dreaming baby dreams in the nursery. I was in the study, seated in one of the tall leather armchairs that faced the hearth, enjoying the warmth of the roaring fire while I brought Aunt Dimity up to date on recent events.

"Peggy offered to donate a second curio cabinet to the museum," I said, "but I don't think we'll need another cabinet anytime soon."

Have the villagers lost interest in metal detecting?

"They're strictly fair-weather detectorists," I replied. "When winter sets in, they stay in. James is still out there, though. He's scanning the pasture behind Ivy Cottage. So far he's found a soup can, three horseshoes, a pair of embroidery scissors, and a gold-rimmed monocle."

The monocle must have belonged to Mr. Perry. He lived in Mr. Barlow's house when I was a girl, but he and his wife were bird-watchers, and the pasture behind Ivy Cottage was one of their local haunts. It took an entire month for Mr. Perry to replace his precious monocle—he had an unusual prescription— but his wife continued bird-watching without him. At least, she said she was bird-watching. The scissors could have slipped out of her pocket when she was . . . bird-watching. I'm afraid the lost monocle didn't help their marriage one bit.

I burst out laughing, then shook my head helplessly.

"I love your stories, Dimity," I said. "James would love them, too, and Lilian would find them riveting. It's a shame that I have to keep them to myself."

I suppose it would be difficult to explain how you came by them.

"Lilian and James would think I'd gone soft in the head if I told them about you," I reminded her.

Perhaps you could bend the truth a little, as you did in London. You could tell them that you heard my stories from your mother.

"I did hear your stories from my mother," I said, "but none of them mentioned Mr. Perry and his monocle."

Are you certain? Isn't it possible that you forgot Mr. Perry's story, but it returned to you when you learned of James's discovery?

"Dimity," I said, wagging a finger at the blue journal, "I believe you're leading me down the path to perdition."

Don't be melodramatic, Lori. I'm merely attempting to give James Hobson pertinent information about the monocle he found. I'm sure it would make him happy.

"James seems to be at his happiest when he's figuring things out for himself," I said. "He may be able to identify Mr. Perry through his unusual prescription."

If he doesn't, please feel free to use the story I've devised for you.

"Well," I said, "the story you concocted about Carrie Osborne's cream buns kept Sally Cook from blowing her stack, so I'll keep the monocle story in my back pocket."

How is the new churchyard wall coming along?

"The weather has not cooperated," I declared, "but Mr. Barlow thinks it'll be finished by Christmas."

A fine time of year to consecrate a grave.

"Spiritually, yes," I allowed, "but if we get any more snow, we'll need a horse-drawn sleigh to get to the grave. Bess wouldn't mind. She thinks snow is the best thing since puréed carrots."

You'll attend the consecration, then, regardless of the weather?

"Everyone will attend the consecration," I said firmly. "The villagers may be fair-weather detectorists, but they'll brave a blizzard for poor old Dave Dillehaye. It was snowing like mad when Lilian unveiled his name on the war memorial, but everyone was there."

I wish my family had been as attentive to him while he was alive, but we weren't aware of his troubles until after he died. My parents fell out with the vicar when he refused to bury Dave in the churchyard. We stopped attending services at St. George's until a new vicar replaced the old one.

"Where did you attend services?" I asked.

St. Leonard's in Upper Deeping. It cost my father a small fortune in petrol to drive there every Sunday, but he was willing to make a small sacrifice to honor Dave's much greater sacrifice. We all were.

"Your parents were ahead of their time," I said. "I'll ask the vicar to say a prayer for them during Dave's memorial service."

Thank you, Lori. Has the vicar set a date for the memorial?

"Not yet," I said. "Lilian's waiting for Mr. Barlow to finish the wall. Whenever it's held, I'm sure it'll draw a standing-room-only congregation. The piece Lilian wrote about Dave for the museum has gotten a lot of attention."

She's an excellent writer. Speaking of which, did you remember to deliver the copies of Peter Pan *to Morningside School?*

"I did," I replied. "One copy per student to read during Christmas break. The teachers explained that the money from the books helps sick children at Great Ormond Street Hospital. As it turns out, one of the twins' classmates had been *in* Great Ormond Street Hospital, so the books meant more to the school than I'd thought they would."

Perhaps they'll put on the play next year.

"If they do," I said, "I know two little boys who will jump at the chance to fly."

The Christmas holiday began yesterday, didn't it?

"Yep," I said. "Will and Rob spent all day playing in the snow. I thought I'd need a blowtorch to thaw them out, but hot chocolates did the trick. Bill and I took them to see the history museum after church on Sunday. They were too busy stuffing their faces with Sally's profiteroles to look at it on opening day."

And?

"And they were disappointed by the lack of bugs," I replied. "They told Lilian all sorts of things about the horseshoes, though, and they were chuffed when she jotted their comments in her notebook."

I suspect a revised caption is in the offing.

"Our museum will always be a work in progress," I said. "Contrary to what most people think, history doesn't stand still."

Very true. There's always more to learn about the past.

"I've certainly learned a lot about your past in the last few weeks," I said. "I feel as if I should write a thank-you note to the Hobsons' movers. If those klutzes hadn't broken the blender, I wouldn't have found the armlet, and if I hadn't found the armlet, you wouldn't have told me about your life in London during and after the war."

Am I really so reticent?

"Not at all," I said. "You're just so interested in other people that you forget to talk about yourself."

Now that you mention it, I've been meaning to ask you about Adam and Sarah and everyone else you met in London.

"See what I mean?" I said, smiling. "You can't help yourself. You'd rather talk about anyone but you."

Indulge me, then. Tell me if Adam and Sarah are still good friends.

"Adam and Sarah are well on their way to living happily ever after," I said, "with Carrie's wholehearted approval, I might add. I don't expect to see Chocks, Ginger, and Fish again until the spring, but Carrie tells me they're doing well. And as you know, Badger continues to be remarkably healthy."

I still find it hard to believe that you brought Bess with you when you last visited him. What happened to your fear of London?

I shrugged. "I don't know if I've changed or if London has— maybe it's a bit of both—but the big scary city doesn't scare me anymore. After all, it's just a collection of villages. And I know how to handle myself in a village."

You most certainly do.

"I don't want Bess and the boys to be as stupid as I was," I said, "so I'm going to take them to London much more often. The boys can hardly wait to start our grand gala Christmastime walking tour of Bloomsbury."

There's no place quite like London at Christmas, especially if you wander off the beaten track.

"Adam and Sarah are coming with us," I said, "so we can wander as far off the beaten track as we like."

Will you visit Badger?

"The man has a library full of scarabs," I said. "We can't *not* visit him. Besides, he's promised to tell the boys spooky stories about the pyramids while they're guzzling his hot chocolate. Will and Rob may not love him when we walk into the town house, but they'll love him by the time we say good-bye."

Badger's easy to love.

"Do you ever wish you could have loved him?" I asked. "And I'm not talking about loving him like a brother."

I know what you mean, Lori, and I hope you'll forgive my reticence, but I believe I'll keep my answer to myself. In the immortal words of Peggy Taxman: Some things are best left buried. Good night, my dear. Sleep well.

"Good night, Dimity," I said. "I always sleep well in winter. Except on Christmas Eve."

Naturally!

As the graceful, old-fashioned handwriting faded from the page, I thought of the many treasures I'd encountered since the Hobsons had moved into Ivy Cottage. One was made of gold and garnets, while another was nothing more than a bit of ribbon attached to a bronze-colored metal disk. The most valuable were made of flesh and blood, but the most mysterious were buried deep within the heart.

"The buried treasures of the heart," I murmured. "You needn't guard them from me, Dimity. I won't come looking for them. But I may ask to you help me pick out a Christmas present for Badger. Something tells me you'll know what he likes."

Smiling, I closed the journal, returned it to its shelf, kissed Reginald on the snout, and went to rouse the treasure of my heart from his slumbers.

Eggless Fruit Cake

Lightly adapted from the original recipe in the 1941 edition of Rational Recipes *by Gertrude Baker*

Recipe

½ pound flour
pinch of salt
1 level teaspoon bicarbonate of soda
¼ teaspoon mixed spice
3 ounces margarine
¼ pound sultanas or currants
3 ounces moist brown sugar
2 ounces mixed peel
milk to mix

Method

1. Sieve flour, salt, and bicarbonate of soda into a bowl.
2. Add mixed spice to dry ingredients.
3. Rub fat into dry ingredients.
4. Add fruit, sugar, and mixed peel to dry ingredients, and mix with milk.
5. Place mixture in a greased and floured loaf pan.
6. Bake in a moderate oven for about 1 hour. Allow to cool.

Note to readers who don't know what "mixed spice" and "mixed peel" are: Both can be purchased at a well-stocked British specialty shop.